THE BILLIONAIRE WHO WASN'T

BETH ORSOFF

ISBN: 979-8-9887329-3-8 (paperback)

www.bethorsoff.com

ALSO BY BETH ORSOFF

Romantically Challenged

Disengaged

Honeymoon for One

Girl in the Wild

Vlad All Over

Vlad to the Bone

Game Changer

Boy Toy

Fall From Grace

The Lies We Tell

The Truth of It

There are many kinds of love—the love between a parent and a child, the love for a sibling or friend, romantic love. The one thing they all have in common is how easily they can be betrayed.

1

J*ust breathe*, I remind myself as I drive my borrowed car into the parking lot of the nondescript industrial park. I circle until I find a space, then check the clock on the dash. Traffic in Los Angeles is as bad as they say, so I always leave extra time. Sometimes I still arrive a few minutes late. But usually, like today, I'm early. I use the bonus time to reread my resume. I have several versions depending on the job I'm applying for and whether I found the posting on my own or was referred by a friend. Not that I have many of those anymore. When your father's an international pariah, I've discovered, it can negatively impact your relationships.

I force myself to wait until five minutes before my appointment time before I reach for the rearview mirror. Lipstick still on lips and not teeth? Check. Mechanically straightened hair still straight? Check. Mascara and eyeliner still in their proper place? Check. "You can do this," I say and fist-bump my reflection before opening the car door.

I smile at the receptionist, who looks as bored as I know I would be if I were stuck sitting in a windowless office all day. That was one of the things I loved about my former job—I was constantly on the go, indoors, outdoors, and traveling too. *Don't go there*, I remind myself for the first time this morning, which is pretty good considering I've been up for hours. *Your old life is gone. Accept it and move on.*

It's the mantra I repeat to myself at least twice a day, which I consider progress. Six months ago I used to remind myself of this hourly and I still cried all the time. Now I only succumb to tears once or twice a week.

"Nina Roth to see Michael McKenzie," I chirp.

I've become really good at faking happiness these last few months. Sometimes I even fool myself.

"Have a seat," Bored Receptionist says and nods to the gray fabric chairs lining one wall. "I'll let him know you're here."

As I faux-confidently stride across the reception area, I can't help but notice the truly cringe-worthy painting hanging on the wall. It's a picture of a woman staring out at what I presume is meant to be a stormy sea. The gray in the painting is an exact match for the gray in the seat cushions, which complements the gray industrial carpet. *That must be the reason Wine World's decorator chose it*, I muse. Then I laugh at my own ridiculousness. Wine World sprung for a decorator? I don't think so!

Wine World, *The Southland's Largest Wine Retailer!* according to all of its advertising, as well as the ten-foot signs affixed above the entrance to each of its twelve retail stores, doesn't waste money on decorators. I'm guessing the office manager chose that painting. Or maybe the owner's wife.

I pull my phone out of my purse, not because I think anyone is trying to reach me but to give myself something to do. I don't look up again until the receptionist asks in a slightly awed voice, "Are those Louboutins?"

I follow her gaze to my foot, which I'd been nervously jiggling. I uncross my legs so both feet are now planted firmly on the carpet and the telltale red soles of my black Louboutin pumps are hidden from view. "Um, I'm not sure."

Bored Receptionist transforms into Nearly Hysterical Receptionist. "You're not sure? How can you not be sure? I would know if I'd spent five hundred dollars on a pair of shoes!"

Seven hundred, but I keep that observation to myself. "They were a gift," I lie. "I thought they might be knock-offs."

The receptionist pushes back from her desk and charges into the waiting area, and I dig my soles into the low pile. From the look of determination on her face, I'm afraid she might actually rip the shoes from my feet. But she just drops into the chair next to mine and leans down. "No way are those knock-offs," she says, reverently stroking the black patent leather. "I'm three credits away from getting my associate's degree in fashion design," she offers by way of explanation. "I know a knock-off when I see one."

I realize this woman is not going to be the person who decides whether or not I get this job—a job I really, really need, by the way—but I still don't want to contradict her, especially since she's right. But nor do I want to fess up to the fact that I'm wearing a pair of shoes that probably cost more than her weekly salary. I'm saved from having to respond by her buzzing phone. She runs back to her desk to answer it, then nods and says, "I'll bring her right down."

"CALL ME BIG MIKE," Michael McKenzie says as I shake his outstretched hand. The moniker suits him since he is several inches past six feet tall and well over two hundred pounds. I immediately imagine him playing football in his younger days, and now, in middle age, with thinning hair and an ample belly, watching the game from the comfort of his Barcalounger, a cold beer in one hand and the TV remote in the other. When he releases his grip, he motions to the chairs across from his desk. "Take a load off."

The chairs in his office are clones of the ones in the reception area, and I smile to myself as I realize Wine World must've gotten a discount for ordering in bulk. It seems fitting since that is their retail strategy as well.

I sit down and cross my legs, making sure the hem of my skirt is as close to my knees as possible and the sole of my raised shoe is pointing behind me. Not that I think Big Mike would recognize a Christian Louboutin, or even know what a Christian Louboutin is, but I'm not taking any chances.

I notice my resume sitting on his desk, but instead of scanning it in front of me as most of my previous interviewers have done, he leans back in his chair, folds his arms across his man boobs, and says, "So, Nina Roth, tell me why I should hire you."

I hate this question, but I'm prepared for it, having answered it at least ten times in the last six months. I launch into my well-prepared answer: "I have a degree in viticulture and enology from one of the best winemaking programs in the country, and I spent a year working at a vineyard in Sonoma. I doubt you will find another applicant who knows more about wine than me."

He unfolds his arms, but his shirt remains stuck to his chest, and I realize that his boobs may be bigger than mine. Sad, mostly for me. "I'm sure that's true," Big Mike says. "But this position is *selling* wine, not making it, and you've never worked retail before."

That's not entirely true. I didn't just *work* at that vineyard in Sonoma, I *owned* that vineyard, or my father did. But I always leave that fact off my resume. It prompts too many questions I don't want to answer. Instead I give him my stock reply: "I worked in the tasting room on weekends. I can track inventory, run a cash register, and I'm great with customers."

Big Mike smiles knowingly and finally reaches for my resume. "Yes, tell me a little more about Platinum Hills Winery. What exactly *was* your position there? Your resume doesn't say."

I swallow hard. This is the point in the interview where it always gets difficult. I don't want to lie, but I can't tell the whole truth either. I paste the smile onto my face and hew to my preplanned (and admittedly sexist—forgive me, feminists, but I *really* need this job) answer: "I guess you could say I was a bit of a Gal Friday. I worked in the vineyards, the cellar, the warehouse, the tasting room, wherever they needed another pair of hands. I'm sure you realize that my passion is for the winemaking, but I can absolutely handle the business side too. I negotiated all of our deals with distributors, and I'm sure I could handle negotiations with suppliers too," I add, assuming that would be most relevant for this job.

Big Mike smirks. "Normally those are all separate positions. It's very unusual for one person to be involved in everything."

"Yes," I acknowledge, mostly because I have no choice, "but Platinum Hills was a small winery, so we all pitched in."

And then it's as if someone watching us has flipped a switch because everything starts moving in slow motion, and we've become animated characters too! I'm no longer me; I'm a tiny mouse. And Mike is a hungry cat eyeing me as his next meal. I watch as a sly grin spreads across his face, then he licks his lips and pounces (metaphorically, of course). "I know who you are, Ms. Roth."

Fuck!

2

———

"Or should I call you Ms. Rothberg?" Big Mike continues.

My whole body sags under the weight of the truth. I don't know why I thought I could pull this off, but I had. Blind hope, I guess. Or maybe just desperation. *There's always Starbucks. Everyone says I make a great cappuccino.*

Then I mentally slap myself. *You will not give up. If you want this job, then fight for it!* I lift my chin and suck in my gut, forcing myself to sit up straight. "It's Roth now, Mr. McKenzie. Legally. But please, call me Nina. And please allow me to explain."

"Okay, Nina. Shall we start over, with the truth this time?"

I struggle to keep from busting out into a grin. I can't believe that actually worked! Normally when people find out who I really am, they tell me to get lost, or worse.

Big Mike reaches for my resume again. "Dalton, Columbia, a semester at the Sorbonne. None of that comes cheap, Nina."

"I know, Mr. McKenzie, but you have to believe me that I had no idea about my father. I swear it. I thought—"

"It's Mike, or Big Mike if you prefer."

Six months ago I wouldn't have believed that anyone would call him Big Mike to his face, but I've since learned just how rude people can be. "Mike, you have to understand. Everyone I knew skied in Aspen and sailed in St. Bart and went to private schools. I had no reason to suspect. No one did."

"You don't have to explain to me," he replies.

But clearly I do. I have to explain to everyone. This is the legacy my father has left me.

He tosses my resume onto his desk and leans back in his chair. "I don't hold the sins of the father against the son, or in this case, the daughter. My own father"—he pauses, as if searching for the right description, before settling on—"wasn't exactly the most reputable character. That's probably why I've gone in the opposite direction. I'm honest to a fault. And I expect total honesty from all of my employees. You make a mistake, you fess up, and we fix it. You lie to me or try to cover it up, you're fired on the spot. Is that going to be a problem for you?"

Oh my God, is he actually going to hire me? I sit up even straighter. "No problem at all, sir."

"Mike," he corrects.

"Mike," I parrot back.

"Here's the deal, Nina. This isn't a winemaking position; it's a wine *selling* position."

I'm about to interject when he holds his hand up and I quickly shut my mouth.

"I don't normally hire prep-school educated, Ivy League grads. Although to be fair, I don't normally get too many resumes from them. In fact, yours may be the first." He chuckles before turning serious again. "This position is for our Westside location, the crown jewel in Wine World's empire. And we need a certain kind of person."

A certain kind of person? "You mean someone with my winemaking knowledge and experience?"

He tries to tamp down on his smirk but can't quite pull it off.

"Let me be blunt. The customers at our Westside location are snobs with a capital S—and I have a feeling you'll fit right in."

He hadn't exaggerated his "honest to a fault." I'm slightly shocked, but only because he said it to my face. That's normally the kind of thing you hear whispered behind your back. I've actually been called much worse than a snob since my father's crimes have come to light, especially on social media, which I now studiously avoid.

"No disrespect intended," he continues. "In this instance, your background is an asset. You can talk the talk with all the pretentious, Tesla-driving assholes who only eat organic and only send their kids to private school. Hell, you used to be one of them!"

I swallow hard and force the smile back onto my face. *Suck it up, baby, you can't afford to be offended.* Besides, he's right. I did used to be one of them. Although I drove a Range Rover, not a Tesla.

"As I mentioned," he keeps on as if he hadn't just insulted me and every person I grew up with, "the Westside store is the crown jewel in Wine World's empire, and the owner wants to make it the premiere wine-buying destination even for people like you, who wouldn't be caught dead shopping in a big box wine store. It's the only location that stocks premium wines from around the world, and the only store that offers weekly tastings. And now the owner wants to set up monthly food-and-wine-pairing events at local high-end restaurants too. We need someone who can coordinate all of that, in addition to the usual day-to-day management of a retail wine shop. Does that sound like something you might be interested in?"

"Absolutely!" With the grand sum of twenty-nine dollars in my checking account, I'm interested in any job; the fact that this one is in the wine industry is just a bonus.

"Good. It pays thirty-eight thousand to start, which I know

isn't great, especially not for someone like you, but we offer excellent benefits, year-end bonuses, and for the right person, there's room for advancement. Still with me?"

"Definitely." If we'd been having this conversation over the phone instead of in person, I'd have already broken into a happy dance.

"Terrific. When can you start?"

"Tomorrow?"

"How about tonight? There's an in-store wine tasting scheduled for seven o'clock, and I'd really rather spend the evening at my son's baseball game than chatting up a bunch of pretentious a-holes." He nods at my little black dress and matching jacket, the closest I own to an interview suit. "What you're wearing now is fine for tastings and the restaurant events, but you'll want to tone it down for work days. Slacks, or skirts if you prefer"—he gives my legs an appreciative glance—"but there's no need to get fancy. Any questions?"

I know I should be asking about the practical details— Hours? Parking? When does the health insurance kick in?—but instead I ask the one question I'm dying to know the answer to: "How did you know who I was?"

I'd darkened my hair from honey blonde to chocolate brunette (although that was as much because I can no longer afford the every-six-weeks salon touch-ups as me trying to disguise my appearance), legally changed my last name, and moved to a new city where I knew no one and I thought (hoped) no one knew me.

Big Mike leans back in his chair and smiles like the hungry cat. "Remember that little check box at the bottom of the online application?"

No. I'd filled out hundreds if not thousands of online applications in the last six months. But I nod anyway.

"You agreed to a background check."

Sneaky. Everyone knows no one reads those online checkbox terms. Plus, isn't it a bit extreme? "You run background checks on candidates even before interviewing them?"

"Not normally, no. But I made up my mind about you the day I received your resume. I've been following your father's case since the beginning."

Ugh. I'm almost too afraid to ask. "You weren't one of his clients, were you?"

"Ha! I only wish I had that kind of money! No, I'm strictly a mutual fund guy. But my father was a crook too. Not as successful as yours—"

"Mine wasn't so successful in the end."

He shrugs. "Maybe, but I didn't get to go to a fancy prep school, and I paid my own way through community college while working two jobs."

"I'm really sorry"—a phrase I utter all the time these days—"but I swear to you, Mike, I didn't know."

"And if you had known, Nina Roth*berg*? What would you have done?"

3

———

What would I have done if I'd known the truth about my father?

It's a question I suspect most people are dying to know the answer to but are too polite to ask—except Big Mike, of course. God knows I've asked myself that question hundreds of times in the last eighteen months. I always tell myself I would've turned my father in, or at least threatened to turn him in to force him to confess. But he swore to the very end—even after he was convicted of twenty-two counts of fraud, perjury, money laundering, and a slew of SEC violations—that he was innocent. He claimed it was his business partner, who'd cut a deal with the government to testify against him in exchange for a lighter sentence, who'd orchestrated a Ponzi-type scheme without his knowledge and absconded with billions of dollars. And, despite the overwhelming evidence against him, I wanted to believe he was telling the truth.

I still want to believe. I want to believe that the loving, generous, outgoing man I called Daddy isn't, or wasn't, the ruthless swindler the media has made him out to be; that my whole life up until now hasn't been a lie.

THE BELL on the front door tinkles and I look up. I've only been working at Wine World for three months, and it's already an automatic response, like Pavlov's dog. But unlike Pavlov's dog, it's not food that I'm salivating for, it's a break from the monotony of the endless paperwork: tracking sales, tracking inventory, tracking online traffic, tracking everything!

Then I mentally readjust my attitude. I'm grateful for this job and grateful to Mike McKenzie for giving me this opportunity. Yes, the paperwork is tedious, but I love interacting with the customers and I get to do a lot of that too. I don't find them snobby and pretentious as Mike warned; they're just normal people. When I told that to Mike yesterday, he laughed in my face. "I knew you'd fit right in," he'd said. But before I could get too insulted, he informed me of the reason for his impromptu visit. He'd stopped by to congratulate me in person—sales at the Westside store have increased almost fifteen percent since I started working there, and the margins are even higher for the weekly tastings. "The owner's thrilled," he'd told me, and I was too. I finally had a marketable skill!

Not that I'm looking for another job—I'm not. I'm just hoping that somewhere down the line I'll be able to transition out of all of the paperwork and into sales full time. In fact, I'm sitting here fantasizing about having that exact conversation with Big Mike at my six-month review when the bell on the door tinkles and the past I've been so desperately running from finally catches up with me.

4

————

"Nina!" my half sister, Tiffany, shouts as she sprints toward me.

I'm perched on a barstool at the corner of the huge wooden tasting bar and I freeze in place. I actually have an office—a desk and a file cabinet in a windowless room I'm convinced used to be a supply closet (it even smells like cleaning fluid!)—but I rarely use it. After my first week on the job, I asked Big Mike if it was okay for me to do paperwork while sitting at the tasting bar. I'd switched to using my own laptop, instead of Wine World's ancient desktop computer, my first week, so in theory I could work anywhere. Although my fellow employees make it clear that they don't like having me out on the sales floor all day. No doubt they think I'm checking up on them since, technically, as store manager, I am their boss. And Big Mike probably thinks the same, which is why he'd given me an enthusiastic yes when I'd asked. But the real reason I spend my days working on my laptop at the tasting bar or walking around the sales floor redoing displays or writing up placards explaining the history, flavor concentrations, and best food pairings for each of the store's hundreds of wines, or one desperate day even reorganizing boxes in the warehouse for eight hours straight, is because if I sit in my windowless, airless, ammonia-infused office for more than a few minutes, I immediately start to sink into a deep depression—and I fear someday I won't be able to pull myself out.

So I'm easy to spot when Tiffany sprints into Wine World in her platform sandals, too-short skirt (even by miniskirt standards, this is a microskirt), and low-cut tank top that highlights her naturally big boobs. At fourteen her cleavage was twice the size of mine. Now at seventeen it's at least triple, although I'm not sure how much to attribute to nature's bounty versus her push-up bra.

I slide off my stool and allow her to embrace me, which has the effect of involuntarily burying my face in her naturally blonde but unnaturally stiff hair. I've tried for years to break her of her hairspray habit. I thought I'd prevailed when we'd lived together again briefly during my father's trial. But that was nine months ago. Without me in the bathroom ripping the can of designer label Aqua Net from her hand, she's regressed to her former ways. Or maybe it's her mother's influence.

"What are you doing here?" I ask when she finally releases me.

"Visiting my sister!"

I notice Jennifer, one of the sales clerks, openly staring at us from the sparkling wine section, so I pull Tiffany behind the bar and lower my voice. I've successfully avoided discussing my personal life with any of my coworkers for the past three months and I don't want to start now. "I told you this wasn't a good time. You can't stay. You have to leave." The sooner, the better.

"Why?" Tiffany's voice booms. "I just got here."

"Because I have a job now," I say through clenched teeth, "and I work a lot of hours."

"So? I don't need a babysitter. I'm fine on my own."

Fine on her own? Obviously she hadn't looked in the mirror this morning. If I dropped her off on Hollywood Boulevard, she'd be arrested for solicitation.

"Great. Which hotel are you staying at? I'll stop by for a visit."

She places both hands on her cellulite-free hips. "How am I supposed to pay for a hotel? You know the Feds cancelled all my credit cards."

I do know since they cancelled all of mine too—but only the ones that were in my father's name. I have one credit card in my own name and it's still active, although I rarely use it. Mainly I rely on my debit card. It's amazing how much less you spend when you're limited to the amount of money you actually have in your account.

"That's not my problem, Tiffany."

"You're a shitty sister, you know that?"

Half sister, but I don't bother to correct her. I know she hates when I point that out, and she's already on the verge of making a scene. "Maybe if you had called first—"

"I did call. Last week."

"Yes, and I told you not to come."

"And then you said you'd think about it."

Jesus H. Christ. Even two-year-olds know "I'll think about it" really means "No!"

"I did think about it, and the answer is still no. Maybe later in the summer when I'm more settled, but not now."

I place my arm around her shoulder and try to steer her toward the front entrance, but she quickly realizes what I'm doing and grows roots into the cement floor. I glance behind me and see that Jennifer has moved from sparkling wines to Cabernet Sauvignon, which just happens to afford her a clear line of sight to me and Tiffany. Even if she can't hear what we're saying, she'll be able to read our lips. I glance down at my watch.

It's only twelve thirty. I don't normally leave for lunch until closer to two, but today I'll make an exception.

I drop my arm from Tiffany's shoulder and spin around. "Hey, Jen, I'm going to grab an early lunch today. Can you hold down the fort until I get back?"

"Oh, sure," Jen says casually, as if she hadn't just been caught eavesdropping. "No problem."

"Thanks." I grab Tiffany's arm and drag her with me out the door.

It's not until we're both standing on the broiling-hot asphalt that I spot my nemesis.

5

I raise my voice for the first time since Tiffany appeared. "You brought *him* with you?" I say, nodding toward the man I hate more than I've ever hated anyone else in my entire life, times ten. "What the fuck were you thinking?"

"I didn't *bring* him," Tiffany says. "He brought me."

As if that's any better! "I told you not to tell anyone where I was. So not only can you not keep your mouth shut, but the first person you tell is a fucking cop!"

"Now, Nina," Agent Brody says, pushing himself off the hood of the dark sedan. Even unmarked, it's obviously a government-issue vehicle—so generic it stands out in a crowd. "Don't be angry with Tiffany. It's not her fault."

"Not her fault?" I yell.

"Give me a little credit, sweetheart. Do you honestly believe I didn't know where you were all this time?" He shakes his head at me. "You didn't even dump your cell phone."

He looks exactly the same—same cheap dark suit, same ugly tie, same annoying smirk, only now he's sporting knock-off Ray-Ban sunglasses instead of a trench coat. "Love the new hairdo, by the way," he says, running his fingers through his own in-need-of-a-trim brown locks. "It suits you."

"Thanks," I say before I can stop myself from accepting the compliment. Then I turn around and glare at Tiffany.

"It's not my fault," she says. "I had no choice." Then she turns to Agent Brody. "Tell her, Jason."

"Jason! What, are you two BFFs now?"

Agent Jason Brody jumps between us, as if this is a Jerry Springer episode and he's afraid I'm about to take down my own sister. "Why don't I buy you two lovely ladies lunch and we can discuss this like adults?"

"Good idea, *Jason*," Tiffany says, baiting me. "I'm starving."

"Yes, Tiffany, go have lunch with your new *cop* friend, and I'll just go back to work."

"Federal agent," Jason corrects, which of course I know. I'm baiting him too. "And I'm on your side, Nina."

I let out a harsh laugh. "If there's one thing you're definitely *not*, Agent Brody, it's on my side. I know you're only here because you still think I have some clue where the money is, which I don't. If I had billions of dollars at my disposal, do you think I'd be working at fucking Wine World?" *Oh shit.* I turn back toward the store, half expecting to see Jennifer with her ear pressed up against the glass, but thankfully she's nowhere in sight.

"You would if you were smart," Agent Brody says in a hushed tone, "which you are, Nina. You know the minute you touch that money you'll be arrested."

I want to scream or strangle him or lie down in the middle of the parking lot and have a temper tantrum like the toddler twenty feet away from us whose mother is clearly mortified, but who I'm actually grateful for because he's attracting attention away from me. I need to get a grip on myself before *I* destroy my new life. I take a deep breath and lower my voice. "For the hundredth, millionth, billionth time, I do not know where the money is. If you want to find it, you should be talking to my father's former business partner. You know, the man you only sent to prison for five years instead of a hundred and five because he testified against him at the trial."

"We've talked to Chet Owens many times and he's always maintained that your father was the mastermind, and only your father knows where the money's at."

"And you believe him?"

"What I believe doesn't matter. What matters is that we find your father."

"Then start looking at the bottom of the ocean."

Agent Brody smiles, revealing straight white teeth and a small dimple in his cheek. He looks almost human. Almost. "You don't really believe your father committed suicide, do you?"

I don't know what I believe anymore. After my father was convicted, but before he could be sentenced and sent to prison, he disappeared. He left a note proclaiming his innocence, then "borrowed" a small plane from a friend, one who hadn't invested money with him, and crashed it into the Atlantic Ocean. The Coast Guard recovered the plane's wreckage a week later, but my father's body was never found.

He could've been eaten by sharks—there was a heavy concentration of them in the area where the plane went down. Or he could've escaped—that's what Agent Brody and the rest of the world believes. Or he could've disappeared into the Bermuda Triangle. At different times I've believed all three.

I admit suicide would be out of character for my father, although it may have seemed better than the alternative— spending the rest of his life locked in a six-foot-by-eight-foot cell. My father was claustrophobic. He didn't even like taking elevators, and if it was anything less than ten floors, he'd opt for the stairs. Although my mother always said that was just vanity

—climbing steps was his way of staying in shape and showing off at the same time.

But it's been more than nine months since his supposed suicide. If he'd escaped, wouldn't he have found some way to contact me or Tiffany so we'd at least know he was alive? What parent would allow their child to think they were dead when they weren't?

That's why lately I've been embracing the Bermuda Triangle theory. That would mean my father's still alive, somewhere, in an alternate universe or fourth dimension, or maybe even kidnapped by aliens, but with no means of contacting me. That one makes me feel the best. And yes, I realize how pathetic that makes me sound.

I let out a long, heavy sigh. "Agent Brody, why are you here?"

"I'm here because I'm trying to help you."

This time I stifle the harsh laugh. "Help me how?"

"I want to help you prove your father's innocent."

6

And if you believe that lie, I've got a bridge in Brooklyn I'd like to sell you. But it's hot, and my feet are swelling inside my high-heeled shoes, and the thought of sitting down somewhere with strong air conditioning and a cold drink is too compelling to ignore. So I take Agent Brody up on his offer of lunch. Buying me a meal is the least that man can do for me.

He drives the three of us to a café six blocks away. If this were New York, we would've walked, even in uncomfortable shoes and high temperatures. But this is LA, so we drive. My environmentally conscious side feels a pang of guilt, but my blistered feet cheer.

We order at the counter—Greek salad for me, grilled chicken for Tiffany (she's obviously over her vegetarian phase), and a cheeseburger and fries for Agent Brody—then grab a booth by the window. Tiffany and I sit down across from each other, which presents a dilemma for Agent Brody. He doesn't want to appear to be literally choosing sides. He solves it by pulling over a chair from a nearby table and sliding it onto the end of our booth. I give him props for diplomacy.

I'm forced to wait until he returns to the counter for a refill

on his Coke before I can question Tiffany. "Why did you bring
him here? And keep your voice down," I admonish since he is
still within hearing distance.

"I told you. I didn't bring him; he brought me. He even paid
for my ticket. Then he picked me up at the airport this morning
and drove me straight to you. I had no idea where you worked,
but he knew all about your job."

I'd follow up with more questions, but I spy Agent Brody
walking back.

"I didn't know what flavors you girls liked," he says, setting a
plate down in the center of the table containing three giant
cookies, "so I bought one of each." Tiffany grabs the chocolate
chip before I can, so I take the peanut butter, and Agent Brody is
left with the oatmeal raisin. I don't feel the least bit sorry for
him. He deserves much worse.

"Everyone feeling a little calmer now?" he asks.

Neither of us can answer because our mouths are full of God
only knows how many fat-filled calories of delicious goodness,
but Tiffany nods and I shrug.

"Good," he says, breaking off a wedge of his own cookie but
keeping it in his hand. "Let's talk about the next step."

I swallow my bite of peanut butter cookie and wash it down
with a swig of iced tea before I say, "Simple. You take Tiffany to
the airport so she can catch the next flight to Philly, and I go
back to work." I've already been gone almost an hour.

Unsurprisingly, they both object.

"I am *not* going back to Pennsylvania. If you don't want me,
then I'll crash with Agent Brody."

The half-terrified, half-shocked expression on his face is
almost worth the near calamity of having Tiffany show up at my
workplace unannounced. Under any other circumstances he
likely would be thrilled to have Tiffany sharing his bed—most
men would. But she's the daughter of a convicted felon, one

whose case he worked on, and under eighteen too. That wouldn't look good in a performance review.

After a beat Agent Brody says, "Tiffany, you can't stay with me."

"Why not?" she demands.

"For one thing, I don't have my own place. I'm crashing on a friend's couch. And for another, it would be inappropriate, for *many* reasons," he adds before she can ask.

Only the first part surprises me. "A friend's couch? I thought the Bureau always put you guys up in cheap hotels."

"There are no cheap hotels in Los Angeles," he says, then finally pops the bite of cookie he's been holding into his mouth.

"There's that place on La Cienaga that rents rooms by the hour. Surely they must not be too expensive."

He gives me his trademark look—part stare down, part scowl, with a dash of evil eye. Clearly I am meant to be intimidated. And just as clearly, I am not. The man has already destroyed my life. There is nothing more he can do to hurt me. After a thirty-second glaring contest, he looks away. "Nina, the obvious solution here is for Tiffany to stay with you."

"I don't think so," I shout as Tiffany says, "I agree." Of course she does.

Then all three of us start yelling at once and don't stop until the assistant manager sidles up to our table on the pretext of clearing away our plates and whispers, "I'm sorry but you're disturbing the other customers. I'm going to have to ask you to leave."

For some reason I find this incredibly funny. Eventually Tiffany starts laughing too. But the assistant manager doesn't see the humor in it, nor does Agent Brody, who remains stone-faced, even as the other customers clap as we exit the front door, which just about sends me into spasms. *A year ago I was dining at Michelin-starred restaurants and now I'm being thrown*

*out of a third-rate café. If only my prep school friends could see
me now!*

Agent Brody drives us back to Wine World but won't let me
out of the car until I agree to meet up with him and Tiffany at
the end of my shift. I finally acquiesce because I have no choice
—I can't unlock the childproof locks and I've already been gone
from work for over an hour—but I have no intention of keeping
my word, a fact Agent Brody is no doubt aware of. The man may
be a jerk, but he's not an idiot.

I know I need to stay one step ahead, so before my shift ends,
I sneak out to my car and move it from the store's parking lot to a
nearby residential street. Then when I lock up for the night, I
leave through the warehouse entrance in the back. If Agent
Brody knew where I worked, he must know where I live too. So
instead of driving straight home like I usually do, I stop at a
fifties diner I've passed dozens of times but never eaten at
before. Their sign claims they have the best milkshakes in LA
and I decide tonight is the night to see if that claim is true.

I'd just ordered my Nutella ice cream shake and BLT
sandwich platter (I gave up counting calories when my father
was arrested—the constant stress keeps the weight off now)
when Agent Brody slides into the booth across from me.

7

Despite the precautions I'd taken, I can't say I'm surprised. Evading the law is new for me, but Agent Brody's been tracking down bad guys for a dozen years. He grabs the plastic-coated menu I'd just returned to the slot behind the condiments and asks, "What's good here?"

"I have no idea. This is my first time. But you should know that, shouldn't you? Haven't you been following me around LA for months?"

He bites down on his smirk, then turns his attention to the menu while I take a sudden interest in the Formica tabletop. Neither of us speaks again until the waitress stops by our table to take his order (western omelet and coffee). "I missed breakfast," he says when she departs.

As if I care what the man eats for dinner! "Where's Tiffany?"

"At a hotel," he says, scanning a text that just popped up on his phone.

"The Bureau will spring for a hotel for her but not for you?"

He returns his phone to his jacket pocket before I'm able to read the message. Deciphering upside down texts is not in my skill set—something I obviously need to work on. "The Bureau's not paying; I am."

"How chivalrous of you."

"Chivalry has nothing to do with it. It's called self-preservation."

Now it's my turn to smirk.

Then he clasps his hands in front of him and smiles. "I know you don't believe me, Nina, but I really am on your side."

How stupid does this man think I am? After he arrested my father, he interrogated me dozens of times. He asked me the same questions over and over and over again until I wanted to scream, spent months tracking my every move, testified against my father at his trial, and now all of a sudden he's on my side?

"What do you want, Agent Brody?"

"Please, call me Jason."

I glare at him in reply.

"I want to help your father." He raises his hand before I can object and says, "You know as well as I do that your father's still alive. That suicide was staged. We can at least agree on that, can't we?"

He takes my silence for acquiescence.

"Good, we're making progress."

I roll my eyes at him, then blow out a long sigh. I'm so tired. So very, very tired. I can't remember the last time I've slept for more than a few hours in one stretch. It must've been sometime before my father's face became a regular fixture on cable news. At first it was just the business channels—they had to fill that twenty-four-hour news cycle somehow. But then the story got picked up by the mainstream media and seemingly overnight Harold Rothberg became a household name. I suppose that's not surprising when you're accused of running one of the largest Ponzi schemes in US history and defrauding investors out of billions of dollars.

For months leading up to the trial, I couldn't turn on the TV or access the Internet without seeing my father's face, usually half-hidden by a baseball cap, staring back at me. At the time I thought the trial itself would be the worst of it. How wrong I was.

At the insistence of my father's lawyer, Tiffany's mother and I dutifully attended court each day wearing dark clothes and somber expressions. "Dress like you're going to a funeral," the lawyer had told us, and we did. It seemed appropriate since each day I felt like I was watching my father's execution happening in slow motion before my eyes. With each new witness, each new piece of evidence, each new argument by the prosecution, the man I knew disappeared, replaced by a heartless monster.

Tiffany wanted to attend court too, but my father insisted she go to school instead. (Another reason to believe he's innocent. Wouldn't a guilty man have wanted his gorgeous daughter to sit behind him in the courtroom every day to make him look good? There were eight men on that jury!)

I would've gone to court every day even if the lawyer hadn't required it, but I wasn't so sure about Tiffany's mother, my father's second wife. She wasn't really a stand-by-your-man kind of woman. *Gold digger* is a sexist term, so let's call the second Mrs. Rothberg an *opportunist*. If it isn't obvious already, she and I don't really get along. But I try not to hold that against Tiffany.

After a six-week trial, my father was convicted and again I thought the worst was over. And again I was wrong. Maybe if my father had actually gone to prison, the media would've moved on to the next scandal, but his suicide note and disappearance only fueled the story more.

Is he really dead or is he in hiding? was the lead-in on every news program for a week— until the wreckage was discovered *without* my father's body strapped to the pilot's seat. Then even those few commentators who'd at least publicly claimed they were undecided joined the majority who declared that my father's suicide was staged, and the media frenzy reached new heights.

"Too convenient," the US Marshal who was spearheading the worldwide manhunt for my father proclaimed on TV.

Which made me wonder . . . "Why are you still working on this case? I thought the Marshals were handling it now."

Agent Brody stretches both arms out along the back of the booth and I can see the sweat stains in his dress shirt. Yuck. He could be an attractive man if he made an effort—he's tall, well-built, with a decent face and thick dark hair that I imagine some women (not me) wouldn't mind running their fingers through. But it would be surface attractiveness only. The man is a first-class prick, and no personal stylist can fix that.

"It's been nine months with no leads. It's not their top priority anymore."

"But it's *your* top priority?"

"Yes."

I try to ignore the armpit stains and focus on his face. Why does this man have such a hard-on for my father? He hadn't known him or been one of his victims or had any friends or relatives who were. He arrested my father, assured he was convicted, and even got him sentenced to one hundred and five years in prison (the judge wasn't buying the suicide note without a body either). This is obviously personal for him, and I want to know why. So I ask.

Agent Brody stops fingering the crack in the vinyl seat back and stares across the table at me. "Because I believe your father's innocent."

If this is another one of his tricks to try to get me to tell him where the money is, it's a good one. Because the only thing I long for more than actually seeing my father again is someone (other than Tiffany) telling me they think my father's innocent too. And Agent Brody knows that. "Since when?" I ask.

He seems like he's about to reach for my hand so I pull it back. Instead he splays both of his palms down on the table. "Since now. Truly, Nina, I've never been more sure of anything in my life."

8

———

Whoa. All at once my head is spinning, my mouth is dry, and I'm having trouble remaining upright. A federal agent, a man who hounded me for information day and night, actually believes my father is innocent?

I barely acknowledge the waitress when she drops off our beverages. "Your food will be right up," she says before disappearing again.

"That looks really good."

For a moment I have no idea what Agent Brody is referring to. Then I look down at the creamy chocolate confection topped with a generous dollop of whipped cream sitting in front of me. I push the fountain glass across the table. "Take it. I'm not hungry."

"Are you sure?" he asks, but he's already unwrapping one of the two paper straws the waitress tossed onto the table before leaving. Apparently she assumed we were sharing.

I can't focus on food when he just turned my whole life upside down. *Again.* As much as I didn't want to, at some point I'd had to accept that my father might be guilty. Not at the very beginning, of course. Being a dutiful, loving daughter, when my father proclaimed his innocence, I believed him. But the evidence against him is *so damning*. And he never really had a good explanation for how all that money had disappeared. Whenever I asked, he always swore that he oversaw thousands of legitimate trades every day, and that Chet had duped him along with everyone else. The problem is, I can't really envision my father as a patsy. It seems even less likely than him committing suicide. But to her credit, Tiffany has never doubted our father. She's always believed he's innocent, even after he disappeared.

I shake my head and start and stop speaking multiple times before I'm finally able to form a coherent sentence. "I don't understand. You've spent the last two years telling anyone who would listen that my father is a criminal mastermind who cheated widows and orphans out of their life savings, stole funds from needy charities, and tortured puppies in his spare time. Now all of sudden you think he's innocent?"

Of course the waitress takes that moment to return with our food, and then I have to wait for Agent Brody to spread his napkin across his lap, sprinkle salt and pepper onto his omelet, and squeeze ketchup onto his plate from a very gassy-sounding bottle before he answers me.

"I never accused him of torture," he says as he spears a forkful of fried potatoes and dips them into the pool of ketchup oozing dangerously close to his omelet, "least of all, puppies." Then he smiles at me before he shoves the fork into his wide-open mouth.

I roll my eyes at him. "Fine. You never accused him of torture. But you know the rest is true. I think an explanation is in order, don't you?"

He shrugs his shoulders and shovels a chunk of omelet into his already-full mouth.

"I expect an answer, Agent Brody!" I hadn't intended to yell and immediately regret it. Only two of the nearby tables are occupied, but the diners at both stop their conversations and turn around to stare at me.

Agent Brody covers his mouth with his hand, saving me from a front-row view of his half-chewed food, which I appreciate, and says, "Start calling me Jason or I won't say another word."

I blow out my breath, loudly so there's no mistaking how angry I am, then lower my voice. "*Jason*, if you would like to continue *breathing*, I suggest you start talking. *Now*."

He swallows with a loud gulp and smiles at me. "Nina, did you just threaten a federal officer? Because that's a crime punishable by a sizable fine and up to six years in prison."

"You wouldn't dare."

He arches his eyebrows. "Wouldn't I?"

"No, because you know I have no money to pay a fine, and if I'm in jail, then I won't be able to help you find my father. That's why you're here, isn't it? You think for some crazy reason that I know where he is, even though I don't, and you brought Tiffany with you because you figured if *you* couldn't convince me to help you, that *she* could."

He stares at me a beat too long before he finally says, "Am I really that transparent?"

"Yes!"

He throws his head back and laughs, then reaches for my shake, which is now his shake, and takes a noisy slurp. "God, that's good," he says before sliding it across to me. "Have some before it's gone."

"I told you I wasn't hungry." But I could feel myself salivating at the sight of all that rich ice cream, and after fifteen seconds of pointless defiance, I reach for the second straw. He's right; it's delicious. Possibly the best shake I've ever drunk. The thought that my father really is innocent and that maybe someone can actually prove it and set him free no doubt boosts its flavor.

Yes, somewhere between threatening his life and sharing a shake with him, I decide to believe Agent Brody.

9

———

Agent Brody won't tell me exactly what evidence he's found that's made him change his mind about my father. When I push, he claims disclosing it could compromise the investigation and my father's ability to later use that information in court. But he hints that it's something Chet told him that made him take another look at the hundreds of thousands of pages of documents they confiscated before the trial.

"So my father was telling the truth?" I ask between bites of BLT. My appetite returned as quickly as it disappeared and I'd already sucked down the rest of our communal shake. "It was Chet all along?"

"Nina, I told you I can't divulge anything specific. Don't you want me to preserve the sanctity of the evidence for your father's appeal?"

"Of course, but—"

He holds up both hands as if he can physically shield himself from my barrage of questions. "No buts. No more questions. I've told you all I can tell you at this point. Now we need a strategy for moving forward."

I set down what's left of my sandwich and wipe the mayonnaise off my lips. "I'm listening."

"I was hoping you were going to do more than just listen."

"I told you, Agent"—I see the arch in his eyebrows and correct myself before he can admonish me—"Jason, I have no idea where he is. None. I don't even know if he's still alive."

"I thought we agreed the suicide note was bogus."

"Probably." It's the first time I say it out loud and I suddenly feel extremely disloyal. "But that doesn't mean his escape plan, if that's what it was, worked either. He could've been killed in the plane crash or drowned afterward."

"If he died, we would've found a body."

"Not necessarily. What if he was eaten by a shark?"

He gives me the arched eyebrows again, so I don't even bother mentioning alien abduction in the Bermuda Triangle.

"Let's assume for our purposes that your father did survive the crash," he continues. "Where do you think he'd go?"

After his disappearance I spent many sleepless nights pondering this same question. "Honestly, I have no idea. Someplace without an extradition policy?"

"It's extradition treaty," he says, "and that's no guarantee. There are plenty of places that don't enforce it anyway. Does he like cold weather or warm?"

"Both. He likes the change of seasons."

"Does he speak any foreign languages?"

"A little French and Spanish, and maybe a couple of words in German, but I wouldn't say he's fluent in any of them."

"Hobbies?"

This one requires some thought. I always considered my father something of a workaholic. "Golf, sport fishing, the occasional scuba dive."

"So he prefers warm-weather activities?"

An image of my father and me building a snowman together

pops into my head and I can't help but smile. It was so long ago —before Tiffany was born, when my parents were still married. I couldn't have been more than six or seven at the time. But the memory disappears as suddenly as it arrived and I'm once again staring across the table at an FBI agent who destroyed my and my family's life. "I wouldn't say that. We used to go skiing every Christmas."

This time Jason is the one to blow out a long, slow breath. "Nina, you're not being very helpful."

"I'm trying, but I honestly don't know anything. I did tell you that."

He stares at me a beat too long again, as if making up his mind about me, then nods his head. "Yes, you did. I'm sorry. I don't mean to badger you."

"That's a first!" The words rush out of me before I can stop them. I assume he'll be offended (even though he shouldn't be since they're true) but he just laughs.

"I did used to enjoy questioning you."

I knew it! He always looked way too happy every time he summoned me to the FBI's offices for another "chat" about my dad. "Nice, Agent Brody, real nice."

"What's wrong with a man enjoying his work?"

The jerk actually winks at me! "At the expense of an innocent woman? A lot, I'd say."

"Not *that* innocent." He smirks. "Did I ever tell you how much I appreciated your little video?"

I feel my face heating up and know that I'm now the color of a ripe strawberry. It was one sex tape! My first, and definitely my last. And I only agreed to record it because it was my boyfriend's birthday. I knew girls in college who'd made so many sex tapes they could've been porn stars and none of them ended up with their bare ass in front of the entire white-collar criminal division of the FBI. Life is so unfair.

I try to look innocent when I say, "I have no idea what you're talking about."

Agent Brody winks a second time and his smile grows even wider. "Sure you don't."

Prick.

I WAKE the next morning from the ringing telephone. The caller ID shows it's someone buzzing the apartment from the entrance to the building. Fed Ex and UPS don't normally deliver until the afternoon. OnTrac maybe? I'm trying to remember if I purchased anything online recently, and if so, what, when the phone rings a third and then a fourth time. I grab it the moment before the voice mail kicks in.

"About time," Tiffany says. "I was starting to think you spent the night with a 'friend.'" I can hear the air quotes.

As if. I have no "friends," or even any no-air-quote friends for that matter. I used to have friends, a boyfriend too, and many acquaintances. But that was before my father was accused of swindling them, their parents, siblings, and assorted relatives out of millions, and in some cases tens of millions of dollars. Now all I have is Tiffany—and we're related, so I'm not sure she counts as a friend.

"What are you doing here?" It's too early in the day for niceties.

"Let me in," she says. I'm about to say no when she adds the magic words: "I brought coffee."

I buzz her up and pull on my bathrobe. I still have my toothbrush in my mouth when I open my front door.

"You brought *him*," I say, nodding toward Agent Brody, who is standing behind Tiffany carrying a cardboard drink holder with three tall paper cups.

"No, he brought me," she says as she waltzes into my combination living room/dining room/kitchen and gives it the once-over. "Cozy."

She's not being sarcastic—well, maybe a little sarcastic—but I can't fault her reaction since mine was the same when I first arrived. My current abode is one-tenth the size of the apartment we lived in with our father. But that one is now owned by a Japanese businessman who bought it at auction after it was confiscated by the Feds. This one is owned by my mother's second husband and, before I moved into it six months ago, was used by them twice a year as a West Coast pied-à-terre. It's the only reason I can afford it—I live here rent-free, at least for the moment. My stepfather keeps threatening to start charging me. But I don't think it's really about the money. He lost a few million dollars investing with my father, and he's looking for someone to punish. Since my father's not available, he's had to settle for me.

"Good morning to you too," Agent Brody says and hands me one of the three coffee cups.

I spit my toothpaste into the kitchen sink and take a sip, immediately regretting it. "Yuck. You forgot the sugar. And the milk."

He pulls a wad of pink, yellow, and green sweetener packets out of his jacket pocket and tosses them onto the breakfast bar. Then he reaches inside another pocket and comes up with a wooden stirrer and two nondairy creamers.

"Aren't you a boy scout?" I say, reaching for the pink sweetener packet.

"Once upon a time," he says and walks into the apartment without waiting for an invitation—smart on his part since I wasn't planning on extending one. Even if we are ostensibly on the same side now, that doesn't mean I want him inside my apartment, especially not first thing in the morning when the only item of clothing standing between me and my birthday suit is a slinky bathrobe. The clingy black fabric doesn't hide much, but I tighten it around me anyway. I know he's seen much more of me on my sex tape, but that was a recording. I'm not about to give him a live show.

After I dump two sweeteners into my coffee, I add a splash of milk from the container in my fridge. "Breakfast?" I ask, hoping at least one of them turns me down. All I have left from last week's grocery shop is a blueberry yogurt and half an onion bagel.

Tiffany shakes her head and Agent Brody says, "I ate already."

I grab the yogurt and a spoon. No reason for me to go hungry. "So why are you two here at this ungodly hour?" Have I mentioned I'm not a morning person?

Tiffany spins on her gladiator sandals, which pair nicely with her brown leather miniskirt. She almost looks like an actual gladiator when she glares at Agent Brody. "You said she agreed to this?"

"She did," he replies. "In broad strokes."

I swallow my mouthful of yogurt. "I don't remember agreeing to anything involving Tiffany, in broad strokes or otherwise." I turn to my half sister. "What did he tell you?"

"That I could live here with you until we find Dad."

10

———

Of course I said no, no, and no again. But apparently I'm a giant wuss since it only took the two of them twenty minutes of badgering to get me to agree. In my defense, I was still on my first cup of coffee.

Hours later when I pull into the Wine World parking lot, I'm once again grateful to Big Mike for hiring me. Not only does this job provide me with a source of income but also a much-needed distraction. Something to think about besides my father and what he did (or didn't) do. And it now also provides me with a place to go to get away from Tiffany. I love my half sister, I really do, but I prefer her company in small doses. When I left the apartment this morning, she and Agent Brody were still trying to fit all of her crap into the den closet. Good luck with that! When I heard the words "Bed Bath run," I sprinted out the door.

So when I happily saunter into Wine World this morning and see Big Mike leaning against the tasting bar, I smile. Unfortunately my smile is not returned. I glance at the giant clock hanging on the wall above his head. It's only 11:50 a.m. so I know I'm not late—my shift doesn't start until noon. Then I catch a glimpse of Jennifer dusting bottles in the chardonnay aisle. As soon as we make eye contact, she looks away.

I don't have to play dumb. I am legitimately clueless as to what is going on here, so I just go with it. "Hi, Mike, I'm glad you stopped by. I was going to call you. Have you heard about that vineyard in Portugal with *three* varieties scoring over ninety points with *Wine Enthusiast*? I think we should consider stocking them. They're getting too big to ignore."

"Nina, we need to talk. Can we go to your office?"

I'm not sure the two of us can fit in my office, but I'm not going to argue the point with my boss. "Of course," I say and turn toward the back of the store.

I know he is following me because I hear the *clump, clump, clump* of his heavy shoes between the *click, click, click* of my heels on the cement floor. Otherwise our walk is silent and I am left to ponder what I did wrong. Because obviously I've done something wrong. The always chatty Big Mike is suddenly mute.

I unlock my office door and am once again struck by the overwhelming scent of cleaning solution. I turn to Mike. "What do you think? Black currant with a hint of tobacco? Or more of a ripe berry with smoky undertones?"

Normally he would appreciate my attempt to poke fun at what some people (including Mike) perceive as the pretentiousness of wine aficionados. But today he doesn't even crack a smile. I give it one more try: "Whatever it is I did or didn't do, I apologize and promise never to do or not do it again. Am I forgiven?"

But instead of a smile, I get a look of sadness, and if I'm not mistaken, a glimmer of pity, as he motions me inside. "Nina, please have a seat."

Shit, what have I done? I rack my brain but can't come up with anything. I took a slightly longer lunch yesterday because of Tiffany, but he can't be this upset about my returning to work five minutes late. And how would he even know? Unless Jennifer . . .

I drop my purse and laptop bag on my desk and leave them there. Normally I'd be stuffing my purse into my bottom desk drawer and booting up my computer before checking the communal kitchen for coffee, but today I do none of that. Today I sit and wait for my charges to be read and my sentence to be pronounced. *Is this how my father felt? If so, I understand why he ran.*

Big Mike reaches for the metal folding chair propped up against the wall of my office, abandoned there by its previous owner and unmoved by me. He pops it open in the small empty space across from my desk and sits down. It creaks under the weight of him, but neither of us comment on the noise. The office is eerily silent, the only sound the hum of the air conditioner, when Big Mike breathes out a long sigh. "Nina, I have to let you go."

It takes me a moment to process that I'm actually being fired. I mean, I was only five minutes late returning from a lunch break. Shouldn't I get a warning first? Was that really a terminable offense? "Mike, it was *one* time. Most of the time I don't even leave for lunch. And it only happened because my sister showed up unexpectedly. And I warned her not to come, but she never listens. My dad was threatening to send her away to boarding school if she didn't start behaving but then all the trouble started and—"

"What the hell are you babbling about? You sound like my wife."

Was that a compliment or an insult? I'm going with insult. "I'm being honest with you. I was five minutes late returning from lunch yesterday. I'm sorry and it won't happen again. But I wasn't trying to hide anything from you. I remember what you said in my interview. If I make a mistake, I fess up and we fix it. If I lie to you, I'm fired on the spot. But I'm not lying. I'm telling you the truth. I was just explaining why it happened. But it won't happen again, I swear."

There's no mistaking his expression this time—pity, definitely. "Nina, this has nothing to do with you being five minutes late from a lunch break."

I voice the only thought running through my head: "Then why am I being fired?"

"It's my fault."

Holding back the tears suddenly becomes easier. Anger has that effect on me. "Your fault? If it's *your* fault, then why am *I* being fired?"

"I never should've hired you. I knew the owner had lost money on account of your father. Not directly, I never would've chanced it if it had been a direct connection, but through one of the feeder funds. To my mind, it's his broker who's the responsible party, but. . ."

I stop listening since I've heard this all before, or variations of it. "I can't hire you because of your father." "A lot of my clients lost money with your dad and if they see you here it would upset them." "What would the neighbors say?" A few of Mike's words manage to penetrate my daze: *anonymous email, furious, good reference*, but mainly I just sit there thinking one thought over and over again: *What am I going to do now?*

Big Mike has an answer to that question. He hands me an empty wine box and tells me to clean out my office. It won't take long. The only personal items I brought in are a few magazines, a bag of pretzels, and a stained coffee mug. I toss them and my laptop bag into the box, which is still only half-full. Big Mike insists on carrying it to my car anyway. After he places the detritus of my short stint at Wine World into the trunk of my car, he hands me an envelope. I'm surprised to find two checks inside.

"You're not eligible for severance because you haven't been here long enough," he says, "but I convinced the owner that, after all your good work for the store, you were entitled to your performance bonus. Prorated, of course."

"Of course," I say and smile, and that's when the first tear slides down my cheek. Frankly, I'm surprised I've managed to hold them back this long. They've been threatening to spill out since the moment he told me I was fired. But now that the dam has cracked, I know the flood will follow, and that's not something I want Big Mike (or anyone) to see. Crying is a private endeavor. "I should go," I say and reach for my car door.

"Nina, I feel terrible about this."

He's not the only one.

"If there's ever anything you need"—he pushes his slightly damp business card into my hand—"my home and cell are on the back."

"Thanks," I mumble as I stuff the card into my purse. I feel the tears flowing and I need to make my getaway. But when I slide into the driver's seat, Big Mike kneels down beside me, wedging himself between me and the car door so I can't pull it closed. I'm stuck.

"Nina, you're a beautiful girl."

I let out something between a laugh and a hiccup. "Yes, I'm sure I look fabulous. I hear raccoon eyes are all the rage this year." I haven't looked in the mirror yet, but this isn't my first crying jag, and in a burst of optimism, I bought non-waterproof mascara at the drugstore last week.

"And people, *men*, always want to help beautiful girls."

I'm still stuck on *men*—don't women want to help other women too? Does he think we're all in competition with each other?—when he reaches out to me with his meaty hand and wipes the tears from my cheek with his thumb.

That's a little weird. I mean, he's not my boss anymore, but he was as of ten minutes ago. I'm still pondering the appropriate reaction to his inappropriate gesture when he slides his hand around to the back of my head.

What the hell?

11

———————

But before I can get the words out, his lips are pushing
down on mine. I try to scream but all that accomplishes is
giving his tongue access to the inside of my mouth. Gross! I
finally bite down, hard. From the pain shooting through me, I
know I've bitten myself too, but I hope the metallic taste
flooding my mouth means I've struck blood, and that not all of it
is mine.

"Aren't you the little spitfire," he says, wiping his lip. The red
liquid immediately reappears so I know I've nicked him too.

"And aren't you the big perv," I say, wiping my open mouth
with the back of my hand, trying to erase not just the blood but
the taste of him.

He laughs in my face. "You know I've wanted to do that since
the day you walked into my office in that short black skirt and
those come-fuck-me heels." He closes his eyes and leans back on
his feet, a look of pleasure crossing his face.

I want to throw up.

"You know how many times I've fantasized about bending
you over my desk?" he continues, still in his semi-trance. "And
that ass."

I need to get away from this man before something *really* bad happens. And to think a few short minutes ago I thought getting fired was going to be the worst part of my day. Since driving is no longer an option, I have no choice but to escape on foot. I have one leg over the gear shift and am sliding my butt across the parking brake when Big Mike grabs my upper thigh.

"Like a ripe peach," he says, squeezing, "and I can just imagine how sweet the juice is."

His fingers are sliding upward and I'm in full panic mode now, when I hear the voice of my nemesis: "What's going on here?"

I look over and find Agent Brody peering in through the passenger-side window, his sunglasses pushed to the top of his head. "Nina, are you alright?"

I've got tears streaming down my face, blood on my lips, my skirt pushed up to my underwear, a man twice my size squeezing my thigh, and I'm straddling a parking brake. Isn't it obvious that I'm not alright? But of course I don't say that. In fact, I am immensely grateful for his appearance—a first, I can assure you.

"Not really," I say as I simultaneously kick Big Mike in the stomach (I would've preferred the balls, but my legs aren't long enough) and attempt to pull down my skirt, which isn't really possible while I'm still straddling the parking brake. I manage to slide my butt into the passenger seat and cover my legs as Big Mike stands up.

"Are you okay?" Agent Brody asks, and I'm about to tell him in detail exactly how not okay I am when I look over and realize that the question was not addressed to me but to Big Mike, who's clutching one arm and swaying slightly.

"Are you fucking kidding me? The man almost rapes me and you're asking him how he's feeling?"

"Almost raped you?" Agent Brody says at the same time Big

Mike says, "I think I'm having a heart attack," before dropping to the ground.

12

───────

"So did he really have a heart attack or was he faking?" Tiffany asks as I relay the story to her over pizza and wine for me, Diet Coke for her (much to her consternation), later that afternoon. Agent Brody already heard it all in the parking lot of Wine World. He wanted me to go to the police station and press charges against Big Mike, but I refused. I want to forget the whole episode, the whole day, maybe the whole year.

"I have no idea," I say, refilling my nearly empty glass. I've never guzzled wine before; normally I savor it. But I've never been fired and almost raped in the same day before either.

"Aren't you curious?" she asks.

Now that I think about it, I realize that I am. That was awfully convenient timing for a heart attack. If I hadn't been concerned that Big Mike was about to die at my feet, I would've been kicking the shit out of him. "I suppose. But I don't know how I could find out. I'm not even sure which hospital the ambulance took him to." And I wasn't about to call any of my former colleagues for an update.

"I thought they always took people to the closest hospital."

"Probably, but I don't even know which one that is." I know

the names of the two big hospitals on the west side, but there could be more I'm not aware of. I've only lived in LA for nine months and thankfully haven't needed to visit any emergency rooms.

"There's an easy way to find out." She reaches for her phone and I think it's so she can ask Siri, but instead she calls Wine World. "Hi, I was at your store earlier today when that man collapsed in the parking lot." Pause. "Three kids, that's awful. Then it's even more important that I find him." Pause. "No, he lost his wallet and I want to return it to him." Pause. "Well, I'm not a hundred percent sure it's his, but it was on the ground near where the ambulance picked him up. Is his name Michael"— she snaps her fingers and I realize she doesn't know Big Mike's last name so I whisper "McKenzie" and she repeats it into the phone. From the huge grin on her face, I know her ploy has worked.

I wait until she ends the call to ask, "Since when did you become such a good liar?"

Tiffany smiles back at me, and for a moment her resemblance to our father is unnerving. "When Dad started enforcing my curfew," she replies and we both laugh. "Miss Jennifer-How-Can-I-Help-You told me Big Mike is at Saint Sebastian's."

"Condition?"

"I didn't ask. I didn't want to push my luck."

I agree with her strategy, but that still leaves us without an answer. "I guess we could call the hospital and ask for his room. If they admitted him, then we know he wasn't faking."

She snorts. "We can do *much* better than that." Then she picks up her phone again.

I listen with awe as Tiffany lies to several hospital employees pretending to be Big Mike's daughter, wife, and ultimately his personal physician who is vacationing in Paris with her family and just trying to find out if her long-term patient is dead or alive before the last train for Versailles leaves for the day and her family misses this once-in-a-lifetime experience.

"He wasn't faking," she says, finally shutting her phone. "It's possible that it was only angina and not a heart attack, but they won't know for sure until they get the results of the blood work back. But his blood pressure is through the roof, so they're concerned about that too."

"Wow. I hope it's not serious."

"Don't you dare feel sorry for him! He attacked you today. And fired you. Who knows what would've happened if Jason hadn't shown up when he did. He could've killed you."

"I don't think Mike would've killed me. Forced himself on me, possibly, but—"

"Definitely. He wanted to taste your juice, Nina. What do you think that means?"

I can't believe my baby sister is lecturing me about sex. I have to laugh. "I know what it means, Tiffany. I'm not a virgin."

She laughs too. "I know. I saw your sex tape."

I'm no longer laughing. Now I'm stunned. "How the hell did *you* see it?"

She laughs even harder. "Oh my God, Nina, my entire school saw it. It was on YouTube for a while until they took it down. It got over three hundred thousand views before they pulled it."

I bury my face in my hands. I was sure this day couldn't possibly get any worse, and it just had. "Do you know if Dad saw it?"

"He wouldn't watch it."

"But he knew about it?" He never mentioned it. Although it's not the kind of thing one would normally bring up in conversation. *Hi, sweetheart, how was your day? Make any good sex tapes lately?*

She nods, then looks away. "Someone sent it to him. Anonymously."

"He talked to you about it?" I couldn't believe our father had discussed my sex tape with Tiffany but not me. Not that I *wanted* to talk to my father about my sex tape. But I always thought he and I had a closer relationship than he had with Tiffany.

"No," she says, taking a sudden interest in the living room rug.

At first I don't understand how she could know so much about what my father knew if they had never discussed it, then realization smacks me in the head. "It was your mother, wasn't it?"

"I'm really sorry, Nina. If I knew she was going to send him the video, I never would've shown it to her."

I'm gobsmacked. Again. "You mean *your mother* was the one who sent it to Dad 'anonymously,'" I say with the air quotes.

Tiffany finally looks up from the rug. "Yeah, what did you think I meant?"

"I thought your mother was the one who told you that someone had sent it to Dad, not that your mother was the anonymous sender!"

"Oh," Tiffany says and returns her attention to the rug. "Sorry."

"I don't understand. Why would she do that?" I know the woman doesn't like me; and the feeling is mutual. As far as I'm concerned, she's the person most responsible for my parents' divorce. Not an unreasonable belief since she and my father started seeing each other while he was still married to my mother. But I still never thought she would *intentionally* set out to hurt me.

Tiffany shrugs, still refusing to look up. "I think she was mad about something your mother said about her to the press."

I remember that day. I had just moved back into my dad and

Raylene's apartment because the trial was starting in a few weeks and I wanted to be there for my father in case he needed me. Some reporter had caught my mom coming out of the hairdresser's and supposedly she said something along the lines of my father being an honest businessman when *she* was married to him, sort of implying that he turned to criminal activity on account of Raylene, or at least that was the headline of the story that appeared everywhere later that day. Raylene went ballistic and threatened to sue my mother for slander. My father reminded her that they had enough legal troubles (and legal bills) and didn't need to add any unnecessary litigation to the mix. Eventually Raylene dropped it, or so I'd thought. Apparently she just took her revenge out on me. She was probably the one who uploaded the sex tape to YouTube. *Fucking bitch.*

I'm so angry I can barely see straight. "I think you need to leave."

Tiffany looks up at me, all doe-eyed innocence. "Why?"

Does she really have to ask that question? Is it not obvious?

"Is this about what my mother did?" she continues.

"Yes, this is about what Raylene did. And what you did too. I can't even stand to look at you right now. Just get out."

13

"You know she didn't do it on purpose," Agent Brody says. I didn't invite him over, but that has never stopped him before and didn't today either. At first I refused to let him in, but after he buzzed my apartment for ten minutes straight, I relented. I told him he had five minutes and then I was kicking him out. He'd already been here fifteen. "She knows what Raylene's like. Why do you think she doesn't want to live with her anymore?"

Agent Brody takes another sip from his wineglass. Since I was still drinking when he'd arrived, I'd felt obliged to offer him some too. I'd thought he'd turn me down since he was on duty, but he'd eagerly accepted. "I think that has more to do with Raylene's new boyfriend. Have you ever seen him with Tiffany?"

For the first time in the two hours since I'd kicked Tiffany out, I stop being blindingly angry with her. "He didn't . . ." I can't bring myself to say it. I don't even want to think about it. I know Tiffany doesn't look like a child, and I'm almost positive she's not a virgin anymore, but the thought of Raylene's new boyfriend, who is more than double my age, doing to Tiffany what Big Mike tried to do to me makes me want to puke. Luckily

I make it to the bathroom before my stomach catches up to my head.

"You okay?" Agent Brody calls from the other side of the locked bathroom door.

"Yes," I call back. With my stomach now empty, I actually do feel a little bit better. After splashing water on my face and brushing my teeth, I rejoin him in the living room. The wine has disappeared, replaced by two glasses of water.

"Drink this," he says, handing me one of the glasses. "And in answer to your previous question, no, I don't think he forced himself on her. Not yet at least. But Raylene was concerned enough to want her out of the house."

"Concerned for Tiffany? Or concerned that Rich Boyfriend might decide he prefers a younger model?"

"You know Raylene. Draw your own conclusions."

The latter, of course. The only person Raylene is ever concerned about is herself. If it came down to a choice between her daughter's well-being and her own, I have no doubt which one she'd choose. She isn't about to let Tiffany come between her and her new sugar daddy. "God forbid the woman should actually go out and get a job like the rest of us."

"Come on, Nina, be realistic. What kind of job do you think Raylene could get? You think she's going to go from being the pampered wife of a Manhattan billionaire to ringing up diapers at Walmart?"

An image of Raylene with her expertly highlighted hair and evening makeup, wearing six-inch heels and a skintight dress (just the way my father liked her), standing in front of a cash register with a plastic name tag pinned to her breast pops into my head, and I laugh. "I don't think that woman has ever changed a diaper in her life. That's what nannies are for."

"My point exactly. Women like Raylene don't get jobs; they get rich men."

I would normally feel obliged to defend my sex, but in Raylene's case it's true. And Agent Brody's disdain for her is so obvious that it actually makes me like him the tiniest bit.

I gulp down the rest of my water, then lie back on the couch. The events of the day must be catching up with me because I'm suddenly exhausted. "So where does all this leave Tiffany?"

"That's up to you."

"You're not going to force me to take her back?"

He shakes his head. "You are your own person, Ms. Rothberg. No one can force you to do anything."

I can barely keep my eyes open, but I manage to say, "It's Roth now, remember?"

"How could I forget?"

His words are innocuous; it's his tone that concerns me, as if he knows something I don't. But I'm too tired to think, too tired to do anything but slip into a dreamless sleep.

I WAKE TWELVE HOURS LATER, still lying on the couch but with a dry mouth, a stiff neck, and a blanket someone has placed over me. The sun hasn't risen yet and the apartment is still dark. I kick off the blanket and head to the kitchen. I never did make it to the grocery store yesterday. I'm even out of yogurt, normally a staple in my fridge. I down a glass of water, drop the last half bagel into the toaster oven, and power up the Keurig. Then I head into the bedroom to change out of my slept-in clothes. I freeze in my tracks when I notice the lump in my bed.

14

"What the hell are you doing?" I shout at Agent Brody, who's snuggled under my duvet.

His eyes flash open and he sits up, and I'm glad to see that he is at least wearing a T-shirt, although in the semidarkness I can't discern if it's his own or one of mine. For a moment he appears panicked, as if he doesn't know what he's doing in my bed either, then his shoulders relax and he yawns. "What time is it?"

"Time for you to get the hell out of my house. Who told you it was okay for you to sleep here? And in my bed no less!"

"You were passed out on the couch and Tiffany's sleeping on the pull-out in the office. I didn't think my getting arrested for driving under the influence would help your father's case, so I decided to spend the night here and this was the only bed left. Would you have preferred I left it empty and slept on the floor?"

"I would've preferred you get the hell out of my life. Just take Tiffany and leave already."

"This again?" He sighs and lies back down. "It's too early in the morning to fight with you. I haven't even had my coffee yet."

"Then go get your coffee and don't come back."

"Can you two keep it down in there?" Tiffany shouts from the next room. "Some of us are trying to sleep."

I lower my voice. "And who the hell told Tiffany she could come back?" I know it wasn't me.

Agent Brody rubs his fingers up his face and through his hair, making his bedhead even worse. "Nina, please. Can't the three of us just sit down and discuss this later when we're actually all awake? Not all of us went to sleep at six o'clock, you know."

And that's another thing that's bugging me—I never go to bed that early, and certainly never sleep for twelve hours straight! "Did you drug me?"

"Drug you? You can't be serious."

"I was fine until you handed me that glass of water and then—"

"You were far from fine. As I recall, you were drunk off your ass, then puking your guts up in the bathroom."

"I wasn't drunk. A little buzzed maybe."

"Ha! Try three sheets to the wind. If I had given you a Breathalyzer test, I guarantee you would've been at least twice the legal limit."

"So what? I wasn't driving. Now it's a crime to drink in your own home?"

He lies back down and sighs again, as if my mere presence *in my own bedroom* is an annoyance to him. "Can we *please* talk about this later?"

I stride across the room, reach for the corner of the duvet, and yank it down to his knees. My glance is involuntary, but I'm very thankful that he's wearing underwear, and in a dark color too. I can't make out any unsightly bulges although I know they're there. "Sure, right after you get out of my bed." Then I stalk off into the bathroom and slam the door shut.

I silently fume as I take a long, hot shower and loofah my

body until I'm sure every last dead skin cell has dissolved down the drain. By the time I open the door again, the bathroom is filled with steam and Agent Brody is gone. He pulled up the covers and tossed the throw pillows on top in a clumsy attempt to make the bed before he left, but I strip it down to the mattress. I know I can't remove Agent Brody from my life, not yet anyway, but I can remove all traces of him from my bedroom.

I'm kneeling in front of the washing machine, stuffing in sheets and pillowcases, when Tiffany taps me on the shoulder and I nearly jump out of my skin. I forgot she was still in the apartment. I thought I was alone.

"Need some help?" she asks.

"Do you even know how to do laundry?" I have no right to be so condescending since I didn't learn to use a washing machine until I left for college. Before that I'd leave the dirty clothes piled up on a chair in my bedroom and they would magically reappear clean and folded in my dresser or hung up in my closet.

"Carmen barely speaks English and she can do it. How hard can it be?"

I slam the door shut and turn the knob, and the machine whirs to life. "You can do the next load," I say, nodding at the duvet cover. It's too big to fit with the sheets.

I head to the kitchen next and Tiffany follows. In my fury at finding Agent Brody in my bed, I'd forgotten about my toasting bagel, which is now cold and black. I dump it into the garbage and pop a K-cup into the coffeemaker. For the next sixty seconds the only sound in the kitchen is the whirring and hissing of the Keurig machine. Tiffany waits until I'm stirring in milk before she asks, "Can I have some?"

I shrug and take my coffee into the living room so I can be alone. A minute later Tiffany joins me, steaming mug in hand. "So are you going to talk to me or not?"

I don't answer, obviously choosing "or not."

"I said I was sorry," she continues. "I don't know what more you expect me to do."

"Well, for starters you could get the hell out of my apartment."

"And go where, Nina? I don't know anyone else in LA."

"Then go back to Pennsylvania."

"I can't," she says. "Raylene kicked me out."

The story Agent Brody told me last night comes flooding back to me and I finally look at my half sister. This morning, in duck-themed pajamas with no makeup and her hair pulled into a sloppy bun, she actually looks like the teenager she is. I want to hear her version of what happened, so I feign ignorance. "Why? What did you do?"

"Nothing," she says and tears start trickling down her cheeks. "I mean, it's not my fault Raylene's boyfriend likes me."

"Tiff, did he try something?" Agent Brody said he hadn't, but Tiffany may not have told him the truth. Although I wouldn't put it past her to lie to me too. Before yesterday's performance on the phone, I might've said I'd know if she was lying, but now I'm not so sure.

She shakes her head, but the tears start flowing harder. "No, not really."

"Not really?"

"We didn't, like, have sex or anything if that's what you're asking."

I'm relieved but still wary. "Did you do other things?"

"Just kissing, mostly."

"Mostly?"

"I gave him a blow job once, but—"

"You gave your mother's boyfriend a blow job! Are you insane?"

"It was just one time. And Raylene was out of town that week."

"You think that makes it alright?"

"No, it was awful. He took *forever* to come. All the other guys I've been with were quick, but with him it just went on and on. I thought I was going to be sick. I don't know how Raylene can stand it."

I can't believe what I'm hearing. I don't even know where to begin. I start pacing the small living room, starting and stopping speaking several times before I can finally deliver the words calmly, or semi-calmly. "Why on earth would you give your mother's boyfriend a blow job?"

She shrugs. "I don't know. I was curious."

"About what? You've obviously done it before."

"Yeah, but only with guys my own age. And one of the girls at school said older guys are better lovers."

"She probably meant guys in their twenties or thirties, not their sixties!"

"Yeah, maybe. I think her boyfriend is, like, in college or something."

"So that was it? You just gave him one blow job?"

"Yeah. The BJ kind of killed it for me."

Killed it for her? "So you were actually *planning* on doing more but you didn't because he took forever to come?"

"Well, that's not the *only* reason. His skin was all wrinkly too. And he kept grabbing the back of my head and, like, pushing me into him, which was just gross. The other guys I've been with just kind of sat there and I did what I wanted. I like that a lot better."

We were definitely getting into TMI territory. "So Raylene found out about the blow job and kicked you out?"

"God, no! If she ever found out I gave her boyfriend a blow job, she'd kill me."

"Then why'd she kick you out?"

Tiffany shrugs and tears start trickling down her cheeks again. "She said she was doing it for my own good; she was afraid Jimmy might try to 'take advantage of me.'" She adds the air quotes. "As if. I got a thousand bucks out of it. I'd say I'm the one who took advantage."

I feel like my head's about to explode. "He *paid* you?"

"Don't say it like that. I didn't ask for the money. He just gave it to me to be nice."

"You think he gave you a thousand dollars to be *nice*?" Could she really be that naïve? Possibly. She's only seventeen.

"Yes, *nice*. He cares about me, Nina. He told me I was very special to him and that I should use the money to go buy myself something beautiful because beautiful women deserve beautiful things."

I shake my head. "Oh, Tiffany."

"What? You think I was wrong to keep the money?"

This whole situation is wrong on so many levels I don't even know where to begin.

"I don't regret it, you know," she continues, "even if it was kinda gross."

I'm almost too afraid to ask. "Because he gave you money?"

"No. I mean, the money was great. After what happened with Dad, Raylene cut my allowance down to next to nothing, so I really needed that money."

I don't ask what she "needed" it for. I take a leap of faith that it's not drugs, and assume she needed it for clothes and Starbucks.

"It's because I know that Jimmy really cares about me, you know, as a person."

"You think he cares about you because he paid you for a blow job?"

"No, because he wanted to . . . do other things that day. And I was nervous because I'd never done those things before and he said that was okay, he only wanted me to do what I was comfortable with, and that's when I gave him the blow job. He really does care about me, Nina. I know you don't think so, but it's true."

For the first time in my life, I agree with Raylene. Getting Tiffany away from Jimmy is the best thing for her. Of course, Raylene could've, and should've, just broken up with the letch when she realized he was after her seventeen-year-old daughter. But Raylene's concern for Tiffany's welfare only goes so far; it would never rival her concern for her own.

I collapse onto the couch and sigh, and Tiffany immediately scoots over to me so our thighs are almost touching—it was a game we used to play when she was a little girl, how close she could get to me without actually making contact. I am reminded again that even though she looks like an adult, she's still a child.

"I guess you could stay here for a little while. At least until we figure something out."

She smiles wide. "Really? You're not kicking me out?"

I shake my head. How could I after what she just told me? "But don't get too comfortable. This isn't permanent. It's only until we figure out your next move."

"Oh, I've got that covered."

That surprises me. "You do?"

"Yeah. You and I and Agent Brody are going to find Dad, prove he's innocent, and then we'll all move back to New York and be a family again."

Sometimes the girl breaks my heart.

15

───────

"Absolutely not," my mom says. She's shouting so loudly I have to hold the phone away from my ear.

"But Mom—"

"It's not up for discussion, Nina. And frankly I'm surprised you would even suggest it." She finally lowers her voice. "I'm not going to mention this to Richard because it'll just upset him. His blood pressure is already higher than it should be. If he found out that your father's daughter was staying in his apartment while your father is out there somewhere spending all of his money—"

"We don't know that, Mom. We don't know what happened to Dad. We don't even know for sure that he's guilty." So far I've only told her about Tiffany. I haven't yet gotten to Agent Brody and his revelations.

"Don't start that again, Nina. He was convicted."

"But innocent people get convicted all the time." My mom used to be a paralegal before she married my father. After their divorce, she flirted with the idea of going to law school. But then she met Richard and decided she'd rather be a rich housewife again.

"No, Nina, they don't. The few who do are poor minorities with inadequate representation, not rich white men with high-priced defense attorneys."

"You don't know that. You don't even work anymore. All you do is plan dinner parties and summers in the Hamptons."

"That is not all I do and you know it."

It's true. My mother does a lot of charity work too, mostly fundraisers for museums and public school art programs or the latest artistic cause du jour. She's a frustrated artist at heart.

Her voice softens. "Listen, honey, I know you're still upset about your father. And I don't blame you. He had us all fooled."

I know there is no point in telling her that Agent Brody now thinks Dad is innocent. Her mind is made up about him, and it was long before he was convicted.

"But regardless," she continues, "you need to get Tiffany out of that apartment. Today, if possible, and absolutely no later than tomorrow morning. Richard's real estate agent is stopping by tomorrow afternoon to give us an appraisal, and I do not want Richard finding out about this. It would be bad for all of us if he did. Do you understand me?"

I understand. There's no one my mother's second husband hates more right now than my father. In the old days, when my father was consistently earning Richard a ten percent return on his money, he tolerated him. But once my dad was arrested—and Richard's millions disappeared—so did the veneer of politeness. Their war has been public ever since. Richard even offered to testify against my father at the trial, but the government turned him down because he had nothing useful to offer. I think that made Richard even angrier, which I hadn't thought possible. My mother said it was because it made him feel impotent. I didn't ask if that extended to the bedroom. I didn't want to know. I'm not sure how she persuaded him to let me stay in this apartment rent-free. I don't want to know that either.

"What am I supposed to do with her, Mom? I can't send her back to Raylene. She's not just dating Jimmy, she's living with him." I hadn't told my mother everything Tiffany had told me, but enough to know that it would be a very bad idea for Tiffany and Jimmy to reside in the same house.

"That's not my problem, Nina. And it's not yours either. She is *Raylene's* daughter; *Raylene* needs to find a solution."

"But Mom—"

"No buts, Nina. It was an uphill battle getting Richard to agree to let *you* live in the apartment until he sells it. He will never agree to Tiffany's staying there too. And I can't say that I blame him. You need to think about what your father's done to him. To all of us."

Does she think I don't? For months and months that's all I've thought about. It's still the first thought that enters my mind when I wake every morning, and during those middle-of-the-night arousals too. "Tiffany's not responsible for what Dad did, and neither am I."

"I know that, sweetie, and I didn't mean to imply otherwise. I'm sorry if you took it that way."

"Well, how else am I supposed to take it? You tell me you had to beg Richard to let me stay in an *empty* apartment because he's pissed at Dad, and you won't even ask him if Tiffany can stay too because you think he'll flip out."

Her voice rises to match mine. "You need to look at this from Richard's perspective. Your father stole millions of dollars from him and put his entire business, a business he spent thirty years building, at risk. Richard had to lay off half his work force. Think about that, Nina. Think about all those people, some of whom had worked for Richard for their whole careers and are now unemployed because of what your father did. Those people have families too. Your father . . . he destroyed a lot of lives."

Mine included. And Tiffany's. But at least I have a roof over my head (until the apartment sells) and food to eat (until my savings from Wine World runs out). "I know, Mom. I feel terrible for all those people. I'm sorry if you think I don't care, because I do. I just don't know what I can do about it."

"Nothing, honey, it's not your responsibility. You did nothing wrong. And I'm sorry about Tiffany. She's a sweet girl. But I just can't ask Richard to let her stay there. It would be too much for him. I hope you understand."

I do understand. But I have no one else to turn to.

16

I send Tiffany to the store to buy staples—coffee, milk, yogurt, and bagels—so I can have privacy when I call Raylene.

"Tiffany is older than I was when I left home," Raylene says. "She'll figure something out."

"You want her to start stripping for a living?"

Before today I'd only hinted that I knew how my stepmother had begun her so-called modeling career, a career she gave up the second my father proposed, which he didn't do until she told him she was pregnant with Tiffany. He was infatuated with Raylene, but he still had enough brain cells left to hire a private investigator to run a background check on her. Coming from humble beginnings himself, he wasn't put off by Raylene's past, but he chose not to share that information for obvious reasons. I only found out a few years ago when I stumbled upon the file in his desk while I was searching for a clean pad of paper.

There's a sharp intake of breath on the other side of the phone line, but Raylene doesn't rattle easily. "Tiffany has a great figure. I'm sure she would do very well as a dancer. And she's in LA now. She could get into acting."

"Don't you think she should finish high school first?"

"You're such a snob, Nina. You *and* your father. You think prep schools and fancy degrees are what matter."

For the record, I'm the only one who went to prep school and has fancy degrees. My dad attended a third-tier state college, which he chose because they offered him a track scholarship. Then his father died in his senior year and he dropped out because he needed to get a job to support himself and his mother. He promised my grandmother he'd go back to school and get his degree someday, but he never did. He was making too much money as a stock broker. I'm actually the first person in my father's family to graduate from college.

"Yes, Raylene, I think a high school diploma is an asset. If that makes me a snob, then so be it."

"Degrees help, I don't deny that," she says. "But what really matters is what you do with your God-given talent. And Tiffany has both beauty and brains. She'll be fine. You both will."

I hate to admit it but I preen at the backhanded compliment. There is much to despise about Raylene, but I cannot deny that the woman always lands on her feet, and at this moment I long for that talent. So I ask myself, *What would Raylene do if she were me?* The answer is obvious. "No one can live on love alone, Raylene. We need money."

She actually laughs. "Yes, I suppose that's true. But as you're well aware, Nina, what your father didn't take with him, the Feds did."

I can't believe I'm about to say this but somehow the words leave my mouth. "And what about Jimmy? I hear he's very fond of Tiffany. Surely he would want to help her if he could." Being a bad person isn't so hard after all. I only feel a tiny bit guilty.

I can practically hear the gears clicking in her brain as she calculates the odds of Tiffany or me contacting Jimmy directly and what that would mean for her if we did. Surely she told him that Tiffany left of her own accord. If he finds out that Raylene kicked her out, he won't be pleased. Not when he could be banging both the mother and the daughter too.

"How much?" she asks.

17

"You should've asked for more," Tiffany says when she returns from the store and I relay my conversation with Raylene.

"Sorry, I'm new to blackmail. I'll try to do better next time."

Tiffany laughs, but I'm actually worried. Did I just commit a crime? Could I go to jail for this? I'm tempted to call Agent Brody and ask him, but I don't want to give him any more ammunition to use against me. I'll Google it later.

And what I don't tell Tiffany is that I did ask Raylene for more. A lot more. Eight thousand dollars more, to be precise. But she told me all she could get her hands on without Jimmy noticing was two grand. And Tiffany isn't going to last long on two thousand dollars, not if she has to pay rent too.

I suggest an early lunch and Tiffany readily agrees (neither of us had eaten breakfast). I drive us to a nearby Chinese restaurant that advertises inexpensive lunch specials: soup or salad, a main course, and dessert all for $5.99! When we arrive a few minutes after noon, the place is already packed with senior citizens.

"What are you getting?" Tiffany asks as she peruses the menu.

"The chicken." I always get the chicken.

"Which one? There are, like, twenty chicken dishes on here."

That's because she's reading the main section of the menu instead of the daily specials, which are printed on the back page. I turn her menu over and point to the listings: kung pao chicken, beef with broccoli, or shrimp lo mein. "Choose one," I say.

"But I don't want any of those. How about we order a bunch of dim sum instead?"

"You're broke, Tiffany. You can't just order what you want because you want it. You have to buy what you can afford."

"I'm not broke! You just said Raylene is sending me two thousand dollars."

"The money's not here yet."

She laughs. "You don't think she's good for it? Jimmy's loaded."

I know she's good for it, mostly because I made it clear to her that if the money didn't arrive by the end of the week, my next phone call would be to Jimmy. "No, I'm sure she'll send it. But I don't know if or when she'll be sending more, so you need to make that money last."

Tiffany dismisses my concerns with a wave of her manicured hand. "If she doesn't, then I'll just go out and get a job."

"Doing what?"

"I don't know. What did you do at that wine store?"

It's the first time I've thought about my current unemployment since Big Mike had attacked me. The thought of having to look for a job again makes my stomach clench. "My situation is different than yours. I have a master's and work experience. You haven't even graduated from high school yet."

"So? I could be a hostess. Or a bartender. I hear bartenders make great tips."

"You're not even old enough to drink!"

She rolls her eyes at me. "Fine, then I'll just be a hostess. Or a barista. I'm old enough to drink coffee."

"And you think you can support yourself on a hostess's or a barista's salary?"

"Sure, lots of girls do it."

"No, Tiffany, lots of girls do not do it. Not unless they're doing something illegal too. Do you have any idea what the rents are in this neighborhood?"

"I'm not paying rent. I'm living with you."

I haven't yet told her about my conversation with *my* mother, only about my conversation with hers. "Yeah, about that . . . Richard is selling the condo. The Realtor is coming tomorrow to appraise it. We need to get your stuff out tonight."

"Why? And why is Richard selling? I mean, the place is tiny but the location's great. I can walk to all the stores and restaurants, and the beach is only a few blocks away."

"He needs the money." I pause but decide she needs to hear it. "Because of what Dad did."

"What everyone *thinks* Dad did. But we know the truth."

I want to believe that. I really, really do. And since Agent Brody arrived proclaiming my father's innocence, I've decided to believe it. I just wish I could be as certain as Tiffany. But I still can't quite wrap my head around the idea of our father as a patsy. Of course, it took me a long time to wrap my head around the idea of our father as a criminal too. Maybe I'm just slow to shift gears.

"Right," I say. "We know the truth, but the rest of the world still doesn't."

"Not yet," she says, pointing her fork at me. "But we're going to change that."

"Yes, that's the plan. But at this moment Richard still thinks

Dad is responsible, so we need to clear you out of the apartment."

"Why? He knows *you're* staying there, right? It's not like he thinks the place is empty."

I was hoping to avoid this part of the conversation. "Yes, Richard knows I'm living there."

She's silent for a moment as she realizes what I'm not telling her, then her bottom lip starts quivering. "Richard doesn't want me there, does he? He told you to kick me out."

I reach across the table and squeeze her hand. "Don't feel bad. Richard doesn't want *me* there either. I know he's selling because he needs the money, but I'm sure the decision was a lot easier for him knowing he could hurt me too."

"But where are we supposed to go?" Her lower lip is really trembling now, but she's still managing to hold back the tears.

I shake my head. "I have no idea."

AFTER LUNCH—WE compromised, I ordered the $5.99 special and she ordered dim sum and we split them both—we return to the apartment and start cleaning. I save the den, which used to be tidy when I was the only one living in the apartment and now looks like a bomb went off in it, for last.

"How the hell did you get all this in your suitcase?" I ask Tiffany as I stare at the piles of clothes, shoes, and purses scattered around the room.

"Well, it's not like I brought just one," she says and opens the accordion closet doors, revealing three pieces of matching Louis Vuitton luggage. She reaches for the duffel on the top shelf and it comes tumbling down, bringing a Neiman Marcus shopping bag with it. I hear the shatter and am afraid to look. My mother stores her crystal vases in that closet.

"Oops," Tiffany says and I know it wasn't one of her items that broke. If it had been, she'd be a lot more upset.

I look down and see fragments of colored glass scattered across the hardwood floor. Of course the bag couldn't have landed on the thick Persian rug, where the items inside might have survived the fall.

"I'll get the DustBuster," Tiffany says and escapes down the hallway before I can tell her we don't own one.

I kneel down to pick up the larger shards of glass and realize that this isn't the remains of one of my mother's vases. This is from an item I haven't seen in years.

18

"I couldn't find the DustBuster so I brought a—" I look up at Tiffany who is standing in the doorway holding a broom and a roll of paper towels. "What *is* that?" she asks.

I hold up the wedge of cut glass in alternating stripes of light and dark blue. "It *was* a sculpture. It used to live on a side table in the living room of our old apartment, but that was ages ago." I can't help but laugh at the irony. I'd always wanted to play with that sculpture when I was little because I thought it looked like a fish, but my mother wouldn't let me because she was afraid I'd break it. I guess she was right.

"How did it end up here?"

I shake my head. "I have no idea. My mother must've brought it out here at some point." It's the only explanation.

"If she liked it so much, then why did she keep it hidden away in the closet?"

I shake my head again. "No clue. I thought she'd gotten rid of everything my Dad had given her when they divorced." I remember well the argument my parents had the night my father told my mother he was leaving her for Raylene. They thought I was sleeping, but I wasn't. I heard every word. It would've been hard not to with all the screaming. I'm surprised this sculpture survived. There was a lot of smashing of glass that night.

"Are you going to tell her you broke it?"

"*I* didn't break it; you broke it."

"No, I didn't. It was an accident. Besides, I thought your parents aren't supposed to know I'm still here."

It's not worth explaining that my mom already knows, and knows why she's staying with me, and still wants me to kick her out. "Let's just clean up the mess and I'll worry about what to tell her later—assuming she ever asks. She's probably forgotten the damn thing's even here."

"I doubt that," Tiffany says as she starts sweeping the tiny shards of colored glass into a pile.

"Why would you say that? My mom hates Dad, and that was *before* he lost all of their money."

She stops sweeping and stares at me as if I'm a moron. She doesn't actually say, "Duh," but I hear it anyway. "You don't save gifts from someone you hate. Maybe something valuable, but not this ugly thing."

It hadn't been ugly when it was in one piece. But I doubt it was valuable either. If it had been, it would've been seized by the US Marshals and sold at auction like everything else my mother still owned that was paid for by my father. All the Feds let her keep is her wedding band and engagement ring—the small one my dad had given her when they got married, not the five-carat diamond he bought her as an anniversary present years later. That one was confiscated and sold at auction with the rest of the jewelry he'd given her, the proceeds added to the fund set up by the government to pay back the victims of my father's crimes. Or Chet's crimes, as it turns out.

But Tiffany's right. My mother must've saved that sculpture for a reason. And she probably brought it to the apartment in Los Angeles rather than keeping it at the house on Long Island because she didn't want Richard to know. Which makes me wonder what else she saved that Richard doesn't know about.

19

"Oh my God, look at that computer," Tiffany says. "It's huge!"

We're laughing at a photo of our dad from October 1982 according to the handwritten date on the back. I assume it's a staged publicity photo because he's sitting behind a huge wood desk wearing a serious expression, a dark pin-striped suit, and large round glasses. We found this picture, along with hundreds of others, in a cardboard box at the bottom of the closet. It's filled with mementos too—a matchbox from a restaurant in Panama, a cocktail napkin with a heart scrawled in red ink and my parents' initials inside, a pressed copper coin with a barely discernible depiction of a waterfall—from the many trips my parents had taken either before I was born or when I was a baby. The earliest vacations I remember took place at fancy hotels with expensive restaurants, not places with names like Posada Miguel and Tico's Cantina.

"How about this one?" I say, holding up a photo of my parents at some unknown tropical destination. My mother's tanned and smiling in her yellow sundress, her normally straight hair permed and poufy. My dad has his arm casually draped over her shoulder, a beer in one hand and a cigarette in the other. There's no date on the back, but I realize it must've been taken before I was born because I know my dad stopped smoking as soon as he found out my mother was pregnant with me. I'd heard the story many times.

Tiffany takes the photo from my hand and stares at it. "Wow, your mother was really beautiful back then."

I let out a laugh. "Don't *ever* say that to her face." My mother is having a hard enough time dealing with "the ravages of time," as she puts it. That remark would send her to the nearest plastic surgeon for sure. She's already Botoxing and getting chemical peels on a regular basis.

"Why not? It's a compliment."

Raylene is almost twenty years younger than my mother, so Tiffany hasn't had to deal with aging woman syndrome yet. But she will. Eventually. In the meantime, "Just don't, okay? Trust me on this one."

"Is it because Gail's an old lady now?"

"Oh my God, you are *so* lucky my mother's not listening to this conversation. You'd be out on the street tonight! And for the record, she's only fifty-eight. I think you have to be at least sixty before people get to call you an old lady."

Tiffany laughs. "Sorry. I'm used to Raylene freaking out about forty. Jimmy wants to throw her a big birthday party—he offered to rent a yacht and everything. She told him no and if he tries to make her a surprise party, she'll leave him and never come back. Did you know she tells all her friends she's thirty-five?"

I didn't know but I'm not surprised. Perhaps that's another reason Raylene wanted Tiffany gone. If you tell everyone you're thirty-five, it's harder to explain away a daughter who's seventeen.

Tiffany and I are still laughing at old photos when the home phone rings and I jump. The home phone almost never rings. The only people who call that number are salesmen and the delivery people who buzz the apartment from the downstairs gate. But it's almost nine o'clock at night.

"Pizza delivery," says the muffled voice on the other end of the line.

"Sorry, you've got the wrong apartment."

I'm about to hang up when I hear, "Nina, it's me, Jason. Agent Brody."

I cover the mouthpiece with my hand and glare at Tiffany. "Did you invite Agent Brody here again?"

"Of course not," she says. "I just texted him to let him know I was staying with you, in case he needed to reach me."

"And why would he need to reach you?"

"Nina, we need his help. We're never going to be able to find Dad on our own. I know. I've tried."

I want to ask her exactly what she's done—because her trying to find Dad on her own is news to me—when I hear Agent Brody calling out to me. "Nina, buzz me in already. The pizza's getting cold."

I put my hand over the mouthpiece again, but before I can get the accusation out, Tiffany says, "And I might've mentioned to him that we hadn't eaten dinner yet, in case he wanted to, you know, pick up a pizza." I cross my arms over my chest and glare at her. "I told him spinach and tomato was your favorite," she says as if that makes this all right. It doesn't. "Well, it's better than eating bagels for dinner, isn't it?"

Marginally.

AGENT BRODY STRIDES into my apartment as if I hadn't thrown him out that morning, two pizza boxes in one hand and a six-pack of IPA beer in the other. I'm willing to bet whatever money is left in my checking account that he was a frat boy in college. I can picture him fifteen years ago, a little thinner, a few less lines around the eyes, wearing jeans and a T-shirt instead of an off-the-rack suit, but otherwise the same, sitting around the fraternity house having contests with his "brothers" to see who could belch the loudest or let loose the longest fart.

He disgusts me, but the pizza doesn't. I inhale the heady scent of fresh-baked dough and grab the boxes from his hand. Tiffany grabs the beer.

"Don't even think about it," I say before she can pop the cap off the first bottle.

"Why not?" she asks.

"Tiffany, you're seventeen."

"So? Don't tell me you never drank when you were seventeen. I know better."

She did know better because our dad used to let us drink alcohol at home once we turned sixteen. His excuse was that he knew we were going to drink anyway, so he'd rather it be under his roof, where he could control it. Of course, that took all the fun out of it.

"Those were Dad's rules, not mine. In this apartment we follow the law." I nod in the direction of Agent Brody, who has trailed us into the kitchen. He leans one hip against the counter, crosses his arms over his chest, and smiles. I turn back to Tiffany. "News flash, genius, if you want to do something illegal, don't invite a cop to the party."

"Federal agent," he replies, as I knew he would. This is becoming our routine.

Tiffany pries the top off a bottle and sashays past me to Agent Brody. I think she's going to offer it to him, but instead she brings the dark glass to her lips. "You don't mind, do you?"

"Actually, I do," he says and grabs the bottle from her hand. "Sorry, but I have to side with your sister on this one."

"You two are the most annoying people ever!" she says and flounces from the room.

We both laugh.

"Is she always that dramatic?" he asks.

"Yes!" I say and we both laugh again. It's actually nice having someone on my side for a change. Then I remember who I'm talking to and reinstate my armor. "So why are you here, Agent Brody?"

He lifts the lid on the top pizza box. "Peace offering."

"You think you can bribe me with a pizza?" But I'm undercut by my stomach, which growls loudly enough for him to hear.

"Don't think of it as a bribe; think of it as an apology. I shouldn't have slept in your bed last night, not without your permission. It was wrong of me and I'm sorry."

Chink. Who doesn't like a man who can admit when he's made a mistake and apologize? Of course, Agent Brody has a lot more to apologize to me for than just sleeping in my bed. "And do you make a habit of sleeping in strange women's beds *with* their permission?"

He licks his lips and smiles. "It usually comes in the form of an invitation."

Arrogant jerk. I can just imagine him picking up women in bars—the badge, the gun, the sexy smile. I know women who swoon over hunky law enforcement types. Luckily, I'm not one of them. "As long as you don't expect an invite from me," I say and grab a slice of pizza from the open box.

"I wouldn't dream of it," but his tone says otherwise. Or maybe it's the way he's looking at me, like he's seen me naked. And then I remember he has. Damn that stupid sex tape.

TIFFANY DECIDES she isn't going to skip dinner even if Agent Brody and I are the two most annoying people ever. She and I finish the spinach and tomato pizza, and Agent Brody polishes off most of the pepperoni pie. Tonight I stick with Diet Coke and leave the beer to him. I can't afford another night passed out on the couch. Although I'm still not convinced that it was the wine that did me in last night. He could've easily mixed something into my water glass while I was puking my guts up in the bathroom. Why he would do that, though, I have no idea. Definitely not to take advantage of me, which is the usual reason a man drugs a woman. And not to get me out of the way so he could take advantage of Tiffany either. It's a conundrum.

"Why can't you just put all of her stuff in the closet?" Agent Brody asks when I tell him he needs to leave because Tiffany and I still have a lot of packing to do.

Tiffany slaps the breakfast bar, where we're all still sitting sipping our drinks. "That's what I said!"

"Because real estate agents look in closets too."

Agent Brody sets down his beer. "No, not the den closet, *your* closet. Just mix her stuff in with yours. Who would know the difference?"

Tiffany wears a size smaller than me and favors different designers, so anyone paying attention would know. But presumably Richard's real estate agent will only be looking at the size of the closet, not checking the labels on the clothes. I have to admit it's not a bad idea.

The three of us abandon our drinks and head to the den to gather up Tiffany's belongings. "What's all this?" Agent Brody asks, pointing to the old photos we left scattered on the floor.

"A trip down memory lane," I say as I scoop up a handful of pictures and dump them in the cardboard box that still holds an album we hadn't gotten to yet. Tiffany does the same, but a few photos are left peeking out from under the couch and Agent Brody reaches for those. But instead of tossing them into the box, he studies them.

He holds one up to me and Tiffany. "Do you know where this was taken?"

It's a picture of our father and Chet, his former business partner. They're standing on either side of a huge fish that presumably one of them has caught. Based on their trim waistlines, apparent since they are only wearing bathing suits, and the lack of gray in either of their full heads of hair, I'm guessing this photo was taken at least twenty years ago.

Tiffany shakes her head. I shrug and offer a guess: "Florida?"

I recall my dad going on several business trips to Florida when I was young. He once brought me back a giant Mickey Mouse stuffed animal and I cried because I thought he'd visited Disney World without me. He finally admitted that he purchased it at the gift shop at the airport on his way home, and promised to take me to Disney for my next birthday, but by then my parents had divorced. My mom and Richard took me a few years later.

"Definitely not Florida," Agent Brody says and taps the picture. "Look at that fish."

Tiffany and I lean in. It looks like a fish. A very large and strange-looking fish, but still a fish. "Why does it have spikes coming out of its head?" Tiffany asks.

"Not spikes. That's its dorsal fin. It's a roosterfish. They live in the Pacific, not the Atlantic."

"So you think the picture was taken in California?" I ask.

"Farther south," he says. "Mexico or Central America. Possibly even South America."

I've never seen him this happy before. He's practically giddy.

"And that's good?" Tiffany asks, also noticing the shift in Agent Brody's mood.

He pumps the air with his fist. "It's fucking fantastic!"

Tiffany and I glance at each other. She's as bewildered as me.

"It's a lead," Agent Brody says, "to your father."

"You think our dad is hiding out in Mexico because he went on a fishing trip there twenty years ago?" I ask, incredulous.

He shakes his head. "No, not Mexico, Panama. And no, I don't think he's living there, although he could be. But do you know what else they have in Panama besides big sport fishing?"

"Good Mexican food?" Tiffany asks. "Oh, wait, that's Mexico. Good Panamanian food?"

"Presumably," Agent Brody replies, nodding to the photo. "But I was referring to their world-renowned banking industry. They're known in the trade as the Switzerland of Latin America."

"I'm assuming that's not because of the chocolate," I say.

"No, it's because of their secrecy."

20

———

Agent Brody explains that anyone can go to Panama and hire a local lawyer to set up a corporation or foundation with an accompanying bank account, then transfer money both into and out of the account, including into and out of the country, with no taxes paid and no questions asked.

"If this is such a well-known place to hide money," I say, "then why didn't you look there already?"

"We did," he says. "But we can't get any information out of the Panamanian government, and according to the immigration department, neither your father nor Chet ever traveled to Panama."

"Then why do you think they were there?" Tiffany asks before I can.

"Just because they didn't go there under their own names doesn't mean they were never there." He holds up the photo again. "And now I have a clue."

We leave Agent Brody riffling through our old family photos while Tiffany and I move her clothes to my closet, or try to. We manage to fit about half of her wardrobe in with mine, and that's with barely being able to move the hangers in and out and doubling up the shoes on the shelf. I finally convince her to stuff the other half of her wardrobe back into her suitcases.

"We can leave them in the trunk of my car," I say, reaching for her carry-on bag.

"I'm not leaving them in the trunk of your car! Someone could steal them."

I'm about to tell her she's worrying for nothing since I park in a gated garage, but then I remember my neighbor complaining that the wheels were stolen off his car last month *while* it was parked in the garage. He went down to leave for work in the morning and found his Mercedes up on blocks. When he filed the police report, the cops told him his was the third set of wheels stolen that month.

I drop the bag, which is small but definitely not light. "Then what do you suggest? Rent a storage space for the day?"

She glances around the bedroom as if a hiding space is suddenly going to reveal itself. When one doesn't, she says, "How about under the bed?"

"They won't fit." I'd thought of that too.

Tiffany's face lights up. "I know! We'll put them inside your suitcases, like nesting dolls."

"That'd be a great idea if they weren't all the same size."

But she's already reaching for my luggage, which I stacked at the top of my closet. It works for the smaller ones, which fit inside my larger cases, but that still leaves her giant suitcase with nowhere to hide. I start dragging it down the hallway toward the front door—the trunk of my car is the only option— with Tiffany screaming that she is not leaving her Gianvito Rossi shoes and her Chloé purses and her outfits from designers I've never even heard of before in the trunk of my car, where anyone with a hairpin could steal them.

"A hairpin? I think you watch too many movies." Surely

someone couldn't break into the trunk of a car with just a hairpin.

She calls to Agent Brody. "Will you please tell my sister—"

"Coat hanger," he shouts from the den. "You unlock the door, then pop the trunk from the inside."

"See?" she says, hands on hips, as if *she* claimed all a thief needed to break into a car was a coat hanger too.

Then Agent Brody appears in the hallway. "But these days most professional thieves just use scanners. It's fast, easy, and no alarm gets triggered, so you can do it in broad daylight. Anyone watching would think it was someone cleaning out their own car."

That's scary, but of less concern to me now than when I actually owned something worth stealing. "And why would someone want to break into *my* car?" Which is really Richard's old Lexus that I'm borrowing. My Range Rover (a gift from my father) was sold at auction by the Feds. "There are brand new Mercedes and BMWs in that garage. Don't you think a thief would go higher end?"

"Not necessarily," Agent Brody says. "The most stolen cars in America are older-model Honda Accords. They chop them up and sell the parts online."

He's *not* helping. "But they don't break into the trunks looking for Manolo Blahniks, do they?"

Agent Brody gives me a blank stare.

I throw my arms up. "It's a shoe!"

Then Tiffany and I both start yelling at once until Agent Brody grabs the suitcase and carries it down to my bedroom. We stop fighting and follow. He pulls my laundry basket, which is filled with two weeks' worth of dirty clothes, out of my walk-in closet and sets the suitcase in its place.

"Oh, that's helpful," I say. "No one will *ever* notice it there."

"I'm not finished," he replies, then reaches for my laundry

basket and dumps its contents on top of the suitcase. "There," he says, gesturing to his handiwork. "Hidden in plain sight."

I'm almost too horrified to speak. "I would never leave a giant pile of dirty clothes just sitting out in the middle of the closet." I'm not a teenager with a full-time housekeeper anymore. And the fact that all my lacy bras and underwear are right on top doesn't help.

"I would," says Tiffany.

"That's because you're a slob," I say as I grab an armload of dirty clothes and toss it back into the laundry basket.

Then the two of us start shouting again until Agent Brody says, "You're both insane," before grabbing the suitcase out from under the pile of dirty laundry. He carries it down the hallway, then slams it down onto the floor in front of the door. "I'll take it with me tonight and bring it back tomorrow after the Realtor's gone."

Tiffany starts to object when Agent Brody pulls his gun out of its holster and we both freeze. I've seen hunting rifles before —Richard took my mom and me glamping once; it was the only type of camping she would agree to—but I've never been in the same room with a loaded handgun before today. He isn't pointing it directly at us, he's sort of waving it around in front of us, but he's an angry man with a loaded gun. Tiffany reaches for my hand and I squeeze it back. *Don't worry.* Wishful thinking, really, as I have no clue how to disarm him.

But Agent Brody is oblivious to our fear, or maybe he just doesn't care. "No one is going to steal your shit from me, Tiffany." Then he stomps into the kitchen and grabs a beer out of the fridge. *Oh great, man with a loaded gun who's drinking too.*

We're too scared to move until he says, "Sit down, both of you." Then we practically run to the breakfast bar. We each take a seat across from him. Tiffany's still holding my hand and I'm still squeezing it back.

He sets his gun on the counter, then takes a long swallow from his beer. Next he pulls three photographs out of his shirt pocket and lays them out in front of us. The first is the one he'd already asked about—the picture of our father and his former business partner with a giant fish between them. The second is a photo of our father and my mother when she was pregnant with me. They're both sunburnt and wearing very little clothes, so presumably it was taken at a tropical destination. And the third is a photo of me and my father sitting on the deck of a boat. This one must not have been taken in a tropical destination since we're both wearing long pants and sweaters. Martha's Vineyard, maybe? I have no memory of ever going out on a boat with just my father, but I was very young in the photo, no more than three or four.

"Let's start with this one," Agent Brody says, pointing to the photograph of my father and me.

21

———

He questions me about all three of the photos. Then he questions Tiffany even though all of the pictures were taken before she was born. When I point that out to Agent Brody, he goes back to interrogating me. I feel like I had before my father's trial when Agent Brody used to ask me the same questions over and over and over again, somehow thinking the answer would be different the hundredth time he asked. Reliving all this again makes me so angry I actually forget about the gun.

"Enough!" I grab the photographs and throw them at his head. But he ducks and they fall to the floor. I don't even inflict a paper cut. "We're innocent. You have no right to hold us prisoner!"

He looks genuinely perplexed. "Prisoner? What are you talking about?"

"You come in here waving your gun at us and—"

"Waving my gun at you? Did you think I was threatening you?" He isn't laughing on the outside, but I have a feeling he's laughing on the inside, or at the very least enjoying our discomfort at the sight of his firearm.

I glance over at Tiffany, who just shrugs her shoulders. "Then why did you bring a gun?"

"Federal agents always carry guns. It's required. I've been wearing one since the first time we met."

"But you never pulled it out before. You always kept it hidden away."

He opens his mouth as if about to speak, then shuts it again and shakes his head. When he finally does speak, he says, "You're right. I'm sorry. I never should've un-holstered my weapon. But I wasn't trying to threaten you. I just wanted to drive home the point to Tiffany that her suitcase was safe with me."

"And you wanted us to stop fighting," Tiffany adds.

Agent Brody smiles at her. "Well, it worked, didn't it?"

She reaches across the breakfast bar and punches him in the shoulder, little sister-big brother style.

He smiles as he points his finger at her. "Assaulting a federal officer is a crime, young lady."

I reach across the breakfast bar and punch him in the shoulder too, but my punch is a lot harder than Tiffany's. "Then you'll have to arrest us both."

He grabs my wrist and stares at me, but it's not his usual trying-to-intimidate-a-suspect glare. I imagine this is his singles bar stare. There's a *dare me* quality to it. Or maybe it's a *let's fuck* quality.

I respond with my own look: *Not interested.*

He lets go of my wrist and says, "I have a better idea. I'm going to bring you with me."

"Ooo, where are we going?" Tiffany asks as I say, "I'm not going anywhere with you."

"Stop being such a dud," Tiffany says before turning back to Agent Brody. "So where are we going?"

But he ignores her question and addresses me. "I thought you wanted to help your father?"

"*I'll* help," Tiffany says. "I always knew Dad was innocent, but nobody believed me. Not even Nina."

"That's not true! But you weren't at the trial, Tiff. You didn't hear all the evidence against him. And whenever I asked him about the money, he could never explain."

"That's because Chet took it. He didn't know what Chet was doing. No one did. Right, Jason?"

"Tiffany, I told you, I can't get into specifics. This is still an active investigation and I need to preserve all the evidence for the new trial. That's the best way we can help your father. That and to *find him*. He needs to come forward in order to exonerate himself."

"And I will help you in any way I can," I say. "But I'm not going to go traipsing across the globe looking for him."

"Why not?" they both ask.

"Because I'm broke! And so are you, Tiffany. We can't afford to go anywhere."

"But the FBI will pay." She turns to Agent Brody. "Won't they?"

Agent Brody hems and haws but eventually admits that no, the FBI is not going to pay for me and my sister to travel around the world looking for our father. "But I can," he says. "Not first-class," he adds, looking directly at Tiffany. "But if we travel smart, keep our expenses low, then I've got enough money to cover this."

"And why would you spend your money on us?" I ask.

"Because I happen to think having you there will be an asset."

"How? I don't know the first thing about finding someone who doesn't want to be found."

"I do," Tiffany says. "I'm great at finding out things I'm not supposed to know."

"If you're so great at it, then why haven't you found Dad already?"

"Because no one would ever let me look for him before," she says, then flicks her hair at me before turning to Agent Brody. "Forget her. *I'll* go with you."

"I can't take you, Tiffany." He holds up his hand to head off her budding objection. "Not *just* you. You're a minor."

"But you can take me if my sister comes too?"

"And your mother consents," he says.

I don't think any of us doubt that Raylene would consent, and certainly not if I'm there too, probably even if I'm not.

Tiffany clasps her hands together and turns back to me. "*Please*, Nina. We *have* to do this. For Dad."

"Tiffany, *we* can't help Dad. Only Agent Brody can. He's the one with the know-how. We'll just get in the way."

"I disagree," he says.

Of course he does.

"The FBI and the US Marshalls have been looking for your father for months and we've come up with nothing. One day with you two and I already have a clue," he says, holding up the photograph of my father and Chet.

"A twenty-year-old photo from a fishing trip is a clue?"

"It's a place to start," he says, "which is more than I had before."

I drop my head in my hands. I'm so confused I don't know what to do. My gut is telling me to stay put. To find a new job and make a new life for myself. Let the FBI track down my father and exonerate him. They're the ones who convicted the wrong man. This is their problem to fix, not mine.

But am I being selfish? This is my dad we're talking about. Even if I don't think I can help, if Agent Brody does, then shouldn't I go? And what about all those people who lost their life savings? And all the schools and charities that had to close down because they lost their funding? If my going with Agent Brody has even the slightest chance of helping them get their money back, then shouldn't I? Don't I owe them that, not as someone who committed any crime against them, but just as a fellow human being?

But if going is the right thing to do, then why is my head screaming at me not to? It sounds like the robot from *Lost in Space. Danger, Nina Rothberg, danger.*

22

———

"It's late," I finally say. "Let me think about it overnight." I don't say sleep on it because I know there will be no sleeping with this decision hanging over my head.

"What is there to think about?" Tiffany shouts. "We have a chance to save Dad."

"Your sister's right, Tiffany. This is a big decision. It could be dangerous."

Ha! My internal robot was right.

"How could it be dangerous?" she asks. "We're just looking for our father."

"Because we may not be the only ones," Agent Brody says.

That gets my attention. "Who else is looking for him? You said the Marshalls put this on the back burner, that they've got other fugitives to find and can't spend all their time searching for my dad."

"Not the government," he replies.

"Then who?" Tiffany asks.

Agent Brody studies the label on his beer bottle. It's ripped in the corner and he's trying to seal it back in place.

"Jason" —I call him by his first name because I know it will get his attention—"please tell us. If we're going to be putting ourselves in danger, then we have a right to know."

"Your father, or his business partner," he adds for Tiffany's benefit before turning back to me, "didn't just steal from good people. They stole from some very bad people too."

Tiffany's eyes go wide. "The mob?"

"This isn't a movie, Tiffany!"

Agent Brody says, "No, but she's not far off base. There've been whispers of a Russian crime syndicate. They can't come forward as legitimate victims, of course, but we think one of their money-laundering fronts invested with a feeder fund that your father did business with. It's still a bit opaque because of all the shell companies."

"Why didn't this come out at the trial?" I was there every day. I would remember.

He shrugs. "We couldn't prove it at the time. We still can't."

"And Russian crime bosses aren't the most sympathetic victims," I say. *Not like all the disabled kids and senior citizens they trotted out in the penalty phase. Two were even in wheelchairs.*

"I don't care," Tiffany says. "I'm not scared of those guys."

"Well, you should be," Agent Brody tells her. "They're scary guys. But our goals here are similar. They want to find your father and the money and so do we. As long as we're careful, we'll be okay. If I wasn't confident I could keep you both safe, I wouldn't have asked you to come."

"And you're basing that confidence on what exactly?" I ask, because I'm anything but confident.

"A dozen years of field experience and this," he says, holding up his weapon.

The sight of his gun has the opposite effect on me.

~

"ARE YOU OUT OF YOUR MIND?" my mother screams.

I don't need to have the phone on speaker. I can hear her just fine holding the handset a foot away from my ear. She called to tell me the Realtor would be arriving at eleven instead of twelve thirty, and to make sure I'd cleaned the apartment and gotten rid of Tiffany. I told her yes to everything (which was true since I'd already sent Tiffany out shopping—but not buying!—while I did all the last-minute straightening). Then I told her about Agent Brody's offer.

"I didn't say yes. I'm just considering it."

"What is there to consider? If this Agent Bradley—"

"Brody."

"I don't give a flying fig what his name is. If this idiot suddenly thinks your father is innocent, then he can prove it himself. He has no business involving two young girls in this mess."

"But Mom—"

"No, Nina, there's nothing to discuss. Richard and I had a long talk last night and we both agree it's time you came home."

"I don't have a home, remember? Richard is selling it."

"That apartment was never your home. It was a lark. And we've indulged you long enough."

"It wasn't a lark! I had a job and I was making friends." Well, the first part is true. "I was doing great until the owner found out whose daughter I am."

"And it'll happen again, Nina. No matter how many times you change your name and your hair color, you'll always be Harold Rothberg's daughter. Which is why you need to come home and work for Richard. He's already agreed to find a place for you at his company."

"Selling aluminum siding?"

"You can't afford to be choosy. Those days are over." She sighs and lowers her voice enough that I actually have to place the phone next to my ear again to hear her. "Sweetheart, I know this isn't the life you envisioned for yourself. Trust me, it's not the life I envisioned for you either. But you can't keep acting like you're a billionaire's daughter."

"How can you say that to me? I barely spend any money. And I had a job. I was paying my own way. I would've paid Richard rent if he'd asked."

"Honey, you know we'd never take your money."

"Then I would've rented my own apartment. I want to be independent, Mom. I'm twenty-seven years old. I don't want to live at home and work for my stepfather. Especially since I know he doesn't want me there."

"That's not true, Nina. Richard loves you and wants to help you in any way he can."

"By selling the apartment and making me homeless?"

I have to hold the phone at arm's length again or risk losing an eardrum. I stop listening until I hear her winding down. "I cannot discuss this with you any further." *What discussion? She's just dictating the terms of my surrender.* "If you want to be treated like an adult, then you need to start acting like one."

"By moving into my childhood bedroom and working for my stepfather?"

"When that's your only option, then yes. You accept reality and make the best of it."

But that isn't my only option. I have another.

23

"I knew you'd make the right choice," Tiffany squeals when I tell her I've decided to take Agent Brody up on his offer. I don't tell her about my conversation with my mother this morning, or our second conversation after the real estate agent called her to tell her she thought the apartment was a perfect size and location for a young professional and asked if it would be okay to bring prospective buyers in to see it the next day. "This place will sell fast," she'd assured my mother, who repeated it to me with a request from Richard that I start packing immediately. He's already readying a cubicle for me directly across from his office.

"It was the only choice," I reply, which is true. Richard isn't a bad person, and he's definitely good to my mom, but if I had to spend all day working for him, then all night listening to him opine on every topic under the sun (and there is no topic on which Richard does not consider himself an expert), I would either kill him, myself, or both of us. Dealing with Agent Brody and the Russian mobsters is actually the safer course of action.

Tiffany and I spend the rest of the afternoon packing our belongings, so when Agent Brody arrives with dinner—a bottle of cheap sake and takeout sushi—we're both ready to leave LA. For Tiffany, the city isn't as exciting as she thought it'd be—"Did you know all the bars here close at two a.m.?" And for me, I feel like a failure and I'm ready to move on.

My mother was right about one thing in her rant this morning—I will always be Harold Rothberg's daughter. I will carry that around with me for the rest of my life. For most of my childhood it was a boon. It provided me with every advantage in life. Only in the last couple of years has it been a burden. But if I can help Agent Brody exonerate my father, then we can all get our lives back. Not our old lives; I know those are gone for good. But new lives where my father isn't an international pariah, and Tiffany and I aren't the daughters of an infamous criminal.

Maybe Big Mike doesn't hold the sins of the father against the child, but the rest of the world does.

"WE CAN'T LEAVE TOMORROW," Agent Brody says. "I need a couple of days to prep everything."

"Prep what?" Tiffany asks. "I have my passport. And Raylene said the money should be in my bank account tomorrow morning. We can stop and get it on the way to the airport."

When Tiffany mentions her passport, it occurs to me for the first time that my passport still says Nina Rothberg. When I legally changed my name to Roth, the first thing I did was get a new driver's license, but it never occurred to me to get a new passport too. I wasn't planning on doing any international traveling. "Is it even legal for me to use my old passport if it has the wrong name?"

"I'm getting both of you new passports," Agent Brody says, then pops a California roll into his mouth. "And new phones."

"Why?" I ask before Tiffany can.

"Did you know all US passports have computer chips in them that make them trackable?"

I didn't know that but, "So what?" Even if the FBI isn't paying for us to travel with Agent Brody, surely they know he's taking us with him... Then it occurs to me that maybe they don't. "You haven't told your boss you're bringing us, have you?"

"How could I?" he says through a mouthful of rice and avocado. "I just found out myself five minutes ago."

"But you're not planning on telling your boss either. Otherwise why would we need new phones and passports?"

"You mean you're getting us *fake* passports with new names and identities? Cool," Tiffany says.

"Not cool," I say, then turn back to Agent Brody. "Isn't it a crime to travel with a fake passport?"

"Yes," he says, "when it's used in furtherance of criminal activity, but not when it's used by law enforcement as part of a criminal investigation."

"So cops can break the law, but the rest of us can't." Figures.

He shakes his head. "If a police officer is speeding down the freeway trying to catch a criminal, is that a crime? No, the officer is doing his job. But the criminal speeding down the freeway is committing a crime, multiple crimes. See the difference?"

I suppose. "But we're not FBI agents, only you are. So aren't we still criminals?"

He downs his shot of sake in one gulp and slams his glass on the table. "Christ, Nina, do you think I would ask you to do something illegal? I'm a federal officer, for God's sake."

"Ignore her," Tiffany says. "She's just a Goody-Two-shoes."

"I am not a Goody-Two-shoes!"

"You are too." She turns to Agent Brody. "She never even cut school. Not once her entire life."

"I did too." That's a lie. I faked being sick and my mom let me stay home.

"When?"

"In high school."

Tiffany snorts *and* rolls her eyes.

"What do you want, an exact day and date so you can call the school to verify?"

"Yes," Tiffany says, "that would be very helpful."

"Screw you!"

Agent Brody holds up his hands. "Ladies, please. This is not something we need to fight about. Nina, I think it's great that you're a Goody-Two-shoes."

"I am not a Goody-Two-shoes!" I shout and they both burst out laughing.

"We're just teasing," Tiffany says. "Lighten up."

Brat. I turn to Agent Brody to see if he's in on this too.

"Sorry," he says, "I was just playing along. But I do think it's great that you're a law-abiding citizen. Our country needs more of them."

"I think most of us are law-abiding citizens, Agent Brody. Maybe your line of work has skewed your perceptions."

"Perhaps," he says, then dives back into his sushi.

AFTER A FEW SAKES (only Agent Brody is drinking because I hate sake and neither of us will give any to Tiffany), Agent Brody admits that I was right—he's not going to tell his boss that he's bringing me and Tiffany with him to Panama.

"Tiffany's under eighteen," he says. "My boss would never allow it."

"And me? I'm twenty-seven."

"Taking a fugitive's children is—"

"Illegal?"

"I was going to say unorthodox. But I'm an unorthodox guy. That's how I get results."

"And your boss is a Goody-Two Shoes?"

He shrugs. "My boss likes to play it by the book, which is what we've been doing for the last nine months. And your father slipped through the net. Now it's time to take a different tack."

I don't disagree. At some point if what you're doing isn't yielding any results, you have to change your methods. It's the same with winemaking. "But why do we need fake passports?" It still makes me uneasy. Other than rolling through a stop sign, for which I had to pay a three-hundred-dollar ticket and go to traffic school, I've never broken the law before.

"You're still worrying about that? What do you think happens to people who use fake passports—and I mean criminals, not people like you?"

I shrug. "I don't know. I assume they put them in jail."

Agent Brody laughs. "I have *never* seen anyone go to jail for using a fake passport who didn't commit some other crime too. If you're trying to get into the country, they won't let you. And if you're already here, they might deport you, but you're an American citizen, so that won't happen to you. In the worst-case scenario, you will have a hearing and I will come and testify on your behalf that I forced you to travel under a fake passport because I was trying to keep you safe, and the judge will—"

"Keep me safe?"

"Yes. The government is not the only one who can track a person's movement through their passport. Criminals can too. Not legally, of course, but—"

Holy cow. I didn't even think of that. "You think the Russian crime syndicate is spying on us? You think they're tracking our passports?"

"I don't know," he says. "But I'd rather not find out."

24

———

Tiffany pushes her Prada tote higher up on her shoulder and crosses her arms in front of her chest so she won't accidentally touch anything. "You expect me to stay in this dump?"

I want to strangle her—from the fit she threw when Agent Brody told her she could only take one suitcase on this trip (which she negotiated to one checked suitcase, one oversized carry-on, and the Prada tote), to her insistence that she had to have the aisle seat on the plane (forcing me into the middle seat next to the overweight guy who hogged the armrest and spent the entire flight farting out the sausage sandwich he'd brought on board for lunch), to the nonstop bitching about the weather since we'd landed (which, to be fair, did suck—even at ten o'clock at night it's hot and humid)—but I remind myself to *just breathe.*

"Tiff, you're the one who wanted to come on this little adventure. Did you think we'd be staying at the Four Seasons Panama City?"

"Ooo, do they have a Four Seasons here?"

Before I can finish saying, "I have no idea," she's already searching the Four Seasons website on her new phone.

"Buenos Aires, Costa Rica, and ooo, two in Bogota. Maybe we should go there."

"Sure, next time I'm hunting for an international fugitive, I'll be sure to add Bogota to my itinerary."

"No need to be sarcastic," she says as she stuffs her phone back into her please-rob-me tote bag.

I wait until I'm calm again, or calm-ish, before I say, "Tiffany, if you hate it here so much, you should just go home. I'm sure Agent Brody will understand."

"I'm not going home. Dad needs me."

"Then stop whining already and suck it up." It's not like I'm happy with the accommodations either, but when Agent Brody said we'd be traveling on a tight budget, I understood what that meant. I spent the last nine months living on very little money, so I have some practice at it. Tiffany is still learning.

"I'm not whining. You're the one who spent the whole cab ride bitching about that guy from the plane."

It wasn't the *whole* cab ride. Maybe five minutes. Maybe. "Because he practically asphyxiated me."

"Oh, please. It wasn't that bad."

"How would you know? You got bumped up to business class." The man who switched seats with her decided he'd rather sit next to his wife and two daughters in coach than alone in business class, or his wife decided that for him.

"Ladies," Agent Brody says, lowering his voice as he joins us next to the potted palm. "We talked about this, remember? We need to keep a low profile."

"I'm not the problem here," I whisper through clenched teeth.

"Puh-lees," Tiffany replies and flicks her humidity-frizzed

hair at me. "You're just as grossed out by this place as I am. Admit it."

Agent Brody places an arm around each of our shoulders and squeezes. Hard. "Unless you want to go back to your mother's lecherous boyfriend," he says, nodding at Tiffany, "and you want to go live with your pompous ass of a stepfather," he adds, looking at me, "you'll both start behaving." Then he lets go of our shoulders and slaps me on the ass.

"What the hell?" I shout, forgetting I'm supposed to be keeping a low profile.

"We're in Latin America now," he replies, grabbing both my suitcase and his. "Me man, you woman."

"Me *American* woman. Slap me again and I'll break your arm." Then I pull my suitcase out of his hand and start wheeling it across the lobby to the elevator.

"You go, girl," Tiffany says, then realizes I'm leaving her behind and calls out, "Hey, wait for me."

But before she can hoist her carry-on bag on top of her four-wheel suitcase, the desk clerk is at her side doing it for her. I have no doubt he would haul all of her luggage, even without the wheels, across the city if that's what she wanted, but Agent Brody says something to him in Spanish, which doesn't include any of the ten words I learned from our former Guatemalan housekeeper, so I don't understand. But the clerk's lustful smile doesn't require translation. He's obviously mistaken our innocent trio for a not-so-innocent threesome.

"What did you say to him?" I demand when it's just the three of us again.

But before Agent Brody can answer, Tiffany says, "He told him he was still breaking me in and he wanted me to carry my own luggage."

Agent Brody and I both stare at her.

"What? They teach Spanish at Dalton too. It's not all French and Latin, you know."

"They teach *Latin*?" Agent Brody is incredulous and I realize it must not be a common offering in public schools.

"I thought Dad made you take Chinese." I can still recall their argument. It was during a family dinner and Tiffany got so mad she threw her glass at the wall and Dad grounded her for a week. Of course, she snuck out to meet her friends the same night.

Then Tiffany smirks and I feel like I'm looking at our father. After his arrest he became infamous for his smirks. "I dropped it after the first week. I convinced him that Spanish would be just as useful."

Looks like she was right about that.

The elevator creaks and groans but eventually deposits us onto the fifth floor of the Hotel Gardenia (which contains no gardens, unless you count the two potted palms in the lobby), where we follow Agent Brody down the dank hallway to room 508. It's not as bad as it could be. The sheets on the two beds (not quite doubles, but bigger than twins) appear clean and nothing on the wood floor is crawling. And while the window air conditioner's motor sounds like it's preparing for lift-off, the room is cool, at least compared to the temperature outside.

When Agent Brody closes the door behind us, Tiffany's eyebrows rise. "You're staying?"

"Of course I'm staying," he says. "This is my room."

"Then where are we sleeping?" she asks.

"Here. This is all our room."

25

———————

Tiffany and I both start shouting at once. We thought we'd be traveling together and working together, not sleeping together too! And neither of us lets up until Agent Brody pulls out his gun—and this time he is pointing it at us. But we've seen it a few times now and it's not nearly as frightening as it had been that first night.

Tiffany rolls her eyes at him. "Oh, are you going to threaten to send us home again if we don't do what you want?"

"No, I'm going to shoot you both in the head and leave you here to die, and no one will even know it's you because you're both registered under your fake passport names. The desk clerk already thinks I'm your pimp, so the local police will just chalk it up to two more dead prostitutes. Case closed."

That shuts us up quickly. Not that I think he'd really do it but . . .

He sticks his gun back in his shoulder holster and asks, "Do either of you princesses have any aspirin? My head is killing me."

I pull a travel-size bottle out of my purse and toss it to him. He downs two capsules dry. I don't know if it's because he's trying to look macho or if the tap water is unsafe to drink. Then he sits down on the edge of one of the beds, which sinks under the weight of him, but there's nowhere else to sit. The only other furniture in the room is two folding tray tables (which I presume are supposed to be nightstands, even though they contain no lamp, clock, phone, or even a pad and pen), an armoire (which serves as the room's combined dresser and closet), and a television attached to the wall.

Agent Brody rubs his eyes with the palms of his hands and sighs. "This fighting needs to stop, and I mean now. I don't want to hear one more cross word between the two of you for the rest of the trip."

I let out a laugh. "You don't have any sisters, do you, Agent Brody?"

"No, I'm an only child."

"Ah, that explains it," Tiffany says, and I nod in agreement. No wonder he thinks he can just tell us to stop fighting. He has zero experience with siblings.

"What?" he asks.

"Nothing," Tiffany replies, so he turns to me.

"Our father used to threaten us with all kinds of things to get us to stop fighting," I say.

"And it never worked," Tiffany adds.

"Although there was that one time at the zoo when he actually left us there. Remember that?"

Tiffany covers her mouth with her hands. "Oh my God, I totally forgot about that! But he didn't really leave us, you know. He just hid in the car and forced poor Lucinda to stay behind and spy on us. And she hated the zoo, especially the monkey house. She was terrified of them. I think she must've had a bad experience with one when she was a child."

"Really?" I love the monkey house. "Isn't that where we hid out when he left?"

"Yup. She said if I hadn't started crying when I did, she was going to quit because she'd rather be deported than spend another minute with those screeching *monos*."

We both laugh at the memory. "I don't remember her being there when Dad came. I thought it was the security guard who called him."

"It was," she said, "but it was all staged. Lucinda called him first and he told her to stay out of sight because he'd already arranged it with the head of security."

I had no idea. All these years I really thought he'd left us at the zoo because we wouldn't stop fighting. "How do you know all this?"

"I overheard Dad telling Raylene. She didn't care that her four-year-old was traumatized, she just wanted to know why Lucinda could suddenly afford to fly home and visit her family for three weeks. I'm not sure which she was angrier about, her thought that Dad was screwing the nanny or because she would have to take care of me herself while Lucinda was gone."

"You're quite the little eavesdropper," Agent Brody says.

Tiffany shoots him a satisfied smile. "I told you I was good at finding out things I'm not supposed to know."

26

———

I flop down onto the empty bed, which feels like a bunch of old springs with a thin strip of cotton on top, and Tiffany lies down on Agent Brody's bed. Then she nudges him with her toe and says, "And where are you going to sleep tonight?"

Agent Brody pushes her sandaled feet to the side so they are hanging off the end of the bed. "Ha, ha, very funny."

"No, really," she asks, kicking off both shoes. "Where are you going to sleep? Are they bringing up a rollaway?"

Agent Brody laughs and I do too. To be fair, this is no doubt the first time Tiffany has stayed in a hotel without room service. It's probably the first time she's stayed in a hotel rated less than five stars.

"What's so funny?" she asks, which only makes us laugh harder.

Finally I say, "Look around, Tiffany. They don't even have a phone in the room. How are you going to call down for a rollaway?"

"I can use my cell," she says defiantly and reaches for her tote. "What's the number?"

Agent Brody turns to face her. "Tiffany, there's no one to call. It's not that kind of establishment."

"Then what kind of *establishment* is it?" she asks.

"The cheap kind," I say. "Without room service or Frette linens or rollaway beds."

She folds her arms across her chest and glares at me as if I'm the one who chose this dump. "That still doesn't explain where we're all supposed to sleep. There are three of us and only two beds."

"And this one's mine," Agent Brody says, slapping the springy mattress. "You can share with your sister."

I'm not surprised. If he were a gentleman, he would offer to sleep on the floor, or better yet get his own room, but frat boys are not known for their good manners.

"Agent Brody, were you ever in a fraternity?"

"Yeah, in college," he says. "Why?"

Hah, I knew it! "No reason," I say and turn to Tiffany. "Which side do you want?" This will be a first for us, and an experience, to be sure.

"We can't share the bed. Look how small it is." She spreads her arms out wide and the bed's narrow enough that they hang down on either side. "I can barely fit in it myself."

"Then you're welcome to the floor," Agent Brody replies, carefully unlacing his boring black shoes before placing them on a high shelf in the armoire. "But watch out for the scorpions."

"Scorpions?" she screeches.

"And the spiders," he says. "But only a few of them are poisonous."

She jumps from his bed to mine without touching the floor and flattens her back against me. "Please tell me he's joking."

He doesn't look like he's joking. "Are you joking?" I ask.

"Nope," he says, pulling his tie over his head and placing it on a hanger, still knotted, along with his suit jacket.

Now I'm a bit freaked out too. Small insects I can handle. I've seen plenty in the fields when checking grapevines. But spiders, especially the big, hairy variety, are something else entirely.

"So what do we do if we see one?" I ask. "And how will we know if it's poisonous?"

"I wouldn't bother trying to figure out if it's poisonous. Just assume that it is and either kill it or avoid it."

His pants are off now and he's down to gray boxer briefs and a white undershirt. Under any other circumstances, I'd be focused on looking, trying not to look, and appalled that he just undressed in front of us without even giving us any warning, but I can't get past the insects. I'm already starting to feel itchy all over just imagining what might be lying in wait for us under the bed or between the sheets or behind the ugly beige curtains, ready to pounce as soon as the lights turn off.

"You want us to kill a scorpion?" Tiffany asks.

Agent Brody slips in between the sheets of his bed. "Better you kill it than it kills you, right?" Then he rolls over with his back to us.

As if we would just let him go to sleep after dropping a bombshell like that!

Tiffany turns to me, a look of terror on her face. "Nina, do something!"

"What do you want me to do? I've never killed a scorpion before. I've never even seen one in person."

"Just hit it with your shoe," Agent Brody says, his back still facing us.

Tiffany loosens her grip on me. "You want me to ruin a perfectly good pair of shoes on a scorpion? What if I need to wear those shoes? You hardly let me bring anything on this trip."

I know for a fact she brought at least four pairs.

He finally rolls over and punches his pillow, no doubt

wishing it were Tiffany, or me too. "Then use *my* shoe. Now go to sleep already. We have a big day tomorrow."

"What are we doing tomorrow?" I ask.

"Starting the search for your father."

27

———————

But tomorrow is a long way off. We still have tonight to get through. And scorpions and poisonous spiders lying in wait.

"Nina, I can't stay here. We have to move."

I agree, but it's almost midnight and we're in an unfamiliar city in a foreign country and we're not even traveling under our own names. I'm not sure I can even use my credit card to pay for a new hotel if it doesn't match the name on my passport. "We'll just stay one night. We'll look for a new hotel in the morning."

"No, we won't," Agent Brody says. "I paid for two nights in advance."

"*You* can stay here," Tiffany says, "but *we're* leaving."

Agent Brody props himself up on one elbow. "No, you're *not* leaving. We're all staying together. That's the only way I can be sure you're safe. You think *I* want to share a room with the two of you? I'd rather take a bullet. It'd be less painful than listening to the constant whining."

"I haven't been whining!" I think I've been handling the situation gracefully, at least compared to Tiffany, who dismisses him with a flick of her hair and says, "Well, if you feel that way about us, then why did you even invite us on this trip?"

Agent Brody kicks off his covers and sits up. "This isn't a fucking vacation, Tiffany. It's serious business. And it would be helpful if you started treating it that way. The both of you."

This silences Tiffany. I open my mouth to object, then decide not to. He's right, this is serious business. If we can't find our father and prove his innocence, then he'll spend the rest of his life as a fugitive, and we'll spend the rest of our lives as the daughters of the man who committed the biggest fraud in history.

"Okay," I say, "what do you need us to do?"

"Right now I need you to let me get some sleep. We'll work through our next move in the morning."

Tiffany crosses her arms across her chest. "Well, I can't sleep here."

"I don't really give a fuck if you sleep, princess. *I* need to sleep." Then he lies back down and turns toward the wall again.

Tiffany glares at his back, which leaves me in the unenviable position of having to break the stalemate. "Be realistic, Jason." I hope using his first name will soften him up. "We're sharing one room. If we don't sleep, you don't sleep."

He sighs but turns around. "Then what do you suggest?"

And that's how we get Agent Brody to search the entire room with a flashlight, then sit outside the bathroom door (just in case we need him to kill something) while Tiffany and I take turns washing our faces and brushing our teeth, and finally to stand guard while we pull the sheets off the bed and remake it just to confirm there aren't any creepy crawlies lurking there.

"Anything else?" he asks after Tiffany and I tuck ourselves in.

Tiffany pulls her eyeshade down from her forehead. "If you could shut off the lights please."

"Anything for you, princess."
And the room goes dark.
And then it goes light again.

28

———

"It can't be morning already," I mumble. Between Tiffany's constant thrashing, Agent Brody's snoring, and my sudden irrational fear of spiders (my fear of scorpions is completely rational), it took me *hours* to fall asleep.

"Shush," Agent Brody says. Then he flips the light off and the room is plunged into darkness again.

I was right; it's not morning. Or at least not post-sunrise. I hear Agent Brody moving around the room, but it's too dark for me to see. "What are you doing?" I whisper.

"Go back to sleep," he calls back.

As if I can. I reach for my new, not-registered-to-me phone, which I left on the tray table/nightstand, and see that it's 4:32 a.m. I fumble with it until I find a flashlight app, then randomly wave it around the room. I catch Agent Brody heading toward the door. He's still wearing his undershirt, but now he has his pants on too, and his gun in his hand.

"What are you doing?" we both say, but I answer first. "Trying to figure out what the hell you're doing."

"Nothing," he says. "Go back to bed."

"You need your gun to do nothing?"

"I thought I heard something. I want to check it out."

My first thought is of the scorpions. I didn't realize they make noise, but maybe they do. It must be the pinchers. "You're going to shoot a scorpion?"

"What is this obsession you have with scorpions?"

"It's not an obsession. And if it is, it's your fault. You're the one who told me about them."

"You're telling me you didn't know they existed before today? Haven't you ever been to the southwest?"

"Does the Grand Canyon count?"

"Yes, and they're there too. I used to play with them growing up in Arizona."

"You *played* with scorpions? What, do you have a death wish?" Because that's information he really should've revealed before we decided to come on this trip.

"I do not—"

We both hear the crash in the hallway and freeze. It was so loud it even woke Tiffany, who bolts upright, eyeshade askew. "What's happening?"

"You two stay here," Agent Brody says. "And don't open this door for anyone but me." The dim light from the hallway spills into our room, then quickly disappears as he slams the door shut behind him.

I immediately flip the switch for the overhead light.

"Jesus, you could've warned me," Tiffany says, squinting against the unflattering fluorescent bulb. "What time is it?"

"Four thirty."

She flops back down onto the pillow and readjusts her eyeshade so that it's covering both eyes. "What the hell kind of hotel is this?"

"The loud kind." But hopefully not the violent kind too.

It feels like forever but is no more than fifteen minutes when someone knocks on the door and I freeze, except for my heart, which feels like it's about to burst through my chest. Another knock, louder this time, and then I hear Agent Brody's voice. "Nina, it's me. Let me in."

I open the door to the room and he practically falls inside, his hair disheveled, his face covered in sweat, and his undershirt filthy.

"What happened?" I ask as I lock the door behind him.

"Nothing."

"Don't tell me nothing. Obviously something," I say, motioning to everything from the waist up. "And what was that noise?"

But he just ducks into the bathroom and slams the door in my face. The only reason I don't pound on it is because I don't want to wake Tiffany again. I hear the water running—not heavy so it must just be the sink—then it stops and he opens the door. His hair is slicked back, his upper body is covered with droplets, and his filthy T-shirt is balled up in his hand. "Why are you still awake? Get some sleep."

Then he shuts the light off and the room is plunged into darkness again. I hear him open the armoire, probably taking off his pants, then the creak of his bed.

"You're not going to tell me what happened?" I say, louder than a whisper but not loud enough to wake Tiffany.

"It was nothing. A bar fight gone wrong."

I don't remember seeing a bar in the hotel. And when I point this out to him, he says, "Across the street. One of the guys must be staying here."

Maybe that explains the noise, but not his appearance. "And you tried to break it up?"

"Not exactly."

Now it's just getting annoying. "You wake up in the middle of the night and grab your gun, tell me not to open the door to anyone but you, then come back here looking like you rolled around in the mud. You don't think I have a right to know what's going on? Because I do."

He sighs, then says, "If you must know, one of those punks tried to steal my gun and I had to chase him down several alleys to get it back. Happy now?"

I bite my lip to keep from laughing. That's definitely not the answer I was expecting. "Just happy to know you weren't being chased by Russian mobsters," which is where my mind naturally went to after scorpions. Then I feel my way back to my own bed and climb in.

I'm just starting to drift off again when Agent Brody says, "You were worried about me." It's a statement, not a question.

"I was worried about me and Tiffany. We don't know our way around Panama, we have no money, and we need you to find our father, not to mention explain to the judge why it's okay for us to travel on fake passports so we don't go to jail!" I Googled it and it is a crime.

"Right," he says in a tone that implies the opposite.

He can think what he likes. I will *never* admit that I was the tiniest bit worried about his welfare too.

THE NEXT TIME I open my eyes, the light flooding our room is coming from the windows. This doesn't surprise me. What surprises me is that I'm alone.

29

I find Tiffany's note in the bathroom, written in eyeliner on the back of my boarding pass and wrapped around my toothbrush. *Need coffee. Jason thought we should let you sleep in. Call me when you're up.*

I feel like this is the first time I've been alone in days, when I realize it's not just a feeling but actually true. Instead of calling Tiffany, I check the tub. I don't see any creepy crawlies, so I turn on the faucet, which is surprisingly hot and forceful. I didn't pack any bubble bath, and of course the hotel doesn't provide any amenities, so I pour a handful of shampoo into the tub, which produces a light spattering of bubbles and makes the water smell nice too.

I've only been soaking for a few minutes when I hear the door to the room open. I immediately panic until I open my eyes and see that I remembered to shut the bathroom door. *But did I lock it?* I don't have to wonder long because within seconds the door bangs open and I'm staring up at Agent Brody, fully dressed in khakis and a button-down, who is staring down at naked me.

"Get out!" I scream and grab the towel off the toilet seat,

where I'd left it. I don't think about the fact that it is/was the only dry towel in the bathroom and is now sopping wet since I plunged it into the tub to cover myself.

He steps out and slams the door shut behind him but says, "I need the bathroom, Nina. Now."

Fuck him. He can wait. "You'll get it when I'm done with it." He's the one who wanted to share a room.

"No, Nina, now. Or I'm going to shit all over the floor!"

That mental image is even more abhorrent to me than having him see me naked in the tub, so I pull myself out of the bath, wrap my soaked towel around my body, and yank the door open. "It's all yours," I say, but before I can get the last word out, he's already pushed me out of his way and slammed the door shut. But this time I don't mind not being privy to what's happening inside. In fact, I cross to the far side of the room, leaving a wet trail in my wake, just so I don't have to hear him too.

Ten minutes later I'm dressed in shorts, a striped T-shirt, and sandals. My hair is still wet, but I managed to dry the rest of me with the sheet from the bed. I'm about to call Tiffany, who didn't return to the room with Agent Brody, when the bathroom door opens and he emerges sporting a sheepish grin.

"Sorry about that," he says. "It was an emergency."

"Obviously," I reply. "Something you ate?"

"I think you may have been right to pass on those chili cheese fries."

The food truck culture has taken over Panama City too, and at our cab driver's suggestion, we stopped at one for dinner last night. I'm surprised it took Agent Brody this long to feel the effects of his meal. The man must have an iron stomach, or at least one made of stainless steel.

Luckily I brushed my teeth before the bath so there is

nothing I absolutely have to do or get from the bathroom that can't wait until later in the day. "Where's Tiffany?"

"The restaurant next door. They serve a full buffet breakfast for five bucks. If you hurry you can still make it."

"Tiffany's having breakfast at a five-dollar all-you-can-eat buffet?" I find that hard to believe.

He shakes his head. "No, she's drinking the coffee, which is excellent, by the way. Local beans."

My mouth is already watering. A cup (or two or three) of coffee is exactly what I need to get me over my night of too little sleep.

I'm not planning on eating either, but when I see all the fresh fruit platters at the buffet, I pony up my five bucks too. (Luckily they take American dollars in Panama, since I haven't changed any money.) Although I start off eating healthy, piling my plate with pineapple, papaya, and assorted melons, that ends as soon as I discover the *hojaldras*, Panama's version of a donut, which is really deep-fried bread covered in powdered sugar, like a beignet but heavier. After three cups of coffee (Agent Brody was right, it is excellent), a mound of fruit, and God only knows how many donuts (hey, it's an all-you-can-eat buffet!), I'm so full I can barely move. I'm tempted to unbutton my shorts but I know Tiffany would disapprove. And rightfully so.

"Should we go back to the room?" I ask Tiffany. Maybe I'll feel better if I can lie down.

"I thought we agreed we were going to find a new hotel?"

"I know, but we still have to pack up our stuff and check out." Which is true. "And I'm not sure Agent Brody actually agreed to switch." Which is also true.

The busboy stops by our table for the umpteenth time to ask if we want more coffee—or really to ask Tiffany if she wants more coffee. He barely looks at me. We both decline and he returns to the counter, where he and his fellow busboy openly stare at Tiffany. She ignores them, which would be hard for me, but she's probably used to men staring at her all the time. She leans back in her chair and smiles.

"What?" I ask because clearly something's percolating inside that gorgeous head of hers.

"You need to be nicer to Agent Brody."

"I'm perfectly civil to him." I'd told her what happened in the bathroom this morning. I could've given him a hard time about it, but I didn't. Wasn't that nice enough? The man did ruin our lives, after all.

"He likes you."

"He does not." But even as I say it I know it's not true. I can tell by the way he looks at me. Not that I think he wants to be my boyfriend or anything of the sort. He just wants to fuck me. I think watching my sex tape gave him the wrong idea about me. And catching me naked in the bathtub this morning didn't help.

"And if you were a little nicer to him," Tiffany continues as if I didn't just deny his interest in me, "he'd be a lot nicer to us."

"So basically you want me to sleep with him so you can stay in a better hotel."

"So *we* can stay in a better hotel. And I'm not suggesting you have sex with him, although you could do worse. He's kind of cute, don't you think?"

We obviously have different taste in men. "If you think he's so great, why don't you sleep with him? Who knows, maybe he'll put you up at the Ritz."

"Because he doesn't want me; he wants you."

I glance over at the busboys, who are still staring at Tiffany, although when they notice me looking at them, they laugh and turn away. I return my attention to Tiffany and take in her blonde hair, which this morning she's loosely piled on top of her head, and her big boobs, clad only in a tank top and semi-sheer overlay. "Oh, I'm sure you could work your charm on Agent Brody if you tried."

She shakes her head. "Maybe if I were eighteen. I think he's afraid to touch me because I'm underage."

She's obviously given this some thought.

She sets her coffee down on the table and leans in. "C'mon, Nina, he's not that bad. I think you'd actually like him if you gave him a chance."

"Have you forgotten what he's done to Dad? To our entire family?"

She sits up straight. "No, I haven't forgotten. But he was doing his job. And now he realizes he made a mistake and he's trying to fix it."

I let out a harsh laugh. How can she be so worldly in some ways and so naïve in others? "And is he fixing it for our benefit or for his?"

Ever since Agent Brody came to town proclaiming our father's innocence, this has been my constant rumination. He must be getting something out of this, or thinks that he will. I don't for one second believe he's doing this for any notions of justice or out of the goodness of his heart. But I can't figure out what he's after. A promotion? Publicity? A book deal? I know if I ask him he won't tell me the truth, so I don't bother. I'll find out eventually.

"What does it matter why he's doing it," Tiffany says, "as long as he proves Dad's innocent?"

I'd reached the same conclusion, but it still nags at me. "Fine, but I'm not sleeping with him."

"I'm not asking you to. But can you at least call him by his first name?"

.   .   .

"I HAVE A PLAN," Agent Brody says when we return to the room. He's sitting on his unmade bed, pecking at his laptop. The hotel is no frills; however they do provide free Wi-Fi. Go figure. He turns to Tiffany. "But I'm going to need your help."

"You need Tiffany's help but not mine?" Yes, I'm offended. And no, I don't know why.

She flops down on our bed, which bounces in response. "Sure. What do you need me to do?"

He stops typing and looks up. "What you do best. Find out something you're not supposed to know."

30

I'm no longer offended, since Tiffany's skills at lying and eavesdropping are much better than mine. But I'm not thrilled with Agent Brody's plan either.

"She won't be in any danger," he insists. "She'll be wearing a wire and I'll be outside listening the entire time."

"And what if some drunk banker makes a move on her?"

"I think your sister can defend herself."

Tiffany rolls her eyes at me. "I go out clubbing with my friends all the time, Nina. Or I used to before"—she glances at Agent Brody—"everything happened."

I don't bother asking how she got into clubs at her age. I doubt the bouncers even troubled themselves checking her fake ID. "There's a difference between a club and a convention."

"Conference," Agent Brody corrects me. "Latin American Bankers Association Annual Conference, which begins tonight at the Panama City Ocean Club." He turns his laptop around so the screen is facing me and Tiffany. In the center of it is a photo of a fancy high-rise building situated on the waterfront. "Nice enough for you?"

Tiffany reaches for the laptop and starts scrolling through

pictures of luxurious hotel rooms, beautiful pools, and gorgeous people enjoying expensive food and drink. "I could stay there no problem."

"We're not staying there, genius. He just wants you to dress up like a prostitute and mingle with some drunk bankers so you can get information on Dad."

"No, I do *not* want her to dress up like a prostitute because I specifically do *not* want her to be mistaken for one."

"So you're not suggesting she participate in a gang bang to get information on our father? My mistake."

"As if I would!" Tiffany says.

I don't bother explaining that it would likely not be her choice.

"I'm suggesting," he says, matching my angry tone with his own, "that she pretend to be a guest at the hotel having a drink at the bar and to use her physical assets and natural eavesdropping skills to glean information that may help us find your father."

"Yes, because of course our father's disappearance nine months ago is going to be the hot topic of conversation at the Latin American Bankers Association Annual Conference."

"It's my job to see that it is," he says.

"Really? And how are you going to make that happen?"

"And your job," he continues, ignoring my question, as usual, "is to stay in the room and wait for us."

Fat chance of that happening.

31

U nlike me, Tiffany has no qualms about participating in
Agent Brody's plan, but she still makes it contingent
upon us staying at the Panama City Ocean Club.

"One night only," Agent Brody says, removing his clothes
from the armoire and carefully folding them before returning
them to his suitcase. He's the only one of the three of us who
bothered to unpack. All Tiffany and I have to do is to toss our
toothbrushes into our suitcases and zip them shut. "And after
that we move to a cheaper hotel."

Tiffany doesn't answer him, but I know once we check into
the Panama City Ocean Club, we won't be checking out again
until we're ready to leave the city. I think Agent Brody knows it
too, he just doesn't want to admit that he's been bested by a
seventeen-year-old girl.

Tiffany wants to book us into a suite, which Agent Brody
refuses to do. And Agent Brody wants to reserve the cheapest
room available, which Tiffany refuses to do. In the end, neither
one of them has a choice since, with the conference starting that

day, the hotel is nearly full. We end up with the only room available other than the Presidential Suite, which even Tiffany acknowledges is too expensive. Our room comes with one king bed, a couch that doesn't open up, a giant soaking tub (which I'm happy to see since my last bath was cut short), and a partial ocean view.

The bellman also assures us that no guest of the Panama City Ocean Club has ever been disturbed by a scorpion or a poisonous spider, but if Tiffany has "any concerns, any concerns at all," she should call down to the front desk and ask for Diego and he will come up to assist her in any way he can. And I have no doubt that he will.

We all thank Diego, and after Agent Brody tips him, he leaves. "I should travel with you two more often," Agent Brody says, locking the door behind Diego. "I get much better service."

I laugh. "I think you have Tiffany to thank for that."

"Don't say that," he says. "You're both beautiful women."

I'm not normally insecure about my looks, but it's hard to feel attractive when I'm with Tiffany. I know I'm a solid eight, but Tiffany is a ten, and an eight just can't compete with that.

"You don't need to suck up to me, Agent Brody. I'm not the one you're sending into the lion's den."

"I'm not sucking up; I'm telling you the truth. When are you going to start trusting me?"

Never.

When I respond with a blank stare, he shakes his head and walks away. Tiffany leans over and whispers, "And when are you going to start calling him Jason?"

Never to that too.

TIFFANY and I unpack while Agent Brody changes out of his khakis and into his cheap suit. When he slips his badge into his pants pocket and straps on his holster, I ask him where he's going.

"To work," he says. "And I want you two to stay at the hotel. Go to the pool or the shops or something. If anyone asks, tell them you're sisters down here on vacation for a few days. If they push for more details, change the subject."

"You mean like you always do?"

As usual, he ignores my question.

"I programmed my cell number into both your phones and added myself to your favorites. If you need me, call. Otherwise I'll see you tonight."

"And you'll be where exactly?" I ask again.

But he just waves and walks out the door.

I lock it behind him, then turn around to find Tiffany rifling through his suitcase. "What are you doing?" I ask even though it's obvious.

"Well, you want to know what he's up to, don't you? How else are we going to find out?"

"What if he comes back and sees you?" He's only been gone for thirty seconds. It's not inconceivable that he's forgotten something and he'll return to the room to retrieve it before leaving the hotel.

"He can't get in. You locked the top lock so the door will only open a couple of inches. One of us would have to unlatch it for him and that'll give me enough time to put everything back."

I don't know whether to be impressed or appalled. Maybe a little of both. Clearly she's done this sort of thing before.

"Well, don't just stand there," she says. "Go check the bathroom."

OUR SEARCH of his suitcase and toiletries bag turns up nothing, which doesn't surprise me. I didn't expect to find a secret diary outlining his plans. Maybe if he'd left his phone or laptop behind, we might've found something, but he took both of those with him. "Well, that was pointless," I say, rejoining Tiffany in the bedroom.

"Not pointless," Tiffany says. "You did find that pack of condoms. That gives us a clue as to his state of mind."

"They were at the bottom of the bag with his shaving cream. And they expired six months ago. They've probably been in there for years."

"Interesting that you checked the expiration date. I guess that gives us a clue as to your state of mind too."

She raises her eyebrows at me and I laugh. Sex is the last thing on my mind. And if the expired condoms are any indication, sex, or protected sex, isn't high on Agent Brody's agenda either.

With nothing else to do, we tour the hotel, then spend a couple of hours lounging by the pool before heading back to the room to shower and dress. By the time Agent Brody returns at six thirty, we're both ready to head out.

"Perfect," Agent Brody says when he sees Tiffany in her V-neck silver sheath, her hair piled on top of her head in a loose bun, setting off her dangly earrings and making her already swanlike neck look even longer.

Perfect only after I made her change her outfit three times. I had to keep reminding her that the look she was going for was seductive, not slutty. And I admit the tan sandals aren't a perfect match, but I refused to let her buy the six-hundred-dollar pair that she'd spotted in one of the shops in the lobby. She'd withdrawn the two thousand dollars that Raylene had sent her before we'd left LA, but we were saving that for an emergency—and rhinestone-embellished shoes, even if they were on sale and looked fabulous with the dress, were not an emergency.

"And why are you all dolled up?" Agent Brody asks, taking in my black cocktail dress and high heels. "Hot date tonight?"

"You didn't think I was going to let Tiffany do this alone, did you?"

"She won't be alone," he says, taking off his suit jacket and folding it over the arm of the couch. "I'll be there too."

"You won't even be in the room."

"She'll be wired. I'll be outside listening to every word."

"Great. I'll be listening to every word too because I'll be right next to her."

"Nina, I don't want you there."

"Why not?"

He hesitates, then says, "Tiffany speaks Spanish. You don't. You'll stick out like a sore thumb."

"And Tiffany won't? Look at her. She'll have every guy in the room lusting after her."

"Aw, that's so sweet of you," she says.

I glance at her and shake my head. Honestly, I just want to smack her sometimes.

"That's the whole point, Nina. I want men chatting her up."

"I can assure you, Agent Brody, my presence will not deter anyone from chatting up Tiffany." I'd been out with her in public enough times to know that. Even our father's presence never stopped men from flirting with her.

"And what if someone tries to chat you up?" he asks. "Then what?"

"*No habla español,*" I reply in my very American accent.

Agent Brody never acquiesces, but short of handcuffing me to the bed, and I'm not even sure he brought his handcuffs (we didn't find any when we searched his suitcase), he has no choice. He shows Tiffany how to tape the tiny microphone to her body, which easily disappears into her cleavage, tests it with the receiver in his ear, and after confirming that it works, we all head out together.

Since the three of us are alone in the elevator, Agent Brody spends the fourteen-floor ride repeating the instructions he'd already given us in the room. "The opening reception is a cocktail party in the Blue Wave Lounge. I want you to just go to the bar and order a drink. Do not approach anyone. Let them come to you."

"And what if no one comes to us?" Tiffany asks.

Agent Brody chuckles and even I have to smile. "I guarantee you that will not be a problem, Tiffany."

But when the elevator reaches the lobby level, Agent Brody pushes the emergency stop button.

"What are you doing?" I ask as the alarm begins to ring.

"One last thing. We don't know each other. If you happen to see me, ignore me, no matter what. Understand?"

"No, I thought—"

He releases the button and the elevator doors slide open and Agent Brody disappears. I turn to Tiffany. "What was that about?"

She shrugs. "Who cares. Let's go get a drink."

But it's not quite that easy.

32

———

As we approach the Blue Wave Lounge, we spot the sign on the easel next to the door. It's written in several languages, but one of them is English: *Closed for private event.* That alone wouldn't stop us, but there are also two stylishly dressed women at a table in front of the entrance checking in guests and handing out name tags. If it were two men, maybe we could sweet-talk our way in, but that isn't going to happen with two women.

"Now what?" If Agent Brody had a Plan B, he didn't tell us what it was. I'm about to whisper into Tiffany's cleavage on the assumption that he's listening and will find some way to communicate with us when Tiffany grabs my hand. "C'mon, I know another way."

She leads us out to the pool area, which is also roped off with a closed sign, but Tiffany steps around it and I follow. The pool patio backs up to the Blue Wave Lounge. All that separates the two is a wall of sliding glass doors and more ropes and closed signs, but we ignore those.

The door to the lounge opens before we even reach it and three men in dark suits step out onto the pool deck. I guess they're in their late thirties or early forties, and definitely bankers or hedge-fund types. They're each holding a drink and wearing a name tag. They smile and nod at Tiffany and me as we pass, and we smile and nod back. *This is going to be easy.* But as we cross the threshold into the lounge, a very large man, also wearing a dark suit, but a much cheaper one than the other three, steps in front of us.

"*Por favor, señoritas, puedo ayudarlo?*"

"*No habla español,*" I reply before Tiffany can answer him.

"I'm sorry, ladies," he replies in heavily accented English, "but this area is closed for a private party."

Tiffany gives him her pouty face. "But we just want to get a drink."

He looks her up and down and licks his lips and I think he is going to relent, but he says, "My apologies, señoritas, but you can get a drink in the Café Azul Restaurant on the mezzanine level. There are also many fine clubs and restaurants a short walk from the hotel. If you visit the concierge, he can help you find someplace."

"But we've been walking all day and my sister's feet are killing her," Tiffany says, pointing to my high-heeled shoes. "Can't we just have one drink and then leave?"

The bouncer or security guard or whatever they call them in Panama City is unmoved (no doubt he's heard better excuses) but the man standing behind him is not. His back has been to us since we arrived, but now he turns around and I can see that he is an older gentleman, in his late fifties or maybe early sixties, but with a full head of black hair, a trim mustache, and an attractive smile. Although at least half a foot shorter than the bouncer, he puts his hand on his shoulder and says, "Come now, Eduardo, surely we can make an exception for these beautiful ladies."

Eduardo replies to him in Spanish, which I don't understand

but assume is something along the lines of *You're the boss,* because Eduardo steps aside and we're in.

Tiffany and I smile at the older gentleman. He smiles back and says, "Allow me to introduce myself. I'm Enrique Rojas."

I've already read it on his name tag, which includes the words *Banco Internacional.*

I hold out my hand to him and he shakes it limply, evidently not accustomed to shaking hands with women. "Ashley," I say, "and this is my sister, Amber."

"Ashley and Amber," he replies. "That should be easy to remember."

That's what Tiffany and I thought too when we chose our fake identities this afternoon. Ashley is my middle name and Tiffany just likes the name Amber.

"And what can I get you to drink?"

"Oh, that's not necessary," I say. Agent Brody was very clear that he wanted us to sit at the bar and let the men come to us, not be off in a corner talking to some old man.

"I insist," he says and slips his arm through mine. "I understand your feet are sore. I have a table where you can sit down."

He propels us through the crowded lounge to a corner booth on the opposite side. Except for the sign on the table, *Reservado,* it's empty. The only empty seat in the room. "Please," he says, and motions for me to sit down, which I do, and Tiffany slides into the circular booth beside me. Then he holds up his hand and a waiter who must've been lurking nearby appears at our table. "Señor," he says, bowing slightly.

"What would you like to drink?" he asks again.

I'm trying to think of a wine produced in Panama but can't come up with one. I finally say, "What do you recommend?"

"If you like wine, we have a lovely Chilean white. Very

refreshing. Or if you'd prefer a bit of local flavor, we have many wonderful rums."

"Wine, please." Chile does produce some very good whites. And more importantly, wine is something I can sip slowly and savor. I have no intention of getting drunk tonight.

"I'll try the rum," Tiffany says.

I give her a hard stare. I don't want her getting drunk tonight either. But she just ignores me and smiles at Enrique.

"*Dos sauvignon blanc y un mojito*," he says to the waiter, who nods and disappears. He turns back to us and smiles. "Tell me, what brings you ladies to Panama?"

"Vacation," I say.

"We're from the US," Tiffany adds, as if he didn't already know that from our accents.

"Which part?" he asks.

"LA," I say at the same time Tiffany says, "New York."

Enrique's eyes widen and I start to panic, but Tiffany doesn't flinch. "Ashley"—she nods at me and I silently thank God that she remembered to use my fake name—"moved to LA last year after her husband passed away. It was very sudden. We were all devastated."

I'm thankful my wine hasn't arrived yet because I surely would have spit it out all over the table. *My husband?*

Enrique reaches across the table and takes my hand. "My condolences. It's always hard when a spouse dies. But you are young and very beautiful. I'm sure you'll find love again."

"Thank you," I say and pull my hand away. I don't trust myself to say more. I have no idea where Tiffany is going with this story, but I have a feeling she isn't done yet and I don't want to unintentionally contradict her.

"That's why we're here," Tiffany continues. "My sister is having a tough time of it and I thought a little trip might cheer her up. I heard Panama City has great nightlife."

"Yes," he says. "We have many fine discos, and there are several casinos too. I can recommend some if you like."

"That would be great," Tiffany says as the waiter arrives with our drinks.

Enrique holds up his wineglass, so we raise our glasses too. "To happier times," he says, staring directly into my eyes.

I look away and concentrate on my wine. Enrique ordered well. This is an excellent sauvignon blanc. Crisp and refreshing, with a mild citrus undertone.

"You are a wine connoisseur?" he asks.

I panic again, unsure how to respond. I try to catch Tiffany's eye—she's much better at the impromptu lying than I am—but she's staring out at the sea of men filling the room, a few of whom I can't help but notice are quite good-looking. All I can come up with is, "Um."

"It's the way you hold your glass, and sniff and swirl before you taste," he says.

I look down and realize that I had done exactly that. It's second nature to me to taste wine this way, so I didn't consider that it's something my recently widowed alter ego might not know to do. "Yes, my late husband was a wine aficionado so I became one too."

"What did he do?" Enrique asks. "Your late husband."

I'm definitely getting in over my head with this story. I turn to Tiffany again, who is smiling at a hot twentysomething banker who's heading toward our table. "Tif— Amber," I correct myself midstream. "I think we should go."

She turns around and glances at my panic-stricken face. "What's wrong?"

"I, um." My eyes start to well up from the overwhelming fear that we are about to be exposed.

But Enrique naturally assumes my sadness is over thoughts

of my late husband. "I apologize. That was insensitive of me. Let's talk of happier things."

"Thank you," I say, overcome with relief. I would make a terrible spy. I'll cross that off my list of possible new careers. "If you'll excuse me, I need to find the ladies' room." Then I push Tiffany out of the booth, much to the chagrin of her approaching would-be suitor, grab her hand, and pull her with me toward the front entrance to the lounge.

When Tiffany realizes I'm leading her out of the bar—I haven't the slightest idea where the ladies' room is—she stops walking. "What are you doing? We just got here."

"I can't do this. I'm not as good a liar as you. And what was all that BS about my dead husband? We never talked about that."

"I improvised. It's a good story. He totally fell for it."

"Yeah, except now he wants to know what my dead husband did for a living."

"So make something up."

"Like what?"

"Anything," she says. "Tell him he worked in finance."

"This guy's a banker, Tiffany." I motion toward the crowd around us, ninety-five percent of whom are men. "They all are. What if they start asking questions like where did your dead husband work and what was his name? What if they knew him?"

"How could they know him if he didn't exist?"

Then we're both distracted by the commotion outside. I can't see around all the people in front of us, but I can hear raised voices, one of which is familiar to me.

33

———

Tiffany and I push our way closer to the front entrance and spot Agent Brody arguing with two men in black suits—our bouncer from the back door and someone who could be his brother. Then Enrique rushes past us and joins them too. They are so loud that the crowd starts to hush and I can hear Agent Brody yelling at them, mostly in Spanish but with a few words of English (*FBI* and *warrant*) sprinkled in too.

"What's he doing?" I whisper to Tiffany, who can both understand what everyone's saying and has a better view than me.

She stops craning her neck and leans in. "He's trying to get inside but they won't let him. He told them he's FBI and he has a warrant."

If he has a warrant, then why the hell does he need us?

"But Enrique just told him his warrant is meaningless here and he needs to leave."

I hear more unintelligible (to me) shouting and then it suddenly stops. The tall man in front of me, who had been blocking my view of the entrance, moves toward the bar and I can finally see what's happening just as two hotel security guards—distinguishable from the bouncers because they dress in blue suits instead of black ones—forcibly escort Agent Brody away from the door. He turns around once and for a moment we lock eyes. My heart is pounding in my chest and I think I might actually be on the verge of passing out from the stress when he winks at me.

Huh? I turn to Tiffany, unsure if I just imagined that whole scene, and she's smiling. "C'mon," she says and grabs my hand, leading us toward the bar, "the fun's about to begin."

34

Once we're seated at the bar, I realize what Agent Brody was up to. I can't understand most of what's being said around me, but I hear the words *FBI*, *Americano*, and *Harold Rothberg*, so I know the conversation in the room has segued from whatever the hot topic had been—maybe the soccer match playing on the televisions above the bar—to my father.

We're still trying to flag down the bartender to order drinks when Tiffany's would-be suitor appears.

"Much commotion," he says to my sister in perfect English. "Very exciting, no?"

"Very," she says. "Do you know what they were fighting about?"

"*No habla español?*" he asks.

"*Un poco,*" she replies and holds up her fingers to indicate a very small amount. "But I like mojitos."

Subtle? No. Effective? Yes.

"Then you must have one." He calls out to the harried bartender, who he knows by name.

"I'm Amber," Tiffany says, then motions to me, "and this is my sister, Ashley."

"A pleasure to meet you, Amber." I assume from the expression on his face that the sentiment is genuine. "And you, Ashley," he says, giving me the briefest nod before turning his attention back to my sister. "I'm Rafael Abarca." When the bartender arrives, he orders three mojitos, not bothering to ask me what I'd like to drink.

Tiffany tells him we're visiting from the US before he can ask, then starts peppering him with inane questions about what types of food he likes and the best clubs in the area. I glance at my watch and can't believe we've only been talking to Rafael for fifteen minutes. It feels like an hour. At least. I consider going back up to the room—clearly Tiffany doesn't need my help, she's much better at both lying and chatting with men than I am or ever will be—when Enrique Rojas sidles up to me.

"Enjoying your mojito?" he asks.

Not really. I'm not a big rum drinker. But I say, "It's very tasty, although not quite as refreshing as the wine."

"I agree. Shall we go back to my table? We can order a bottle. They also serve a very nice Pinot Noir if you prefer red. Have you eaten?"

Not since breakfast and I'm starving. "Not yet. We just came in for a drink," I add, remembering our cover story.

"They have excellent tapas here. You must try some."

I glance over at Tiffany, who is pretending to hang on Rafael's every word, and he is lapping up the attention like a puppy.

She must've learned this trick from Raylene.

Enrique notices my hesitation and says, "Your sister will be quite safe with Rafael." Then he leans over and says something to Rafael in a voice too low for me to hear. Rafael nods and says, "*Sí, sí,*" in response.

"It is done. Please join me," he says and holds out his arm for me.

I'm starting to understand the appeal of powerful older men. Enrique is at least twice my age, yet his manners and his confidence make him very attractive, maybe even a little bit sexy.

I slip my arm through Enrique's and allow him to lead me back to his table, which is empty again but for the reserved sign. We slide into the booth on opposite sides and he orders a bottle of the sauvignon blanc and an assortment of tapas. This time he doesn't ask me any personal questions. We talk about wine and food and restaurants we've eaten at and cities we've traveled to and I don't even realize that hours have passed and the lounge is almost empty until Tiffany appears at our table, sans Rafael, and says, "I'm exhausted. Are you ready to go?"

"Yes, absolutely," I say, embarrassed by my behavior. I was supposed to be keeping a watchful eye on Tiffany, not enjoying myself on a pretend date!

When I slide out of the booth and stand up, Enrique does too. "Thank you for the wine," I say, "and the company. It was a lovely evening."

"Not half as lovely as you, my dear," then he kisses my hand.

I can't stop myself from blushing, but at least I don't swoon.

"I would very much like to show you the city," he continues.

I would very much like that too, but Tiffany intervenes. "Sorry, she can't. We're leaving tomorrow."

"So soon? That is too bad." I think he genuinely means it. I know I do! This is the most enjoyable evening I've had in ages. "Perhaps you could change your plans," he says.

"Perhaps," I say without thinking. I have no idea what Agent Brody has in mind for us to do next, but presumably it does not include a tour of the city with Enrique.

"I doubt it," Tiffany replies.

Again we're both disappointed by Tiffany's response. Then Enrique pulls a business card out of his jacket pocket and hands it to me. "If your plans change, please contact me."

"Won't you be busy with the conference?" Tiffany asks. She obviously has more information about it, and Enrique's role in it, than I do.

"For your sister, I shall make time."

TIFFANY WAITS until we're alone in the elevator before she starts grilling me. "What was that about?"

"Nothing," I say.

"It didn't look like nothing. It looks like he's really into you. 'For your sister I shall make time,'" she says, mimicking Enrique.

I have to laugh. He is a bit over the top. Maybe it's a Latin thing. Or an older man-younger woman thing. But I can't deny that it was the best date, real or pretend, that I've had in years.

"Did you at least get anything useful out of him?" Tiffany asks.

"Useful?"

"About Dad. You know, the reason we're here."

I'm embarrassed to admit that I hadn't even thought about my father the entire time I was with Enrique.

"Oh my God," she says, "you really like this guy!"

"He was nice, okay? I don't have every man in the world falling all over me the way you do."

The elevator arrives at our floor and we head down to our room in silence. I half expect to find Agent Brody waiting for us, but the hotel room is empty. Although evidently the maid has been there in our absence since the comforter has been turned down and there are chocolates on our pillows.

Tiffany flops down on the bed. "Nice as in just nice? Or nice as in nice," she says in a sexy voice and wiggles her eyebrows.

I laugh as I kick off my shoes. "Just nice," I say as I lie down next to her, even though he's the other nice too.

Then the door bangs open and Agent Brody barrels in. I

assume he'll be happy—we'd done exactly as he'd asked us to do and we didn't get caught—but instead he's angry. "That man is twice your age."

For a moment I wonder how he could know what we were talking about, then I realize that Tiffany is still wearing her wire and he's been listening to every word. "So what? It's okay for an older man to be attracted to a younger woman, but not for a younger woman to be attracted to an older man?"

"So you *do* like him?"

Busted. I decide to take a page out of Agent Brody's playbook and not answer. "Why do you care?"

"I don't," he says, but clearly he does. Even I can see that.

"Should I leave you two alone?" Tiffany asks. She doesn't say "to have your lover's quarrel," but I know that's what she's thinking. It's obvious from the huge grin on her face.

"No!" I say and Agent Brody tells her, "That won't be necessary," before turning back to me. "You know the man's a criminal. And married."

Both of these revelations surprise me, although if I'm being completely honest, I'm more upset about the married part. I hate when married men don't wear a wedding ring. It's like they are purposely trying to dupe the entire female population. If you're looking to cheat, at least be honest about it.

"And you know this how?" I ask. "Because I don't recall him mentioning it."

"No, I imagine it didn't come up in conversation when he was plying you with expensive wine and telling you how lovely you are."

"I barely drank the second glass. I'm not even buzzed."

"Well, your cheeks are pretty rosy for someone who's not buzzed."

I can't admit that my cheeks are rosy because I'm on a good-date high. Or was. The evening's ruined for me now. I can't believe I fell for the Latin charm. I should've known better. Although Agent Brody is obviously jealous, which is actually a little endearing. Plus we still need his help finding my father. So I swallow my pride and say, "You were right about tonight. Tiffany didn't need me there; I was only in the way. I was about to come back to the room when Enrique asked me to have a drink with him and I figured what's the harm. I mean, the man's old enough to be my father!"

I can practically see the light bulb appear above Agent Brody's head. Tiffany notices too. "What are you thinking?" she asks.

"I'm thinking what if Enrique *knows* your father?"

35

I'm sorry I wasn't the one wearing the wire tonight, and Agent Brody is too. He grills me on every detail of my conversation with Enrique, then gets annoyed each time I tell him my father's name never came up.

"Why would I have brought up my father? Enrique doesn't even know my real name. You told us not to tell anyone anything, not to give out any personal information, to change the subject if anyone asked. So why on earth would I have mentioned my father?"

"Because the entire reason we're down here is to get information to help us find your father." He doesn't say "you moron," but it's implied.

"And *you're* the one who's supposed to be getting that information. *You're* the FBI agent. We're just here to help. And we followed your instructions to the letter. If you wanted me to do something differently, then you should've told me. So don't try to blame me when *you're* the one who screwed up."

"I didn't screw up. I had no idea what you were doing. Only your sister was wired."

"And whose fault is that?"

He silently fumes at me. And I glare right back at him. Tiffany's the one to break the stalemate. "Didn't you get anything useful from *my* wire? I definitely heard people talking about Dad after you made that big scene. Bravo on your performance, Jason. Academy Award caliber."

The compliment softens him up, which is no doubt her intent.

"Yeah, they were talking about him, alright. But no one mentioned working with him or having any information about his whereabouts. With half the people at that party loaded, I thought I'd at least hear rumors, but if anyone knew anything, they kept it to themselves."

"So your plan was a bust," I say.

They both shoot me angry looks.

"Well, it's the truth, isn't it?"

I watch as Agent Brody's scowl morphs into a self-satisfied smile. "We're not done yet. Thanks to you we have Enrique. That's a connection we still need to explore."

"And how are we going to do that? Tiffany already told him we're leaving tomorrow," which he should know since he was listening in.

Agent Brody picks up Enrique's business card, which I left on top of the dresser with my purse and room key, and holds it out to me. "Call him and tell him you've had a change of plans. Surely Mr. Rojas will find a way to fit you into his busy schedule."

Apparently Agent Brody is jealous no more. "I thought you said he was a criminal. And married."

Agent Brody flicks the business card at me, then sits down on the couch and stretches his long legs out in front of him. "He is."

"So you want me spending time with a married criminal?"

"You already have," he says, reaching for the television remote.

"Yes, but I didn't know he was a criminal." Or married. Although the married part is becoming less relevant by the second. The man is a criminal! "What if he figures out who I really am and what I'm up to?"

"Then you'll need to make sure he doesn't," he replies as he clicks through the channels on the flat-screen TV.

"And how am I supposed to do that, *Agent Brody*?" Yes, I'm now trying to piss him off.

His eyes roam the length of my body so his implication is clear. "I'm sure you'll find a way."

"Fuck you!" I stomp into the bathroom and slam the door shut. I want to smash something. Agent Brody's face would be my preference, but since that's not possible, I zero in on the bathroom mirror. The hair dryer is already in my hand when I realize that if I break the mirror, I'll have to pay for it, which is bad enough, but then there's that old superstition about seven years' bad luck. That I'm not willing to risk.

I set the hair dryer down and collapse onto the toilet seat.

There's a knock on the door followed by Tiffany's voice. "It's me. Can I come in?"

I unlock the knob and she slips inside, shutting the door behind her. "He's being a jerk."

"You think?" I say, my voice dripping with sarcasm.

"But it's a good plan."

"You mean our only plan." I nod at the door, where my nemesis is relaxing on the other side. "You realize he doesn't have a fucking clue how to find Dad. This whole trip is one big wild goose chase."

She sits down on the edge of the oversized tub and for a while the only sound in the room is the steady dripping from the faucet. When I finally get up to tighten the knobs, she asks, "Will you do it?"

I twist both handles as far as they'll go, but the drip, drip, drip continues. "Do you think it's too late to call housekeeping?"

"Nina."

I know she's waiting for me to respond to her question, but she shouldn't be. She knows the answer as well as I do. Of course I'll do whatever it takes to find our father and prove his innocence, and so would she. What child wouldn't?

"Do you really need me to say it, Tiff? Yes, I'll do whatever I need to do to get Enrique to confide in me."

"You don't have to sleep with him," she says, "not if you don't want to. He might not even try. He seemed very gentlemanly. He did kiss your hand," she adds, and we both laugh.

"That's true. He might actually wait for the third date before he tries to stick his cock inside me."

"Exactly!"

I guess my sarcasm wasn't obvious this time.

"And if you see him tomorrow, that would only be the second date," she continues, "so you're safe. And I'll come too if you want."

Thoughts of a threesome, because that's what I imagine Enrique will be thinking, pop into my head, but I immediately dismiss the idea. He's probably too old for that. But it would be easy enough for him to get rid of Tiffany. "What if he invites Rafael?"

Tiffany smirks. "Leave Rafael to me. There were some advantages to living with Raylene, you know."

I CALL Enrique the next morning and tell him we've decided to stay a bit longer.

"I am delighted to hear it," he says. "Let me check my schedule."

I hear rustling in the background and wonder if he really still uses a paper calendar instead of an electronic one when he says, "It looks like I have a short break late this afternoon."

Perfect. The shorter the better. "I could meet you for a coffee." I'd rather not drink alcohol with him anyway.

"No, no, I want to take you somewhere special. Not to Starbucks."

He laughs at his own joke, so I do too. "Anywhere is fine, Enrique. I know you're a busy man."

"No man is ever too busy to spend an evening with a beautiful woman. There's a dinner tonight for the conference attendees that I need to appear at, but no one will notice if I slip away early. I'll pick you up at your hotel at nine. That's not too late for you, is it?"

"No, but you don't have to pick me up. I can meet you somewhere."

"Perhaps that is how they do it in America, *querida*, but not here in Panama. You are my guest. I will pick you up at your hotel."

But I'm not giving up so easily. The man's a criminal. Agent Brody didn't tell me exactly what crimes he'd been accused of committing, but I can use my imagination. And I would feel much more comfortable meeting him in a public place than being alone with him in his car. "Are you sure about that? I thought Panama City was very modern."

"It is, *querida*, but I am not. I shall be at your hotel at nine."

Fuck!

.   .   .

"STOP WORRYING," Tiffany says as I continue to pace the hotel room—door to window, window to door, repeat. "I won't leave your side, I promise."

"And I'll be following from a safe distance," Agent Brody says.

I want to wear a wire tonight, but Agent Brody refuses. He doesn't think Enrique's quite as gentlemanly as Tiffany does and he doesn't want to take a chance that the evening could turn physical and I'd be found out. When I ask what he thinks Enrique would do if he discovers the mic, Agent Brody won't respond. But I keep pushing until he finally says, "He's a criminal, Nina. Nothing good."

"But you said he's a white-collar criminal." I got him to tell me that much this afternoon. "They're not violent."

"He's not laundering money for the Girl Scouts. He works for some very bad men. Men who would not hesitate to eliminate anyone they considered a threat."

If he's trying to calm my nerves, he's doing a really crappy job. "But I'm no threat to them. I only want information about my father."

He blows air through his nose and lets out a long sigh. "I told you, I'll track you through your cell phone. I'll know exactly where you are at all times."

"Yes, but you won't know what he's doing to me." It isn't sex I'm worried about; it's that I'll slip up and he'll figure out who I really am. I don't know how he'll react to my lying to him, and I don't want to find out.

Tiffany says, "I'll be there too and I won't let anything bad happen. I promise."

I glance at my not-even-a-hundred-and-ten-pounds-when-she's-wearing-ski-boots sister. The thought of her being by my side when Enrique finds out we've been lying to him since the moment he met us only makes me worry more.

· · ·

TIFFANY and I wait for Enrique on a stylishly uncomfortable couch in the hotel's ultramodern lobby. I opt not to wait upstairs because I don't want to give Enrique an excuse to come to our room. Agent Brody isn't there; he's sitting outside the hotel in a rental car, tracking us on his laptop. But evidence of his existence remains—his suit hanging in the closet, his underwear in the drawer, his razor on the sink. If Enrique finds that, this operation will be over before it starts.

As soon as I see Enrique enter the lobby, I rush to greet him.

He air-kisses me on the cheek. "You look beautiful," he says, admiring Tiffany's handiwork. I'm wearing one of her dresses—red and clingy, except in the chest, where it's loose on me. I only brought one cocktail dress on this trip and I wore it the previous night, so I had no choice but to borrow one of Tiffany's. Tiffany also blew-dry my hair and applied my makeup—dark red lipstick and smoky eyes—a look I never would've attempted on my own. I feel like an impostor. I can practically hear the announcer's voice in my head: *Tonight the role of the seductress will be played by Nina Roth.*

Tiffany joins us and Enrique air-kisses her cheek too. "Lovely as always, Amber."

"Thank you, Enrique. I hope you don't mind if I tag along this evening. I had other plans but my friend cancelled on me at the last minute."

If he's upset by this news, he doesn't show it. "Two beautiful women to escort instead of one. I'd be a fool to complain."

He smiles at Tiffany, but when he turns back to me, his smile disappears. "And I am not a fool, *querida.*"

36

———

"Would you excuse us a minute?" I say. I don't give him a chance to respond before I grab Tiffany's hand and pull her down the hallway to the ladies' room. "He knows," I say as soon as the restroom door closes behind us.

"Knows what?"

"Who we are!"

She just laughs. "No, he doesn't. You're being paranoid."

"Didn't you hear what he said to me? He's not a fool."

She laughs again. "Yes, because he's going out with two women half his age instead of one. I think any man would say the same."

I shake my head. "You didn't see the way he looked at me. He was serious. I'm telling you, he knows."

"And I'm telling you, it's all in your head. Now let's get back out there before he really does start to suspect something."

I hesitate but realize I am not going to convince her. And she's right that if we stay in the restroom much longer, he will get suspicious. So I take a deep breath and follow.

Please, God, let this all be okay.

Enrique is standing in the lobby where we left him, only

now he's talking on his cell phone. When he spots us approaching, he ends the call and slips the phone into his jacket pocket. "Ready?" he asks, all smiles again.

"Yes," Tiffany replies. "Where are we going?"

"Just a little out-of-the-way place I know."

I'm envisioning a remote location with no cell service, no street lights, and where no one will hear us scream. But ten minutes later his driver pulls up in front of another downtown hotel-casino, and this one is even more bustling than our own.

Is he screwing with us? Making a joke? Is Tiffany right and I'm just paranoid? Either way, I breathe a sigh of relief when the elevator opens onto the fifty-fourth floor and we are deposited into the vestibule of a crowded restaurant. The room is filled with noisy diners enjoying the food and the view from the floor-to-ceiling windows. I can see the entire city skyline from here, and a more subdued skyline across the bay.

As the hostess leads us to our table, we pass a brightly lit staircase with loud music emanating from above. "The disco," she says.

I've traveled outside the US enough to know that internationally the word *disco* is synonymous with dance club and doesn't necessarily mean a DJ playing Donna Summer and the Bee Gees. But I thought Enrique would choose a more romantic restaurant, or at least a quieter one. Perhaps I misread his interest in me. I unwillingly think back to the day Big Mike fired me and a shiver runs through me. This wouldn't be the first time I've misread the signs.

The hostess seats us at a table with four place settings. I assume the waiter will remove the extra one, but he doesn't. A few minutes later I realize why when a gorgeous twentysomething man dressed in a narrow-cut suit with an open-collared shirt approaches our table. The man elicits stares from everyone in the vicinity, men and women alike. I decide he must be either a model or an actor because no one that good-looking could be anything else. Naturally Tiffany is salivating over him, as is every other woman in the room, myself included. Enrique stands up and says, "Diego, *que bueno verte.*"

The two men hug and converse in Spanish until Enrique suddenly switches to English. "Diego, I would like you to meet Ashley."

When he faces me, I'm lit by his thousand-megawatt smile. Even his teeth are perfect. I'm about to offer him my hand to shake when he bends down and says, "*Mucho gusto,*" and gives me an air kiss on the cheek, so I do the same.

"And this is Amber," Enrique says, nodding at Tiffany.

Diego says, "*Mucho gusto,*" and air-kisses her cheek too, but he allows his eyes to wander from her face to her cleavage, which is barely contained inside her embellished scoop-neck tank top.

When Diego takes the empty chair between me and Tiffany and across from Enrique, the waiter appears with our menus. I wait for Enrique to open his before I open mine, but as soon as he does, he leans over and whispers, "I thought you and your sister might enjoy meeting a local celebrity."

"He's a celebrity?" I just assumed everyone was staring at him because he was so astonishingly good-looking. He doesn't look familiar to me at all.

Enrique nods. "He's the star of a very popular Mexican soap opera, but he is Panamanian by birth. His father and I have been friends for many years. He's my godson."

I immediately envision Enrique as Marlon Brando in *The Godfather* and realize this is who he must've been talking to when Tiffany and I were in the ladies' room. "And you can just call him up and ask him to join you for dinner at the last minute and he comes?" *A favor he can't refuse?*

Enrique must be reading my mind because he laughs and

shakes his head. "I think the English word for it is serendipity. I was speaking to his father earlier today and he mentioned that Diego was visiting. When your sister decided to join us tonight, I thought it would be more enjoyable if she had a companion, so I called Diego. I promised to introduce him to two very beautiful American women." Enrique's gaze shifts to the other side of the table and mine follows. "I do not think he considers it an imposition."

I have to agree with him. Diego is obviously enamored with Tiffany. And although his accent is heavy and his English is grammatically incorrect, Tiffany doesn't seem to care. To be honest, if he were looking at me the way he's looking at her, I wouldn't care either. When Diego notices we're staring at them, he immediately stops ogling Tiffany and turns to face us. "I apologize, my English is very bad."

"It's better than my Spanish," I assure him.

Then Tiffany says something to him in Spanish and he laughs.

But Enrique isn't laughing. "You speak Spanish, Amber?"

I glare at her across the table. She just gave up our only advantage.

She realizes her mistake and immediately starts backtracking. "Just a little. I studied it in school but I *never* speak it. I thought I should practice while I'm here." Then she says something in Spanish, exaggerating her American accent to the point where even I wince.

Enrique smiles benignly. "Yes, you should always take advantage of an opportunity to practice a language with a native speaker. I'm sure Diego would be happy to help."

"*Sí, sí,*" he says, then turns back to Tiffany. He speaks to her in Spanish and she laughs. Then she replies in a mix of English and Spanish, and Diego follows suit. I catch a word here and there—soap opera, *Neuvo* York, *escuela*—and assume they are talking about where they're from and what they do.

Enrique and I might as well be at another table for all the attention they pay us, which I presume was Enrique's purpose for inviting him. But this is advantageous for me too. Now that Enrique and I are effectively alone, I try several times to steer the conversation toward banking—that is the only way I can think of to broach the topic of my father without seeming completely obvious. But Enrique deflects every time.

"I'm sure you would find my work very boring, *querida*. I would like to hear more about what you do."

I try to deflect too—"I'm between jobs at the moment." But apparently I'm not as good at it as he is because he keeps pushing until I finally say, "I'm not really sure what I'm going to do next. Ideally I'd like to work in the wine industry."

"I think that is an excellent idea. You are very knowledgeable about wine. I think you would make a fine sommelier."

I laugh. It's something I'd considered too—for about ten seconds. Only high-end restaurants employ sommeliers and, even if I could get hired without anyone finding out who I really am, as soon as the first patron discovers I'm the daughter of Harold Rothberg, I'll be booted out on my ass. It'd be Wine World all over again, but presumably without the attempted rape.

"Why is that funny? Do you not want to be a sommelier?"

"I'd love to." But since I can't admit the truth, I say, "As you know, though, it's a male-dominated profession. It's very difficult for a woman to break in." That's true too.

He leans back and smiles. "I'm surprised, *querida*. I would not think you would let that stop you."

I glow from the compliment. He's right; I wouldn't let that stop me. But I can't disclose my real obstacle. And again I'm struck by the notion that he knows who I am and he's just toying with me. I glance across the table at Tiffany to gauge her reaction, but she's staring into Diego's dark brown eyes. I doubt she even heard any of my conversation with Enrique.

"I have many friends who are restaurateurs," Enrique continues. "Perhaps I could help you."

"You have friends who own restaurants in the US?" How far did his reach extend?

He shakes his head. "No, here in Panama mostly. Although I know a few investors in Miami. But those places wouldn't be right for you."

"Thank you for the offer, Enrique, but I live in the US—and have no plans to move."

"You live there now," he says, "but you don't have to. You like Panama, no?"

"Yes." For the whole three days that I've been here. With the high-rises, the waterfront, and the constant heat and humidity, I feel like I'm in Miami Beach. "But it's not my home."

"It could be."

It finally dawns on me that he's serious. This isn't a polite "let's do lunch" when it's obvious the person doesn't mean it. "But I don't even speak Spanish."

"You could learn." He glances at Tiffany, who is explaining to Diego that in America *pissed* means angry, not drunk like it does in the UK, then turns back to me. "I'll help you. And everyone here speaks English too. It would not be a problem."

"Enrique, I have no place to live. I'm staying in a hotel."

He leans in and reaches for my hand. "I could help you with that too, *querida*. I'm a wealthy man. And a generous one. I like to make women happy."

Oh my God. Did he just offer to make me his mistress?

37

I pull my hand back and reach for my water glass. I'm not thirsty, but I take a long sip to buy myself time to think. I've never been propositioned to be a mistress before. I'm not sure how to respond. Finally I say, "May I ask you something personal?"

"Of course," Enrique replies.

I lower my voice to a whisper even though the restaurant is so loud I'm positive no one else can hear. "Are you married?"

"Yes. And I have three grown children, including a daughter about your age. She graduated from Harvard Business School last year and now works for the IMF," he says with obvious pride. "My eldest son is a doctor here in Panama. My youngest" —he sighs—"is still finding himself." He reaches for his own water glass and takes a sip. "Not unlike you, perhaps."

"And is that why you want to help me? Because I remind you of your son?" I don't actually believe that, but I want to be absolutely sure I'm not misinterpreting his proposal.

He smiles and reaches for my hand again. "No, *querida*, that's not why."

I gulp. For the first time in my life, I actually want Raylene's

advice. She knows much more about these sorts of
arrangements than I do.

"And your wife? Does she live here in Panama?" I thought he
might react to my mentioning his wife, but he's not flustered
at all.

"She spends most of her time at our house in the country.
She breeds horses; it's her passion. I live in an apartment here in
the city, not far from my office."

"And she doesn't mind when you . . . go out to dinner with
other women?"

He gives me an affectionate, almost paternal smile. "I do not
discuss my dinner plans with her, *querida*. She prefers it that
way, and so do I."

I'm not naïve. I know plenty of rich men have mistresses, and
plenty of wives look the other way. I've just never been asked to
participate before. This evening is definitely not going as
planned! "Excuse me a moment," I say and stand up.

Enrique stands too, and then Diego does as well. Tiffany just
looks confused.

"Come help me find the ladies' room," I say and grab my
purse.

"Sure," she says as she joins me.

I use the restroom (I really had drunk a lot of water) while I fill
her in on my conversation with Enrique. I had assumed
correctly that she hadn't been listening. She and Diego were
discussing his acting career while I was being propositioned.

"So what did you tell him?" she asks as I exit the stall and
head to the sink.

"Nothing. Did you think I was going to accept?"

She pulls her lipstick out of her tiny evening bag and turns toward the mirror. "I don't know. He's not bad-looking for an old guy. And according to Diego, he's loaded."

"And how did *that* come up in conversation while he was helping you with your Spanish? Nice save, by the way."

"Thanks," she says and reaches for a tissue to blot the excess color off her lips. "I don't think he actually said his godfather— Oh, did you know Enrique is Diego's godfather?"

"Yes, he told me."

She nods and continues. "Anyway, he didn't come out and say he was loaded, he just sort of implied it. He said Enrique has a huge estate in the country."

"I know. That's where his wife lives."

"How convenient. Then he can go out in the city with his mistress and never have to worry about running into his wife. Did you know Dad and Raylene ran into your mother at a restaurant once? This was when he was still married to your mom. Raylene told me he tried to pretend she was a business associate but your mother wasn't buying it."

I remember hearing that story too, except my mother was shouting it at my father, and he was denying every word.

"Do you think Raylene engineered it?" she asks. "Dad accused her once. He said she'd purposely picked that restaurant because she knew your mother was going to be there too."

I wouldn't put it past Raylene. "But how would she have known? She and my mother were never friends."

Tiffany shrugs. "I don't know. I just always wondered. So did you ask Enrique about Dad?"

"No," I say, slamming my purse down on the counter. "I tried, but he kept changing the subject. It was like he knew exactly what I was trying to do and he purposely steered the conversation in another direction."

"Like you becoming his mistress?" She wiggles her eyebrows at me and giggles.

I don't find his proposal nearly as amusing as she does. "C'mon, Tiff, be serious. I need your help. I can't go out with him again. If I do, he's definitely going to expect sex. If there's any hope of getting information out of him, it has to be tonight."

"Well, we are in a hotel. You could always get a room. You wouldn't have to have sex with him," she adds before I can object. "You could just give him a great blow job and see if he talks. I know Raylene's boyfriend was a lot chattier after I blew him. Of course, he did say I gave him the best BJ he'd ever had. Even better than Raylene."

Her obvious pride over that accomplishment makes me shake my head. Raylene may be her mother, but she's definitely not a good influence. When all this is over, I have to get her away from that woman, no matter what my mother says.

"I am *not* giving him a blow job just so I can ask him about Dad."

"Then what *are* you going to do?"

38

W hen we return to the table, our dinner plates have been cleared and dessert menus are sitting in their place.

"Would you like an after-dinner drink?" Enrique asks.

"No, thank you." I've already had a glass and a half of wine. That's my limit if I want to keep a clear head, and I definitely need to for what I have planned.

Tiffany turns to Diego and says, "Let's go dancing. There's a club upstairs."

That *is* part of my plan. I want to be alone with Enrique, but still in a public place, and I want Tiffany to remain nearby in case we need to make a quick exit. I don't know how Enrique's going to react, but I want to be prepared for all eventualities.

"A wonderful idea," he says and turns to Enrique as if for approval.

Enrique nods his head. "Yes, let's all go dancing."

Let's all go dancing? That's not part of the plan! I place my hand over Enrique's, the first time I have touched him instead of him touching me—and it does not go unnoticed.

He squeezes my fingers. "Yes, *querida*?"

"I thought we could stay here and have coffee. And chat." I

give him what I hope he interprets as a meaningful look. If he thinks I'm going to tell him I want to take him up on his offer, that's okay too. So long as he stays at the table.

"Let's go dancing. And when we're tired of dancing, we can all chat. There's a lounge upstairs that is much better for chatting, I think." Then he signals the waiter for the bill.

THE FOUR OF us head up the staircase together, Tiffany and Diego in front, Enrique and me a few steps behind. The stairs are steep and I hold on to the handrail as I climb, but Enrique stays beside me with his hand on my back the whole time. When we reach the top of the stairway, he says, "*Un momento, por favor*," and disappears into the crowd.

I must look as nervous as I feel because Diego says, "Do not worry. He'll be back soon."

I smile at him and Tiffany clasps my hand. She understands my nerves because she knows what I'm planning to do.

When Enrique returns, she drops my hand and moves closer to Diego. The band, which had been playing something with a salsa beat, switches to a much slower tune. The lead singer grabs the mic and says something in Spanish and Tiffany whispers the translation in my ear: "For the lovers in the room."

Couples crowd onto the dance floor, including Tiffany and Diego.

Enrique watches them as they move with perfect synchrony. "I think your sister's Spanish is improving."

I can't tell if he's joking or serious, but once again I'm struck by the feeling that he's toying with me.

"May I have this dance?" he says next and offers me his hand.

I take it, but the moment we're on the dance floor, he places his other hand on the small of my back and pulls me to him in a tight embrace. I know he can feel every inch of me from my breasts to my thighs because I can feel every inch of him too. *Agent Brody was right. I never could've gotten away with wearing a wire.*

And then it occurs to me that maybe this entire evening is actually part of Enrique's plan. He chose this restaurant. He had to know how loud it is and that there's a dance club attached. And then as soon as we arrive, he disappears and all of a sudden the band is playing a slow song "for lovers" instead of something with a beat. That has to be Enrique's doing. What better way to check to see if I'm wearing a wire than a slow dance? He's not going to pat me down. And he's not going to risk asking me if I want to get a room. A slow dance is the perfect alternative.

I can already hear Tiffany's voice in my head: *Stop being so paranoid!* But am I being paranoid? Surely a man like Enrique can find a local girl to be his mistress. Maybe he even has one already. What if his proposal was just meant to throw me off-balance? To misdirect my attention? What if he knows who I really am and thinks I'm actually here working *for* the FBI? He could've seen Agent Brody wink at me last night. Agent Brody wasn't that discreet. What if Enrique knows Tiffany and I are sharing a room with Agent Brody? He could've followed him after he had him escorted from the lounge last night. Or had him followed. Or had me followed. Or what if Enrique doesn't know who I am, but he thinks the FBI is investigating *him* and that I keep asking him questions about his job because I'm trying to get information on *his* crimes? What if he thinks I'm an FBI agent too? What if, what if, what if. I can't take it anymore!

I pull away from Enrique and push through the crowd, but the room is bursting with people. I need to be alone so I can think. I can't afford to lose my head. I spot an exit sign on the far wall and run in that direction, or more accurately walk as fast as I can in a crowded room while wearing five-inch heels, which isn't very fast. I crash through the exit door expecting to find myself in an interior hallway, but instead I'm standing outside in a rooftop lounge. Heads turn my way but quickly turn back to their companions. Although my entrance was loud, I'm dress and age appropriate. I look like I belong here.

I slow my gait and start walking again. I have no idea where I'm going other than away from where I am. I pass tables filled with happy people drinking exotic cocktails and fancy coffees. It's not until after I turn the third corner that I realize that the lounge is 360 degrees. I soon end up back where I started, only now Enrique is waiting for me.

39

———

"What's wrong?" he asks, but I just shake my head and keep walking. I hear his footsteps behind me and know that he's following, but I don't stop. I realize I'm going around in a circle, but I don't care. I have no idea what to say to him; no idea what to do. I thought I could keep pretending to be Ashley and that maybe if I accepted his offer, or pretended to, that I could get him to open up to me. When I'd talked it through with Tiffany in the ladies' room, it had seemed like a good plan. But now it seems like the stupidest idea I've ever had. This whole evening I thought I was playing him, but now I think it's just the opposite—he's been playing me.

I need to find Tiffany. We can take a cab back to our hotel. Enrique won't stop us. He won't make a scene, not in front of all these people.

I complete my second lap around the rooftop lounge and head toward the same door I entered from. But when Enrique realizes I'm about to leave, he grabs my arm. "Don't go, *querida.*"

Why does he keep calling me querida? *I'm not his* querida. *What does that even mean?*

Then the door opens from the inside and a waitress appears.

She says something in Spanish and then in English asks if we want a table.

"Yes, thank you," Enrique replies. I turn to him but he keeps his hand on my arm. "You're upset. I can't let you leave this way."

"Why not?" I ask, but he doesn't reply. He just steers me in the direction the waitress is leading us, still holding on to my upper arm. His grip isn't tight. I could pull away from him and flee. But I don't want to make a scene either. *We're in a public place. He's not going to hurt you here.*

I take deep breaths as we walk to our table and I feel myself begin to calm down. *Why on earth did I run? That was incredibly stupid of me. How the hell am I going to lie my way out of this now?* And then I realize that I'm not. I'm going to tell him the truth and let the chips fall where they may. I repeat my internal mantra: *We're in a public place. He won't hurt you here.*

Thank God I'm not wearing a wire. Because when Agent Brody hears that I told Enrique the truth, I'm not going to need Agent Brody's protection from Enrique; I'm going to need Enrique's protection from Agent Brody.

The waitress seats us at a table with a view of the bay, but I'm too agitated to enjoy it. Enrique orders a cappuccino for me and an espresso for himself, then the waitress leaves and we're alone again—except for all the other patrons sitting nearby. *We're in a public place. He won't hurt you here.*

"Ashley, please tell me what's wrong. Was it the dance? I didn't mean to upset you. If I did, then I apologize."

It's the "Ashley" that stings me. Maybe that's why he's been calling me "*querida*" all night. Maybe using my fake name bothers him too. Before I can lose my nerve, I take another deep breath and blurt out: "My name's not Ashley."

I'm expecting a reaction to this revelation, but he just stares at me with a neutral expression on his face. *He must be great at poker. My father was (is) too.*

"Aren't you angry?" I ask.

"We all have our secrets, *querida*. I presume you had a good reason for giving me a false name."

"I did. I do." I'm not sure where to begin but my name seems as good a place as any. I swallow hard, then say, "My real name is Nina Roth."

"Nina Roth," he repeats back to me, as if trying it out on his tongue.

"Nina Roth is my legal name. Now. It used to be Nina Rothberg."

I'm sure *this* fact will produce a reaction. It always does. But he just stares at me stone-faced.

And then I realize the truth. "You already knew."

He glances down at his empty hands. "Let us say I suspected."

So I wasn't being paranoid after all. Or if I was, that paranoia was justified. "When . . . did you begin to suspect?" I ask, playing along with the notion that he didn't know for sure, which I don't believe. If he already suspected, it would've only taken him seconds to Google my father's name and find photos of me too. I was at the trial every day.

"Not until this morning when you called. You seemed very eager to see me again."

"Well, why wouldn't I be? I had a nice time last night." No harm in flattering him a little, especially since it's true.

He gives me an affectionate smile. "That's very kind of you, Nina, but as I told you, I'm not stupid. When a beautiful young woman pursues a much older man, there's usually a good reason."

"But I thought that's what you wanted. Or was that offer you made me earlier all part of this cat-and-mouse game we're playing?"

"Not at all. You would make me very happy if you accepted my offer. Are you considering it?"

I'm saved by the waitress, who arrives with our coffee. Or I think I am. When we're alone again, Enrique says, "You have not answered me, *querida*."

Luckily for him he's talking to me, a person who actually answers questions, and not Agent Brody. "I'm flattered, Enrique. Truly I am. But I didn't come down here to be someone's mistress. I'm looking for my father."

"And you brought the FBI with you? Did you think that would help?"

His sudden shift in tone from affectionate to angry gives me a chill. Enrique Rojas is definitely not someone you want to piss off. I don't regret telling him the truth about who I am and why I'm here—he knew anyway. But obviously telling him the *whole* truth would not be a good idea.

40

"I didn't bring that FBI agent with me. Why would I?"

"You tell me, *querida.* It seems an unlikely coincidence that you and he would be here at the same time. Did you know he's been visiting all the big banks, waving his badge around, and demanding information about your father?"

"No, I didn't know that." So that's what Agent Brody was doing the day he left us at the hotel and wouldn't tell us where he was going. He must've been trying to stir up interest in my father, hoping some of those bankers would be talking about it at the conference that night. It wasn't a bad plan.

"And then he appears at the reception with a subpoena even though he knows that is meaningless here. This isn't America. We have our own laws."

His anger is palpable, and understandable, but I need to direct it at Agent Brody and not at me. "Enrique, I know that man. He led the investigation of my father and testified against him at his trial. He destroyed my family, and my life. You cannot possibly dislike him any more than I do. No one can."

"And yet you are down here together."

I shake my head. "I didn't bring him here, Enrique. At least not intentionally. Maybe he followed us. Tiffany and I were careful; we didn't even use our own passports." I wish I had brought mine with me so I could show him, but I left it locked in the safe in our room. "But we're not experts at this." *Far from it.*

"And the false names?"

"All part of our plan to stay under the radar. But obviously our plan failed." That much is true. "Enrique, we just want to find our father. We don't even know if he's dead or alive."

He leaned back and sighed. "I cannot help you, *querida*. I do not know your father."

After all this . . . and he doesn't even know him. I knew it was a long shot, but it was our only shot. Our only hope. Now that's gone too. I lean back in my chair and close my eyes. The tears come involuntarily.

"Please, Nina, do not cry."

"I'm sorry." I really am. I feel like a fool.

He hands me his handkerchief and I laugh, which prompts his questioning look. He's probably wondering if I've lost my mind. I'm wondering too. "It's the handkerchief," I say, wiping my eyes. "I don't know anyone who still uses a handkerchief. It's very *Gone with the Wind*."

He seems to consider this. "Some people have told me I look like Rhett Butler."

That elicits another laugh from me. "I can see the resemblance. I think it's the moustache."

He laughs too and I feel the tension ebb away. We're no longer circling each other like a cat and mouse. We're just two people enjoying each other's company.

The waitress stops by our table to ask if we need anything else even though we've barely touched our coffees. "Do you like flan?" he asks.

"Yes, but I like flourless chocolate cake better," which I'd noticed on the menu downstairs.

He laughs and orders both desserts. When the waitress leaves, we relax into our chairs and sip our coffee.

"I know you want to find your father, but if the FBI finds him too, won't they just extradite him back to the US and put him in jail? He was convicted already, no?"

"Yes, but my father's innocent. That's why we need to find him. He needs to come forward to exonerate himself."

Enrique gives me an affectionate smile. "A daughter's loyalty. Very heartwarming, *querida*."

Obviously he thinks I'm delusional. "This isn't just loyalty, Enrique. There's new evidence. We can prove it was really my father's business partner who masterminded the scam. My father is as much a victim as anyone else."

Enrique sets down his coffee. "And this new evidence, you have it in your possession?"

"No . . . not with me." I need to tread lightly here. We're getting into Agent Brody territory.

"But you have access to it?"

"Back home, yes. Not here. Why?"

He gives me a sad look, like he realizes he has gotten my hopes up and he knows he's about to dash them again. "No reason, *querida*. Just curiosity."

Tiffany and Diego arrive at the same time as our dessert.

"There you are," Tiffany says. "You left so quickly. We didn't know where you went." She begins to drag over an empty chair from the table next to ours, but Diego takes it from her and carries it. Once she's seated, he brings over one for himself too.

"I needed some air," I say and shoot her an I'll-fill-you-in-later look.

"But everything's okay now?" she asks.

"Yes, Tiffany," Enrique says, "everything is fine."

Tiffany's eyes widen when he uses her real name, and poor

Diego just looks confused, but Enrique says, "You must try the flan. It's delicious." Then he grabs a spoon and digs in.

I OFFER to take a cab back to our hotel, but Enrique insists on driving us. Diego wants to come too, so the four of us climb into Enrique's car—Enrique, Tiffany and me in the backseat, and Diego up front with the driver. When we reach the entrance to the Panama City Ocean Club, the driver waits in the car as the two men escort us into the lobby. Tiffany heads toward the elevators and Diego follows, but I stay just inside the revolving door. I want to say good-bye to Enrique in a well-lit public place.

"Thanks for everything, Enrique. And I'm sorry I lied to you."

"You had your reasons, *querida*. I'm not angry."

I'm glad to hear it. I doubt I'll ever see Enrique again, but I still don't want to end the evening on bad terms.

"When are you leaving?" he asks.

"I don't know. Tomorrow, probably. As soon as we can get a flight home." I'm sure Agent Brody will be anxious to leave as soon as possible since he's the one paying for the hotel. "There's no reason for us to stay."

"No reason?" He reaches for my hand and pulls me toward him. "I have very much enjoyed your company these last two days, Nina Rothberg."

"It's Nina Roth now. Legally. That's what it says on my driver's license."

"I would like to see more of you, Nina Roth. And I do not care who your father is."

"Are you planning any trips to the States in the near future?"

"No, although that could change. But I think you should stay here in Panama. No one will care about your past, and I can help you with your future. I have many friends here."

He makes a compelling argument. But then I remember that he's married. "I can't, Enrique. What you want me to be"—I can't bring myself to say the word *mistress*—"is not who I am. Even if your wife doesn't mind, I do."

He nods as if he understands, and I'm sure he does. If it were his daughter who was being propositioned, no doubt he would want her to say no too.

"Then I shall leave you here, Nina Roth." But before he goes, he leans down and kisses me. Not a demanding kiss, but one that is soft and slow and so exquisite that I almost regret that I turned him down.

"*Buenas noches, querida.*"

"*Buenas noches*, Enrique."

I watch him walk out the lobby's revolving door, but he reappears a few seconds later. "If you see my godson, can you please tell him that I'm waiting?" He turns to leave, then pivots back again. "And remind him that I'm not a patient man."

I laugh. God only knows what Tiffany and Diego are up to. "Will do," I say as I head toward the elevators. I'm expecting to find Tiffany and Diego kissing (or more) in the vestibule, but it's empty. When I emerge from the elevator onto the fourteenth floor, however, I find that I was right—I only had the location wrong. Tiffany's back is leaning on the door to our room and Diego is pushed up against her. Presumably he is trying to work his way inside—both the room and my sister—but so far Tiffany has resisted.

I clear my throat loudly as I approach. Diego doesn't even look up, but Tiffany turns and sees me, then pushes Diego off of her.

He tries to cover the bulge in his pants with his jacket, but it's unbuttoned and not quite long enough. "*Hola*, Ashley."

"*Hola*, Diego. Enrique wanted me to tell you that he's waiting for you downstairs, and to remind you that he's not a patient man."

Diego blushes, which just makes him that much more adorable. "*Sí, sí.* I know that about him." Then he turns back to Tiffany. "I must go, *mi amor*, but we shall see each other again very soon." Then he turns on his heel and takes off down the hallway.

I wait until he passes me before I join Tiffany. "I'm surprised you didn't invite him in," I say as I slide the key card into the lock and pull it out again, apparently not quickly enough, though, since the red light doesn't turn green.

"I wanted to. But I knew you'd get mad."

She's right about that. Besides the fact that he is undoubtedly a heartbreaker and she will likely never see him again, Agent Brody's clothes are in the closet and his shaving kit is on the vanity. I would not want to have to explain to Enrique why there's a man staying in our room, and especially not the identity of that man.

I try the key card again without success.

"I'll do it," Tiffany says and grabs the plastic key from my hand. But she tries three times and it won't unlock for her either.

What the hell is going on here?

41

After several more unsuccessful attempts to unlock the door, we head downstairs to the front desk.

"I think there's something wrong with our key card," I say to the clerk. "The door won't open."

He takes it from me and checks it on his computer. "What is your room number, señorita?"

"Fourteen twenty-two. I don't know what's wrong. It worked fine this morning."

"*Un momento, por favor.*" Then he disappears into the office behind the reception desk.

"What's that about?" Tiffany asks.

I shrug. "I have no idea."

The clerk returns with an older man dressed in a tailored suit, but still wearing a name tag from the hotel. "*Buenas noches, señoritas.* I'm Señor Pérez. I understand you are having a problem with your room key?"

"Yes, it's not working. I think if you just give us a new one, it'll be fine."

"I'm afraid it's not that simple, señoritas. The room number you gave us is registered to a Mr. Jason Brody."

I'm surprised Agent Brody registered under his own name. Maybe he had to in order to use his credit card. Unlike the hotel we stayed at the first night, this one isn't cash only. "Yes, we're staying with Mr. Brody."

"Both of you?" he asks.

"We're his nieces," Tiffany replies.

He stares at Tiffany in her tight tank top and short skirt, then glances at me in my slinky red dress, and it's obvious from his smirk that he's come to a different conclusion. "Yes, well, we've been trying to reach your uncle for the past few hours. His credit card has been declined."

"What do you mean his credit card's been declined?" I ask. "We've been here for two days."

"*Sí*, but we bill the card daily. It was accepted for the first night, but when we ran it this evening, it was declined. We've been trying to reach Mr. Brody on the number he left us, but he has not returned any of our messages."

I turn to Tiffany, who appears as bewildered as me. "Give us a minute," I say to Mr. Perez, and we step away from the desk. I pull out my phone and find Agent Brody in my favorites. After several unanswered rings, the voice mail clicks in. I leave an urgent message, then end the call and text him too. I stare down at my phone, but it remains silent.

"Where the hell is he?" I whisper to Tiffany. He was supposed to be following us as well as tracking us, so he should know that Enrique left and it's safe to return. And even if he doesn't know, he should still respond to an urgent voice mail and text message. What if we were in danger?

"Do you think something could've happened to him?" Tiffany asks.

"Like what?"

"I don't know. Maybe he got into a car accident. The traffic here is crazy."

"No worse than Manhattan, and he's used to that."

"Then where do you think he is?" she asks.

"I don't know, but I'm not going to stand around the lobby all night waiting for him." I return to the front desk, where Mr. Perez is still waiting. "We can't reach him either, but I can pay for the room."

I hand him my credit card and he glances at the name. "I will need your passport as well, Miss Roth."

Fuck!

But then I realize I have an excuse. "It's in the safe in the room. The one you locked me out of," I say, raising my voice. There are only a few other guests in the lobby at this late hour, but Mr. Perez glances around nervously. I pull out my driver's license and slam it onto the desk. "That should be good enough. Or do I have to call the US Embassy and have them verify my identity? I can't wait to write up a review of this place on Trip Advisor."

"I think in this case we can make an exception." He smiles at me, then hands my credit card to the clerk, who slides it through the machine. The clerk returns it to me along with a hotel registration card.

"And how long will you be staying with us, Miss Roth?"

"We're leaving tomorrow. I'm not feeling very welcome here." I glare at Mr. Perez to keep up the act.

"I do apologize for the inconvenience," Señor Pérez says. "If there's anything we can do to make your stay more pleasant, do not hesitate to let us know."

"Actually, there is. I'd like a late checkout tomorrow. Our flight's not until the evening." I have no idea what time the flights to the US leave, but I'm not sure how much credit I have left on this card and it looks like I'll be the one paying for our tickets home too.

"That would be our pleasure, Miss Roth," Señor Pérez says

and hands me my new key card. "Have a wonderful evening."

"Thank you," I say in my haughtiest voice before turning to leave.

"Well done," Tiffany says as we head to the elevators together. "You can be a real bitch when you want to be."

"Thanks, I learned it from Raylene," I say and we both laugh.

But we're not laughing when we see who's waiting for us on the fourteenth floor.

42

Agent Brody is slumped on the floor in front of our door. His hair is disheveled, one pant leg is torn, and he has blood dripping from his nose.

Tiffany rushes to his side and I follow. "Oh my God," she says, "what happened?"

He grabs the door handle and pulls himself upright. "Your friend Enrique happened," he replies, nodding at me.

"What are you talking about? He was with us all night. He left maybe half an hour ago. And why didn't you call us back?"

"Because my phone is at the bottom of Panama Bay. I didn't even know you called."

The elevator pings and a well-dressed older couple steps off. They glance at us, then head in the opposite direction.

Agent Brody lowers his voice. "Let's take this inside."

I unlock the door with the new key card, then deadbolt it behind us. "This room is in my name now, by the way. My *real* name."

"What? Why?" he asks.

"Because your credit card was declined for the second night. The hotel said they tried calling you."

He eases himself onto the foot of the bed and lies back. The blood isn't just under his nose, it's dripped down his chin and stained the front of his white shirt too. "Well, obviously I didn't get their message either," he says and closes his eyes. That's when I notice the faint pink bruise on his cheek.

Tiffany heads to the bathroom and returns with a washcloth, which she hands to Agent Brody. "Thanks," he says and holds it under his nose.

"What happened?" Tiffany asks again. "For real."

"Enrique," he replies. "For real. Or someone who works for him. He didn't appreciate my inquiries about your father."

This makes no sense. He would have no reason to do this. He doesn't know anything about my father. "How do you know it's someone who works for Enrique? It could've been someone from one of the other banks you threatened. I'm sure you pissed a lot of people off yesterday. Any one of them could've done this to you."

He sits up and removes the washcloth from underneath his nose and the blood immediately starts to pool above his lip again. "How do you know what I did yesterday?"

"Enrique told me."

"And what else did your friend Enrique tell you about me?"

"Nothing," I say, attempting to quell his anger. "I told him I was looking for information about my father and—"

He jumps up from the bed. "You told him who you were? What the hell were you thinking, Nina? Are you trying to get us all killed?"

"No, I was trying to not get *myself* killed. And I didn't *tell* him anything. He already knew." I proceed to fill in Agent Brody on the rest of my conversation with Enrique, including the part where he said he had never met my father and couldn't help me, but omitting the proposal to be his mistress. I don't think that tidbit is relevant to this discussion, or any of his business. But

Tiffany obviously disagrees because when I'm finished, she says, "Don't forget to tell him about Enrique's proposal," which of course prompts Agent Brody to ask, "What proposal?"

"He offered to help me find a job in Panama."

"And an apartment," she says.

I glare at her, then turn back to Agent Brody. "He wants to help me because I remind him of his son."

He smirks. "Please tell me you're not that stupid."

Jerk. "Why do you even care? You're not the one he propositioned."

"I don't," he says, easing himself back onto the bed and wincing from the pain. He must have bruises under his clothes too. "But purely out of curiosity, did you accept?"

I'm tired of Agent Brody and his insinuations. Tired of his endless threats. Tired of this wild goose chase he's led us on. And tired of him. "You know what, this is my room now and I don't want you here. Go find somewhere else to sleep. And you can buy your own ticket home too."

"Nina—"

But I ignore his entreaties as I stomp into the bathroom and slam the door shut so hard that the robe hanging from a hook on the back falls to the floor. I can hear him and Tiffany whispering in the bedroom and then a knock on the bathroom door, which I ignore.

"Nina, please," he says. "I just want to apologize. I shouldn't have said that."

"No, you shouldn't have," I shout through the closed door. Then I wrench it open and stare up at his bruised face. "But if I had wanted to accept, I wouldn't need your goddamn approval. You don't own me, Agent Brody."

"No," he says, "but I do care about you."

I snort. "Give me a break. All you care about is finding our father and you're using us to do it. What's your real agenda here?

Are you bucking for a promotion? Considering a career in politics? Maybe you think you can sell your story to the tabloids or write a book? I know it can't be for the reward money because you're not eligible." That was my first thought—there's a ten-million-dollar reward for anyone who can provide information leading to my father's capture. But it's only available to private citizens, not law enforcement personnel.

"Believe what you want, Nina, but I have one goal here: justice."

"Yeah, I'm sure it's *justice* that you care about. Where was all this interest in *justice* when you were railroading my father?"

"I screwed up. I've admitted that. And I need to make it right. Why is that so hard for you to believe?"

Why indeed? I didn't used to be such a suspicious person. I guess having your life turned upside down changes you, and not for the better.

IN THE END I allow Agent Brody to spend the night. He offered to get his own room (he said he had other credit cards, and cash too), but it's already one in the morning and my anger at him dissipates as my exhaustion increases. I don't want to fight anymore; I just want to sleep.

I WAKE to the sound of the door to the room opening and slamming shut. But it's still too dark to see. "Who's there?"

"It's just me," Agent Brody replies. "I went to buy a new phone."

He must've been quieter on his way out of the room than the way in because I didn't hear him leave.

Then Agent Brody pulls open the shades and bright morning sun streams in through the windows.

"Is that really necessary?" Tiffany mumbles and rolls over so she is facing away from the light.

"Yes," Agent Brody says and holds up a cardboard carrier with three coffee cups and a greasy-bottomed paper bag. "I brought breakfast."

He hands me two coffees and the paper bag and I notice his previously pink bruise has already started to turn purple, but at least his nose has stopped bleeding and there's no blood on his shirt. I head into the bathroom to wash my face and brush my teeth. When I return to the bedroom, Tiffany is sitting up in bed sipping her coffee and nibbling on a *hojaldras.*

"So what's the plan?" she asks Agent Brody as I slide in next to her.

I take a sip of my coffee, which he remembered to add milk and sugar to, and reach for a donut. The oil and sugar melt in my mouth simultaneously and I moan. If I lived in Panama and ate these for breakfast every morning, I'd be huge. Enrique wouldn't want me as his mistress anymore.

"I'm working on it," Agent Brody says, pecking away at his laptop.

I wipe the sugar from my lips with the back of my hand. "There is no plan, Tiffany. We're going home." I turn to Agent Brody. "Are you searching flight times? I got us a late checkout, but we need to be out of the room by three."

The sooner we leave, the better, as far as I'm concerned. I have no idea what I'm going to do next, but whatever it is, I'm ready to begin. I won't go back to New York and work for my stepfather, that I know for sure. I like California. It's less frantic than New York. Maybe if Tiffany and I both get jobs, we can afford the rent on an apartment. Although hers would have to be part-time since school starts again next month. Maybe Raylene would chip in. I'd be taking care of her daughter for her. It wouldn't be unreasonable to ask her to pay for her support.

I'm still lost in my own thoughts when I hear Tiffany say, "We can't go home. What about Dad?"

"Tiff, we tried. He obviously doesn't want to be found. Short of placing an ad in every newspaper around the world saying, 'Please contact your daughters; they have evidence to set you free,' I don't know what else we can do."

"Then let's do that."

I turn to Agent Brody, hoping he'll shut her down, but he says, "I've heard worse ideas."

"Really? I find that hard to believe." Actually, impossible to believe.

Then there's a knock on the door and we all freeze.

43

—————

At first none of us move. But when whoever wants in knocks again, Agent Brody grabs his gun from the end table, which he was using as a makeshift nightstand, and silently pads into the bathroom. When he's hidden inside, he motions for me to answer.

"Maybe it's housekeeping," Tiffany whispers as I call out, "Who is it?"

"*Flores,* señorita," a male voice replies. Tiffany translates: "Flowers."

Flowers? I unlock the deadbolt but keep the top latch in place so it only opens two inches. I see a teenage boy—he doesn't even look eighteen—dressed in a bellman's uniform holding a huge bouquet of flowers. "I'm sorry, but I think you have the wrong room."

"Nina Roth?" he asks, glancing at a piece of paper in his hand.

At first I'm startled that he knows my real name, then I remember the room debacle last night. "Yes, but I don't think anyone's sending me flowers. I think you must have the wrong person."

Either he doesn't understand me or chooses to ignore my response. "For you," he says and holds out the vase.

I know arguing with him will be pointless, so I run to my purse and grab a few dollars, then open the door. He hands me the vase and I hand him his tip. "*Gracias,* señorita," he says, pocketing the money in one swift practiced movement, then heads down the hallway toward the elevators.

I carry the huge bouquet of tropical flowers into the room and set them down on the desk next to Agent Brody's computer. Tiffany jumps up from the bed. "Those are gorgeous. Is there a card?"

I find the note hiding behind an enormous purple bloom. It's handwritten by someone with beautiful penmanship and I read it aloud.

*Q*UERIDA—

I would have loved for you to stay, but I know that you are anxious to continue on your journey. I hear Nevis is lovely this time of year. Safe travels.

—Rhett

"I'M CONFUSED," Tiffany says. "Who's Rhett?"

I don't bother explaining. If he hadn't addressed me as *Querida,* and signed as Rhett, I would've thought I really had received these flowers by mistake. But I know they're from Enrique. It's the reference to Nevis that's throwing me.

I glance over at Agent Brody, who returned to the bedroom as I read the note and who is now inexplicably beaming. "What are you so happy about?"

"You did good, Nina. Very, very good."

Now Tiffany and I are both confused.

He takes the card from my hand and reads it for himself, smiling even more broadly. Then he glances down at me. "Don't you understand? Your boyfriend just told you where to find your father."

"Where?" Tiffany asks.

"Nevis!" he says as if we're both idiots.

Tiffany's eyes widen. "You mean that's a real place?"

Agent Brody shakes his head. "What did you think, it was Middle Earth?"

"Where's Middle Earth?" she asks. "Is that like the Middle East?"

I catch the Tolkien reference, but I have to admit I'd never heard of Nevis before today either. "Where's Nevis?"

Agent Brody grabs his laptop and starts typing, then he turns the screen to face us. He'd Googled Nevis. The first link is to a tourism site, the second link is to Wikipedia, and the third link is to the Four Seasons Resort.

"Ooo," Tiffany says. "They have a Four Seasons. Leave it to Dad to hide out in luxury."

Our father did love the Four Seasons hotel chain, but, "There is no way he's staying at the Four Seasons. Right?" I turn to Agent Brody for confirmation, but he's scanning his cell phone.

"Pack your bags," he says, not looking up from the five-inch screen. "We're taking the next flight out."

44

———

It isn't quite that simple. There are no direct flights from Panama City to the small Caribbean island of Nevis. We have to wait at the airport in Panama for hours and then fly standby to Miami, where we spend the night sleeping in uncomfortable chairs before taking the first flight out in the morning to Puerto Rico. Then we hang around the airport in Puerto Rico most of the day waiting for the only flight out to Nevis. By the time we arrive on the island that evening, we've been traveling for thirty-plus hours and we're all tired and cranky.

After we clear immigration, we head out to the taxi stand. "The Four Seasons please," Tiffany tells the driver, who reaches for her suitcase.

Agent Brody throws his bag to the ground. "We are not staying at the Four Seasons!"

"That's where Dad would stay. Right, Nina?"

Agent Brody turns to me. I'm sure my father isn't staying there, at least not without a disguise, but that doesn't mean we shouldn't. "He did love the Four Seasons resort in Hawaii."

He shakes his head. "You two are ridiculous. You have no idea how real people live."

I would object—we are real people, we just have more money than most, or we used to—but I'm too tired. At this point I don't care where we stay as long as the room is clean and contains a bed I can lie down on. And air-conditioning would be nice too. The sun is already dipping toward the horizon and it's still hot out.

The cab driver offers to take us to a guesthouse near the center of town, which he declares is the only budget option on the island. After a quick search on my phone, I confirm he's not exaggerating. Nevis is beautiful—green hillsides, swaying palm trees, and aquamarine water—but definitely not cheap. I'm trying to remember if my father ever talked about this place, but I can't recall him mentioning it. If he travelled here before, he did so without me.

The three of us climb into the backseat of the cab. Tiffany and Agent Brody each grab a window seat, so I'm stuck in the middle with the hump under my feet.

"Nevis is a tax haven," Agent Brody informs me as we drive (on the left side of the road, not the right—it used to be a British colony) along the narrow highway leading from the airport to the center of town. "One of many in the Caribbean, unfortunately."

"I wouldn't think a lower tax rate would be my father's main objective at this point," I reply.

Agent Brody laughs. "True. But they also allow wealthy individuals to buy citizenship here."

You can *buy* citizenship? That's convenient. "So you think my father is a citizen of Nevis now? Would that protect him?"

"No, Nevis has an extradition treaty with the US, which I'm sure your father knows. And he wouldn't have been stupid enough to apply for citizenship in his own name anyway."

"Then why would he come here? Besides the obvious," I add, nodding to the sun setting over the white-sand beach.

"Because Nevis is also an international banking center with strict privacy laws. Like Panama. And Switzerland."

"So we'll be heading to the Alps next? You should've told me. I would've packed my ski gear."

My sarcasm doesn't escape him and he laughs again. "I certainly hope not. The exchange rate in Switzerland would wipe me out."

I wouldn't ask, but since he brought it up . . . "So how much money do you have left?" Panama is cheap compared to the US, but we just spent thousands of dollars on airfare. And I know he already had one credit card declined.

"Enough," he says.

"How much is enough? I mean, we have no idea how long this is going to take. Even if my dad is here, who knows how long it will take to find him."

"Nevis is a small island. If he's here, we'll find him quickly." Then he closes his eyes and leans his head back against the seat. Conversation over.

Ten minutes later the taxi drops us off at Will's Guesthouse, which is really just a ten-room motel not far from the ferry dock. There's no pool, but the front desk clerk tells us it's only a short walk to the beach.

"Anyone want to go for a twilight swim?" Tiffany asks as we trudge up the steps (no elevators here) to room number eight.

"Isn't that when the sharks come out?" I say, remembering my Shark Week.

"Don't be such a wuss," Agent Brody says, unlocking the door to our room with an actual metal key. We're greeted by a welcome blast of cold air from a radiator-style AC unit. "Besides, there are no sharks on Nevis. They can't afford it here."

I smile at him but don't respond. Instead I check out our

room, which is dated—lime-green carpeting, floral bedspread, huge square phone (although at least it's push-button and not rotary dial)—but more importantly is clean and has two double beds. And the desk clerk promised to send up a rollaway (for a small fee) so I'll finally be able to sleep alone again.

Tiffany heads to the bathroom while I pounce on the bed next to the window. A bit springy, but after nothing but upright chairs and barely reclining airplane seats for the last thirty-six hours, I don't care. When Tiffany emerges from the bathroom, her minidress has been replaced by a bikini. "Who's coming?" she asks, grabbing a bath towel from the rack.

"I'll go," Agent Brody replies, never taking his eyes from Tiffany's voluptuous body.

I doubt he really cares about swimming; it's just an excuse to keep ogling Tiffany in her bikini. I don't blame him. If I were a man I'd do the same.

"Nina, you coming?" she asks.

I shake my head and stretch my arms and legs out on the bed. "I'm happy here, thanks."

"Don't fall asleep," Agent Brody admonishes. "Or you'll never sleep tonight."

I could probably nap now and still sleep tonight, but it's easier to agree. I have no intention of sleeping anyway.

I WATCH from the window as Tiffany and Agent Brody head off toward the beach. Once they're out of sight, I grab Agent Brody's phone, which he left sitting on a chair with his dirty clothes. He probably thought it was safer to leave it in the room than lying on a towel on the beach where anyone could walk by and steal it. In that respect he was correct to leave it behind. But my goal is different than a random thief.

The phone's screen is black and when I try to wake it, I'm

asked for the password. I should've expected that. I try a few random numbers and am not surprised when none of them work. I realize I know almost no personal information about Agent Brody, not even his birthday (not that I think he'd be dumb enough to choose that as his password). I toss the phone back onto the chair and move to his suitcase.

I pull his laptop out of the front pocket and boot it up. But of course the computer is password-protected too. I'm debating trying a few random combinations, although this password will be longer so I have even less chance of getting it right, when there's a knock on the door.

I panic and slam the laptop shut, only realizing moments later that if it were Agent Brody, he wouldn't have knocked, he would've used his room key.

I stand up to the answer the door when, to my surprise, it opens from the outside.

45

"Sorry," the desk clerk says, as startled to see me as I am to see him. "I thought the room was empty. I knocked, but no one answered."

"I was in the bathroom," I lie. Then I spot the rollaway bed on the catwalk beside him and realize that's why he's here. "Come on in."

He pushes the cot into the corner of the room, then hands me a stack of sheets, a blanket, and a pillow. There won't be any turndown service and chocolates on my pillow at this hotel. I'm heading to my purse, which I left sitting on top of my suitcase, when Agent Brody's phone rings. The desk clerk and I both stare at it, but neither of us move. "You can get that," he finally says. "I'll wait."

I hesitate but realize this may be my only shot. The name "Benny" is lit up on the screen so I say hello to him when I answer.

"Who the hell is this?" he barks into my ear.

"Ashley," I say, adopting my fake persona again. I don't know why other than that he sounds so angry I don't want to tell him my real name.

"Where's Brody?"

"Out." I answered Agent Brody's phone to get information, not to provide it.

"Then give him a message for me."

"Sure, let me just find a pen and paper."

I start scanning the room, but Benny doesn't wait. "Tell him time is running out." Then he hangs up on me.

TIFFANY AND AGENT BRODY return twenty minutes later, wet towels draped over their shoulders and sand covering their feet.

"You should've come," Tiffany says, perching on the edge of the bed in her damp bathing suit, thereby choosing where she'd be sleeping tonight. "The water's beautiful."

Agent Brody, standing in the middle of the room dripping seawater onto the carpet, concurs. Then he notices the rollaway in the corner. "The bed came. Excellent." He turns to me for a response, but I continue to glare at him with my arms folded across my chest. "What's wrong?"

What's wrong? What's *not* wrong? "You tell me. Who's Benny?"

His smile disappears, replaced by a scowl. "You checked my phone?"

"It rang. What was I supposed to do, not answer it?"

"Yes, that is exactly what you're supposed to do when someone else's phone rings. I would've expected this from Tiffany, but not from you. I thought you were better than that."

"Hey," Tiffany says, "I'm standing right here, you know."

We both ignore her.

"Benny asked me to give you a message. He said, 'Time is running out.' Care to explain?"

But instead of answering me, he walks over to his suitcase and pulls out a pair of jeans, a wrinkled shirt, and clean underwear and turns to Tiffany. "I'm showering first." Then he strides into the bathroom and slams the door shut.

As if a closed door will stop me! But the lock does. "Who is Benny?" I shout even though I can already hear the water running.

Not surprisingly, he doesn't answer me. I turn to Tiffany, who is rummaging through her own suitcase, presumably for clean clothes too. "Do you know how to pick a lock?"

"Seriously?" she asks.

"Seriously." I'm tired of having all of my questions ignored. I want answers. Now.

"Wouldn't it just be easier to wait for him to finish? He's usually pretty quick."

"Why are you not concerned about this?"

She shrugs. "Why should I be?"

I realize without context it might not seem so bad. "You didn't hear this guy, Tiff. He sounded angry. Really angry. Like the kind of guy you don't want to meet in a dark alley with a baseball bat. That wasn't a friend calling."

"Then who do you think he was?"

The bathroom door squeaks open and a waft of steam escapes, but the shower is still running. *Was the shower a ruse? Was he eavesdropping on us?* Then Agent Brody steps into the room, dripping wet and wearing nothing but a towel around his waist. "Benny's my loan shark."

46

———

"You have a loan shark?" Tiffany asks, seemingly impressed.

"Well, I couldn't exactly get a bank loan to finance a worldwide search for your father, now could I? I had to find an alternate source of funding."

"Why didn't you just borrow the money from the FBI?" I ask. "They're already paying for you anyway."

"Because it doesn't work that way. And if you ever had a real job, you would know that."

"I had a real job! I was doing just fine at Wine World before you two showed up."

He lets out a harsh laugh. "Not quite, sweetheart. You were fired for lying about who you are and then your boss tried to rape you in the parking lot. Or was that foreplay I interrupted? You do seem to have a thing for older men."

I'm stunned speechless. That was a low blow, even for Agent Brody. But as angry as I am, I can feel the tears welling up in my eyes. No way am I letting that jerk see me cry. I grab my purse and stomp out of the room.

I hear him calling my name from the doorway, but I keep

going—along the catwalk, down the stairs, then across the street. I have no idea which way I'm headed and I don't much care. Nothing I do matters anyway. No matter how hard I try, all of my attempts at a so-called normal life will always blow up in my face. I'm the daughter of Harold Rothberg, guilty until proven innocent, and that will never change.

I've walked for ten minutes and have no idea where I am when someone grabs my arm from behind. I spin around and find Agent Brody. His hair's still wet, but he's wearing more than a towel. "What do *you* want?" The *asshole* is implied.

"To apologize. I never should've brought up ... that situation. I'm sure it was unpleasant for you."

Unpleasant? Yes, I think we can all agree attempted rape is an "unpleasant" experience. Prick. I try to wrench my arm free, but he doesn't even loosen his grip. "You've apologized. Your conscience is clear. Can I go now?"

He releases my arm but says, "We need to talk."

"*You* want to talk? Since when?"

He sighs. "Nina, this would all be so much easier if you just trusted me."

"If you want me to trust you, then you need to start *answering my questions*, and not just walking away every time I ask you something you don't like."

"Fine. But can we not do this out on the street?"

I shrug, but I don't leave.

"I think we passed a bar a couple of blocks back. I don't know about you, but I could really use a drink."

Two rum punches later ("the official drink of Nevis" according to our waitress) and I'm feeling much better about life in general and mine in particular. At my urging, Agent Brody even returned Benny's call and assured me that they had reached an understanding.

"I didn't know loan sharks were so reasonable," I say, crunching the ice of my second cocktail. Agent Brody offered to buy me a third, but I know if I have any more, I won't be able to walk back to the hotel.

He laughs. "They're not. I agreed to up his vig in exchange for another week."

"What's a vig?"

"Think of it as a bonus. He helps me and I help him. Just like with you."

Now I'm the one who laughs. "How exactly are you *helping* me? I *should* be home looking for a new job, and instead I'm off on this ridiculous wild goose chase with you and Tiffany. Not that it hasn't been fun," I say, presuming he'll register my sarcasm.

But he chooses to ignore it. "This isn't a wild goose chase. We're making real progress. When we started, we had nothing. Now we know that your father, or someone in his firm, set up an account in Panama, and the money was transferred out of that account and into an account in Nevis."

The alcohol must be dulling my brain. "How do we know that?"

"Your friend Enrique."

I'm still not making the connection. "But he just suggested we go to Nevis. He didn't say anything about an account in Panama or anywhere else. And he was quite insistent that he had never met my father."

"And that may very well be true. But he wouldn't have had to. Anyone from your father's company could've set up a foundation in Panama with the help of a local lawyer, and then that local lawyer would've opened the bank account. The lawyer passes on the account number, the money gets wired in, no questions asked, and leaves the same way. It's the beauty of Panama's banking laws."

"So if anyone at my father's company could've done this, then why were you so convinced it was my dad?"

"Because of the amount. A low-level employee might be able to siphon off a few million dollars over the course of many years without getting caught. But billions of dollars—that only happens when it's being orchestrated by someone at the top. It had to be your father or Chet. They were the only ones who could've pulled this off."

"And Chet cut a deal."

Agent Brody stares down into his half-empty glass. "He was very convincing. And my boss wanted this wrapped up quickly."

"So you decided it was easier to just believe Chet than to dig up the truth?"

"It wasn't my call, Nina." Then he dials down his anger for a more repentant tone. "But yeah, you're right. We screwed up. And that's as much my fault as anyone else's, and why I need to make this right."

"And of course it was your bright idea to drag me and Tiffany into this."

He nods. "The Marshals had been searching for your father for months and had no leads. We were at a dead end. You and Tiffany were my only hope."

"And you couldn't tell your boss your plan because you knew he wouldn't approve, which is why you had to get the money to bring us along from a loan shark."

"Correct," he says, "except my boss is a she. And if she knew any of this was happening, she'd have my nuts in a vice."

I'm buzzed but not brain-dead. "Wait a minute. You mean your boss doesn't even know *you're* out searching for my father?"

He gives me a sheepish grin. "You said you wanted the truth."

47

My head's spinning and not from the alcohol, although that isn't helping. At first I just stare at him across the lacquered wood table. Then I start to speak several times but I don't get more than a word or two out before I stop. I don't know who I'm angrier at—him for misleading me or myself for believing him.

I toss my straw aside and lift my glass, sucking down whatever remains—rum-flavored water mostly. Then I slam the glass down on the table. "You asshole! You bring us down here pretending to be on assignment from the FBI and they don't even know you're here! The false passports, the new cell phones, the fake names, now it all makes sense. You knew the FBI was watching us, so if they found us here, that means they'd find you too. There never were any Russian mobsters, were there?"

"I told you we could never prove that. But I do think the threat is real. Not all of your father's clients were upstanding citizens. Even if he didn't mastermind this Ponzi scheme, he still made some questionable choices."

"Apparently he's not the only one! I can't believe I fell for your act. You must think I'm a complete idiot."

"You never fell for my act, Nina."

That surprises me. I thought he'd be apologizing again, not going on the offensive.

"You never trusted me," he continues. "Not for a minute."

"Well, I was right not to, now wasn't I?"

"Yes. But don't act as if I duped you into this. You came with me because I was your only hope too. We're just two desperate people working together because we have no other choice."

"Not quite. I may not have a job at the moment, but I still have a family that loves me. I can move back home with my mother anytime I want. And my stepfather has already offered me a job with his company. I have options."

"Crawling home with your tail between your legs and spending the rest of your life kowtowing to that pompous ass of a stepfather? You call that options? I'd rather go to jail."

"Well, I'll probably end up in jail now anyway. I knew I never should've used that fake passport."

He laughs and shakes his head.

"What's so funny? I'm in a lot of trouble because of you."

"You think the FBI is going to prosecute you for helping them find your father? They'll probably give you a medal."

Now I'm confused. "You just said your boss doesn't know you're still searching for my dad. That if she did, she'd have your nuts in a vice."

"If we fail, yeah. But if we succeed, then we'll all be hailed as heroes. You'll see. She'll take credit for my work so fast it'll make your head spin." He waves his hands in the air as if opening a curtain onto a stage. "I can envision the press conference now— she'll be front and center, basking in the glow of the television lights, claiming this whole operation was her idea."

"You think she'd really do that?"

"In a New York minute."

"But what if you told the truth? Or I did?"

"She'll make sure we're on board first. She'll threaten me with my job and then sweeten the pot with a promotion. And she'll threaten you with prosecution for the false passport, then maybe offer you a piece of the reward money or something else that you want that only she can provide. That's her MO—the carrot and the stick."

"She sounds like a horrible boss."

"You have no idea," he says and drains the rest of his cocktail.

We sit in silence. I'm mentally reviewing my options and presume that Agent Brody is doing the same. The reality is that he's right—I have no options. At least none that I find palatable.

I could fly back to LA and hope that no one ever finds out about the false passport. It's worked up until now so there's no reason to think it wouldn't work for one last trip home. But then what? I only received a few thousand dollars when I left Wine World. That won't last long. And if my stepfather hasn't sold the apartment yet, he will soon. Then I'll be homeless too.

Or I could go back to New York with my tail between my legs like he said. Returning to my childhood bedroom and working for my pompous ass of a stepfather would be better than jail, but not by much.

I have no choice but to admit that Agent Brody is right—I came on this trip because it was my only hope. And it still is.

48

———

I toy with my glass even though it's empty. "*If* I agree to stay and keep helping you—"

"And keep helping yourself," Agent Brody says.

I ignore his remark, true though it is, and continue. "And that's a big *if*. Will you promise to be honest with me from now on?"

He considers it for a moment, then says, "Yes, on one condition. If I think you and Tiffany would be safer not knowing something, I'm not going to tell you. I want you both to go home unharmed."

I let out a laugh. "You still think we're being followed by Russian mobsters?"

But Agent Brody isn't laughing; his tone is deadly serious. "Billions of dollars are missing, Nina. Even if your father wasn't the mastermind behind this scheme, lots of people think he knows where the money is. It would be foolish to believe we're the only ones looking for him."

True. "Okay, you can withhold to keep us safe, but no other reason. Deal?"

"Deal," he says and then orders another round so we can

drink to it.

We stumble back to the room and find Tiffany pacing the lime-green carpet. "Where the hell have you two been? I was about to call the police."

"And what would you have told them?" I ask as I careen toward the bed. It would be a lot easier if the room would stop swaying.

"Oh my God, you're drunk!"

Am I? Probably. I was already buzzed when Agent Brody ordered the third round to seal the deal, which was really two rounds because he added shots too. "If you were worried, why didn't you just call me?" I ask before falling face first onto the bed.

"I tried. You left your stupid phone in the room."

Did I? I do sort of remember plugging it into the charger when we arrived.

"And you didn't answer yours either," she yells, I assume at Agent Brody since my eyes are closed. At least he's the one who replies: "I was busy."

"Busy!" she screams.

I reach for the pillow and pull it on top of my head to muffle the sound of the yelling. My brain is already starting to ache.

I wake up hours later with my stomach queasy, my mouth dry, and my head pounding so badly I wish I could cut it off. The room is dark so someone must've shut off the lights. I consider getting up for some aspirin when the bed shifts and I realize that I'm not alone. "Tiffany?"

"No," Agent Brody answers sleepily, "it's me."

Oh my God, what did I do?

49

———

I have no time to think as I feel the bile rise up in my throat. I rush to the bathroom, tripping on someone's shoe along the way, but still manage to reach the toilet in time. I'm lying on my back on the bathroom floor when Agent Brody appears in the doorway. He's stripped down to a T-shirt and underwear, but I notice I'm still fully clothed. Surely if I had slept with him, I wouldn't have bothered getting dressed again.

"Are you okay?" he asks.

"I will be," I say before heaving into the toilet again.

That satisfies him enough that he goes back to bed. Or maybe he just doesn't want to listen to me retching since he shuts the bathroom door on his way out. When my stomach is empty, I pull myself up and look in the mirror. Huge mistake. Most of my makeup is rubbed off except for two big black smudges of mascara under my eyes, I have weird lines indented into one side of my face (from the seams of the bedspread I guess from the pattern), and my hair is matted and slightly damp. I take a whiff of the ends—puke—which sends me heaving into the toilet again.

When I can muster the energy to lift myself off the bathroom floor, I turn on the shower and drag myself in. It helps. A little. At least I smell better than I did. I search Tiffany's toiletries bag (mine is still in my suitcase) until I find a few aspirin and I down them with water from the tap. Then I wrap the towel around me and open the bathroom door.

Someone has turned a light on low—Agent Brody, I presume —and the room is cast in a warm amber glow. His clothes are lying in a heap on the floor and I can see that it's his shoe I tripped on earlier. He's laid out on my bed, lying on top of the bedspread with his forearm shielding his eyes from the light. He doesn't move when I enter the room and I think he's sleeping when he asks, "Feeling better?"

"A little," I say and sit down on the edge of Tiffany's bed, which is still fully made up. "Where's Tiffany?"

"Out," he says. "I don't know where."

I wish my head would stop pounding so I could think more clearly, but it doesn't and I can't. "Maybe I should call her," I finally say.

He moves his arm away from his eyes, and I can see that they're glassy and bloodshot too. Or maybe they just look that way to me because I'm peering at them through my own glassy, bloodshot eyes. "You can try, but she may not answer. She didn't when I called."

I'm going to try her anyway, but walking across the room for my phone just seems like so much work that I have to lie down and rest first. When my towel hikes up to my thighs, I realize I should probably put on some clothes, but that would take more energy than I currently have. Instead I reach for the edge of the bedspread and pull it over me.

"Don't worry," he says. "Nothing happened."

"What makes you think I'm worried?" I answer even though of course I am. Yes, I woke up with my clothes on, but it looks like he took his off in a hurry, which concerns me. And he was in my bed with me, which concerns me too.

He lets out a laugh. "Because I know you, Nina. You're lying here wondering why I was sleeping with you when there's an empty bed three feet away."

I hadn't actually asked myself that question, but I should have. No doubt I would've gotten to it eventually. "So why were you?"

"Because you begged me to sleep with you."

"I did not!" But even as I deny it, a memory begins to float to the surface of my alcohol-addled brain. Not begging exactly, but definitely an offer to have sex with me and a clear recollection of me telling him, "You know you want to." Ugh. I feel like I might puke again, but I can't muster the energy to get off the bed.

"Begging might not be the right word," he says. "But you definitely wanted me."

"So why didn't you give me what I wanted?" I sneer because I have no defense for my behavior.

"I would've, but you passed out on me."

"Passed out? I doubt that."

"Fell asleep snoring loudly, if you prefer."

"I don't snore."

"I don't know what to tell you, kiddo. You did last night."

I remain silent. What is there to say? I'm mortified. I was drunk, yes, and probably still am, but that's no excuse. After a while the silence between us is so oppressive that I ask him, "So why did you stay? Obviously you knew you weren't getting any."

"I was too tired to make up the rollaway, and I was afraid if Tiffany came back and found me sleeping in her bed she might kill me in my sleep."

That gets a laugh out of me. "Weren't you afraid she might get mad if she found you sleeping with me?"

Now he laughs. "I guess you don't remember that part. The

last thing she said before she stormed out was 'You two deserve each other.' I took that as consent."

I laugh again.

Then he rolls over onto his side to face me and I can't help but notice that the bulge in his underwear has gotten a little bigger in the last few minutes. "So. You're awake, I'm awake, what do you say?"

I'm pretty sure I understand what he's asking, but in my current impaired state I think it best to confirm. "Did you just offer to have sex with me?"

"You offered first. I'm just re-offering."

I let out another laugh, which, judging from the expression on his face, is not the reaction he'd been hoping for. "I'm afraid I'm going to have to decline, Agent Brody. But thank you anyway."

"Why? You're obviously attracted to me. And I'm attracted to you too. So what's the problem?"

The phrase *beer goggles* comes to mind, or in my case *rum punch goggles*, but it's not that. Physically, Agent Brody is attractive. But even though we're on the same side now, until a few weeks ago, he was my sworn enemy. That's not something I can easily forget, at least not when I'm sober. Plus, I never go for the frat-boy type, and didn't even when I was in college. I always choose charm and intellect over brawn and infantile behavior.

"We're working together now. Having sex will only complicate an already complicated relationship. We should at least wait until after we've found my father and gotten this whole mess over with. Don't you agree?"

I phrase it that way so he has no choice but to acquiesce— my intent. Not that I plan on sleeping with him after we find my father either. But he doesn't need to know that. As Tiffany keeps reminding me, he'll be nicer to us if he thinks there's a chance he'll get laid.

When the aspirin finally kicks in, I call Tiffany and, as Agent Brody predicted, she doesn't pick up. I leave her a voice mail and send her a text message apologizing for my behavior and asking her to call me. My plan is to pull on pajamas and set up the rollaway bed so we can each sleep alone tonight, but that doesn't happen. Instead I fall asleep exactly where I am.

When I wake up the next time, the light in the room isn't coming from the bedside lamp, it's filtering through a crack in the window curtains. Agent Brody is still asleep in my bed, although now he's under the covers, and Tiffany is standing over me wearing the clingy red dress I borrowed from her our last night in Panama. She must've changed into it after I blacked out.

"Wake-y, wake-y," she says and reaches for the bedspread, which is still wrapped around me. She starts to yank it down, then stops when she realizes I'm naked underneath. I must've ditched the wet towel sometime during the night because it's lying on the floor next to the bed. She smirks as she glances from me to Agent Brody. "Looks like someone had a good time last night."

"I didn't sleep with him if that's what you're implying."

She arches one eyebrow. "Then why are you naked?"

It's too early in the morning to explain. The giant red numbers on the bedside clock show that it's only seven fifteen. "Where did you sleep last night?" Obviously not here. The rollaway is still folded up in in the corner of the room with the extra set of linens stacked on top.

She pushes my legs to the side and sits down next to me, a smug smile on her face. "At the Four Seasons."

I briefly debate whether I want to know the answer to this question. But after what I almost did last night, and would've done had I not passed out, I'm in no position to judge. "Alone or with someone else?"

"What do you think?"

Yeah, dumb question. I'm still suffering from an epic hangover, so I lean my head back against the pillow and close my eyes before I continue. "Was he gorgeous or just rich?"

She waits a beat before she answers. "Neither. But he was extremely helpful."

It's not just her words that grab my attention but her tone of voice, like she has a secret she's dying to tell. I open my eyes and push up onto my elbows. "In what way?"

She glances over at Agent Brody, who appears to still be sleeping. Then she leans in and whispers, "I think I know how to find Dad."

50

"How?" I shout, and Agent Brody stirs, although I'm not convinced he was sleeping anyway. He was probably awake and listening to every word.

Tiffany leans back and crosses her legs, savoring the moment now that she has both of our undivided attention. "Well, I was really mad at you two when I left last night. I mean, I couldn't reach either one of you and I thought something terrible had happened. And then it turned out you were just off drinking together—and you didn't even invite me."

"It wasn't planned, Tiff, you know that. And I didn't mean to walk out without my phone."

"I know," she says, then turns and glares at Agent Brody, and I do too.

Under the pressure of death stares from two angry women, he cracks. "Yes, I'm the asshole who didn't answer his phone—*mea culpa*. Please continue."

She dismisses him with a flick of her hair. "Anyway, I was really angry and hungry too, and I didn't know where to go, so when I saw a cab downstairs, I grabbed it and told the driver to take me to the Four Seasons."

"Wearing that?" I ask, nodding to the clingy red dress, which is a mini on me and a micro on her.

She looks down at her outfit. "What's wrong with it? You wore it to dinner with Enrique."

I don't want us to get sidetracked by yet another discussion (lecture, according to Tiffany) about how easy it is to create the wrong impression with inappropriate attire. "You're right, continue."

"So as I was saying, I went to the Four Seasons, which is beautiful, by the way. And I figured since I was there I'd ask around to see if anyone had seen Dad."

"You're kidding?" Agent Brody says. "You actually thought you could just waltz into the Four Seasons and ask if anyone had seen Harold Rothberg recently?

"I didn't tell anyone who he was or that I was his daughter. I just pulled up a picture of him and my mom on my phone and asked if anyone had seen him there."

Agent Brody and I exchange a glance, but neither of us says anything. Obviously anyone looking at that photo would recognize our father. His face was a fixture on the news for months.

"And did they?" I ask, just to keep the story going.

"No." Her shoulders sag and she suddenly looks like a disappointed teenager.

"Well, you tried," Agent Brody says, uncharacteristically magnanimous, in my opinion.

"But it wasn't a total waste," she says, perking up again. "I went to the bar thinking maybe the bartender had seen him." She turns to Agent Brody—"Dad likes his pre-dinner drink"—before turning back to me. "He said he hadn't seen him, but while I was there, this old dude tried to pick me up."

"How old?" I ask.

She shrugs. "I don't know. Maybe forty."

Agent Brody groans and I let out a laugh. When we were having our little *tête-à-tête* last night, he admitted to being thirty-six—only four years away from being declared "old" by Tiffany.

She ignores us and continues. "At first I was going to blow him off. But then I figured since I was starving anyway, I'd let him buy me dinner."

"And did he?" Agent Brody asks.

Tiffany rolls her eyes at him. "Of course he did. But I insisted we eat at the bar instead of the restaurant just in case some really hot guy walked in."

Agent Brody, who had been lying on his side listening to her story, finally sits up. "So even though this guy buys you dinner, which I'm sure no matter what you ordered wasn't cheap—"

"I had the lobster risotto, which was delicious. And the mojito was even better than in Panama. But then I realized he might actually know something and I stopped drinking. I even made a deal with the bartender to spike his drinks and water down mine so I could, you know, like, take advantage of the situation."

"Wow, Tiff, I'm impressed."

She grins at me. "Thank you. I'm pretty impressed with myself too."

Now it's Agent Brody who's rolling his eyes. "So what did he *know*, Tiffany?"

"Turns out he's a real estate agent on the island and he's telling me how he only deals with high-net-worth clients, blah, blah, blah, and then he says something about citizenship and I remember what you"—she turns to Agent Brody—"said about Dad maybe buying citizenship on the island. So I start acting all interested and asking questions and then the guy just wouldn't shut up."

Agent Brody jumps out of bed. "What did he tell you? Did your father buy citizenship on Nevis?"

"Well, I did ask. But he said he didn't know Dad. Then I showed him the photo and he said he'd never seen Dad on the island—but he recognized Raylene."

51

"**I** knew that bitch was lying," Agent Brody says and starts pacing the room in his underwear.

"You mean my mother?" Tiffany asks.

Agent Brody turns to us and I can tell from the look on his face that he realizes he screwed up. "Sorry, Tiffany, I misspoke. What else did the old guy say?"

"Just that he'd shown Raylene some properties a while back, but she hadn't bought any, at least not from him. But he also said a lot of his clients, especially the ones who buy to establish citizenship, never even come to the island. He said it all gets handled through bankers and lawyers, and then he gets a double commission—one for the sale of the property, and then more when he rents it out to someone else because these guys almost never come down and use it."

"Come down?" Agent Brody asks.

"Yeah, he said a lot of the people who buy are from the northeast—hedge-fund guys and Wall Street types trying to hide assets, he assumed, but he doesn't get involved in any of that. He just sells the property, rents it out, then deposits the money into whatever bank account they tell him to, after he takes his commission first."

Agent Brody starts pacing again, obviously lost in thought, so Tiffany turns to me. "Do you want to hear about the bank accounts?"

This gets Agent Brody's attention. "Whose bank accounts?"

"Well, I'm not sure exactly, but I think it may be my dad's. I mean, wherever he is, he needs money, right? And he can't just go to an ATM machine. But like Joe, that's the real estate guy's name, said, if he rents out property, he can get the money deposited into any bank account, and no one ever has to know."

Agent Brody shakes his head. "It's not that simple, Tiffany. Nevis doesn't allow numbered accounts. There has to be a name attached."

"Are you sure?" Tiffany reaches into her purse and pulls out a piece of notepaper, which she unfolds. "Because I found a bunch of account numbers on his computer."

Agent Brody grabs the paper out of her hand and a huge grin spreads across his face. "Do I want to know how you got this?" he asks.

She matches his grin with her own. "Yes, I think you do."

Agent Brody may want to know, but I'm not sure I do. Tiffany turns to me and says, "Don't look at me like that. I didn't sleep with him."

"I didn't say you did!" But I had been thinking it. "So how did you get it?"

She stretches her long legs out in front of her, savoring the moment again. "I was pretty sure he wasn't lying to me about Dad. I mean, he did admit that he recognized Raylene. But I wanted to take a look at his computer anyway. I knew he had it with him because I saw him using it before he started hitting on me. But he wouldn't let it out of his sight. I mean, even when he went to the bathroom, he took his briefcase with him. It was like his purse. So I suggested we get a room."

Now I know who she spent the night with. "You suggested the two of you get a room together, but you had no plans to sleep with him?"

"I *didn't* sleep with him. I mean, we fooled around a little until the lude kicked in, but it didn't take long. Remember, the bartender was giving him doubles all night."

"The lude?" Agent Brody asks. "Please tell me you haven't been carrying drugs with you all this time."

She shakes her head. "Nah, I bought it off the bartender."

"Sounds like a helpful guy," Agent Brody says.

"Yes, and smokin' hot, but definitely gay."

Which explains why she stuck it out with Joe the Realtor instead of spending the night with the bartender.

"So you and Joe get a room, you drug him, he passes out, and then what?" I ask, equal parts appalled and impressed by my sister's prowess.

"Once he was out, I turned on his computer and started searching."

"No password?" Agent Brody asks.

"No, it had a password," Tiffany replies. "But I got him to tell me that before he passed out."

Neither of us asks how she got him to tell her.

"At first I tried word searches with Mom's and Dad's names, but I either got too many hits—he does know a couple of Harolds and Harrys and even an Evan Rothberg, no relation," she says before Agent Brody can ask. "And no hits at all on Raylene, which surprised me because he said he'd met her."

"She probably gave him a false name," Agent Brody says.

"Why would she do that?" Tiffany asks.

"Privacy," he says. "So how did you find the bank accounts?"

"I got bored reading all those emails about golf dates with

Harold and Harry, so I just started clicking around in his files. He's very meticulous about his money. I wrote down a list of all the accounts he sent weekly or monthly deposits to, thinking those would be the ones where he rented out the properties."

"And none of them had names attached?" Agent Brody asks.

She shakes her head. "Just numbers. A couple had companies, but it was always something something LLC, nothing I recognized."

Agent Brody stares at her. "Something something LLC?"

"Yeah, not like Apple or Coke or some name you'd know. Just random words. Although one was Starlight Partners, which I only remember because my mom told me once that she used to work at a club called Starlight Express and that the brothers who owned it were partners and then one killed the other. When I saw that name, it made me think of that story. I don't know why."

But Agent Brody has already stopped listening. He grabs his phone and makes a call.

52

———

Two hours later Agent Brody is still on the phone, but his excitement has turned into anger. I don't know what caused the change since Tiffany and I both showered and dressed and then went out for breakfast at a restaurant the desk clerk recommended to us. When we left the room, Agent Brody was excitedly asking someone to send him all the information he or she could find on Starlight Partners, LLC and when we return he's shouting, "I don't care about their fucking privacy laws, you're a goddamn hacker, for fuck's sake."

"Bad news?" I ask after he ends the call and hurls the phone onto the bed. It bounces off the mattress and hits the floor, but the carpeting cushions its fall. If it had landed on hardwood, the phone would've broken for sure.

He folds his arms across his chest and gives me his trademark stare.

I fold my arms across my chest too. "What happened to answering my questions?"

"Yeah," Tiffany says. "You're supposed to tell us everything now. That's the deal."

I'd filled her in on last night's conversation with Agent Brody —at least the parts I could remember.

"Unless I think telling you would put you in danger," he says. "*That* was the deal."

Tiffany folds her arms across her chest too, so now all three of us are in this belligerent stance. "And how is telling us about your hacker going to put us in danger?"

The three of us remain locked in a silent battle until one of us—Agent Brody—breaks. "Fine. What do you want to know?"

"Everything," Tiffany says.

"But start with Starlight Partners, LLC," I say. "Are you thinking our father owns the company?"

"I don't know." Then he looks down and suddenly realizes that he's the only one of the three of us who isn't dressed—he's still wearing his T-shirt and underwear from last night. He moves to the bed and places a pillow on his lap before continuing. "But it seems like too much of a coincidence that Raylene came down here to look at properties and then that name pops up on this guy's list of clients."

Tiffany sits down on the opposite bed. "But he said she didn't buy anything from him."

"Not directly. But she could've bought a property from him through an LLC and he would never know. He told you he'd never met most of his clients in person. And the privacy laws in Nevis are so strict it's almost impossible to find out who really owns these LLCs. It can be done, but it would take years of legal wrangling."

"And we've only got a week," I say, recalling our conversation about Benny the Loan Shark.

"Exactly. We need to do this off book."

"So that's why you called your hacker friend?" Tiffany asks.

Agent Brody nods. "Unfortunately he's not as good as I'd hoped."

I sigh. Another dead end. But then I realize . . . "We don't really need to know who owns the company though, do we?"

Agent Brody looks at me like I'm an idiot. "Well, it is generally helpful when tracing money to know whose money it is you're tracing."

I glare at him. "Yeah, I know that." Again, the *asshole* is implied. "But can't we just *assume* it's my dad's company and trace the money anyway? What's the harm? We have no other leads. You're the one who made the leap that Enrique led us to Nevis on the assumption that my father, or someone at his company, set up an account in Panama and then transferred money out of that account and into an account here. Which makes sense, I guess. I mean, Enrique's never even met Dad," I say, turning to Tiffany. "How would he know where he's hiding? But he is a big shot in Panama's banking industry." He admitted that much during our dinner when I was pumping him for information. "It's possible he'd know about the money." I turn my attention back to Agent Brody. "So if we're *assuming* my dad moved money through Panama, maybe when he was planning his escape, why can't we *assume* he moved that same money into and then out of an account in Nevis too? Maybe an account set up by his wife under a fake company name? An account the FBI never knew about it"—until now—"so the money would never be traced."

Agent Brody finally drops the scowl he's been sporting since we returned and breaks into a smile. "I knew bringing you two along was a good idea. Even if you are the biggest pains in the ass I've ever met in my life."

Tiffany snorts. "Yeah, it's obvious you hate having us around. That's why you get a boner every time one of us walks into the room."

The pillow hadn't fooled her either.

But Agent Brody has already stopped listening. He'd

scooped his phone off the floor while she was talking and we can hear the ringing on the other end.

Tiffany and I would stay, but Agent Brody tells us there's nothing for us to do and the best way we can help him is to leave him alone so he can work undisturbed. So we change into bathing suits and head out to the beach. As Tiffany promised, the water is spectacular—warm and clear enough to see the bottom even when it's high over our heads.

We grab lunch at a beach shack, then rent bikes so we can spend the afternoon tooling around the island. There is only one main road that circles the entire isle, so we know we can't get lost. And that road is only twenty-one miles long, so we can cover the whole island in one day even with stopping for photo ops—although after the tenth swaying palm tree, they all start to look the same.

We're biking through Charlestown, which, although it's the capital of Nevis, is only a few blocks long, when Tiffany suddenly veers off the main road and into an alley. I follow her a few feet in and stop. "What are you doing?"

"I just saw Joe the Realtor," she says, trying to hide herself behind a trash can.

I turn around automatically, but I have no idea who I'm looking for. Tiffany had only described him as an "old guy" around forty. I assume all the people passing us on the street are fellow tourists from their sunburned faces and vacation attire, but there could be some locals too. I turn back to Tiffany. "Why is that a bad thing? He probably has no idea you two didn't sleep together"—assuming Tiffany was telling the truth about that. "It's not like you stole his wallet or anything." And then it occurs to me . . . "Did you?"

"No, I did not steal his wallet." Pause. "But I did take some money for cab fare."

"Tiffany!"

"What? He owed me that much after boring me with his stupid stories all night."

I'm about to point out that it was her choice to stay and listen to those stories, and she's the one who encouraged him to get a room, and he did buy her dinner too, but I decide not to waste my breath. "How much did you take?"

"I don't know," she says. "A few hundred maybe."

"A few hundred dollars!"

"Not US," she says and pulls a wad of colorful bills out of her purse.

Although they're dollars according to their lettering, they're closer in size and color to UK pounds. Agent Brody and I have been using US dollars since we arrived and they've been accepted without question, but it makes sense that someone who lives here would carry local currency instead. I count her bills, then pull out my phone to check the exchange rate. "You've got over ninety dollars here, Tiff. How much was your taxi?"

"That's all?" she says, finally coming out from behind the trash can. "I thought it was more than that."

"Well, how much did you think you'd stolen from him?"

"Not stolen. Earned."

Somehow I doubt he'd see it that way. "We can't stay in this alley all day. He's probably gone now anyway."

"I don't think so," she says. "I saw the sign for Sterling Realty, that's his company, just up the road—and the windows face the street."

I shake my head. I still can't believe she stole money from his wallet while he was passed out in bed. Who does that? Tiffany, apparently. I walk my bike to the edge of the alley and peek out onto the main road. I spot the real estate office half a block up, on the bottom floor of a two-story stone building with a row of shuttered windows facing the street. If Joe the Realtor happens to be looking out as we happen to be riding by, there's no way he won't see us. But it gives me an idea.

"Do you by any chance still remember his password?"

53

All I can say in my defense is that it seemed like a good idea at the time. The plan was simple. I would go into the real estate office pretending to be looking for a vacation rental for my family, then Tiffany would loiter in front of the window until Joe spotted her. When he did, she would head off on her bike, he would pursue, and while he was pursuing her (but unable to catch her since he was on foot and she was on a bike), I would log on to his computer and see if I could find out any more information about Starlight Partners LLC. Now that we knew what we were looking for, I reasoned, the search would be quick.

And it would've been. Except neither of us realized that the police station was just up the street. It, too, was in a stone building with shuttered windows and a very small sign over the door. It could've easily been a bank in that building, of which there were an excessive amount for such a tiny town.

At least we both have the forethought to pretend we don't know each other. When the police officer, who happens to be leaving the station as Tiffany zooms past on her bike with Joe the Realtor in pursuit, grabs her, I hightail it out of the real estate office. I bike back to the alley and call Agent Brody because I have no clue what to do. When my call goes straight to his voicemail, I figure he must be talking on the other line, so I return to the hotel.

After he finishes berating me for my stupidity—I take it without complaint since in this instance he's right—he hops on my bike and heads down to the police station without me. When I object to being left behind, he shouts, "I'm not bailing you both out!" and slams the door in my face. I have no good response to that either.

He returns two hours later with a slightly chastened Tiffany. I get the story over an early dinner, which Agent Brody insists we order from a local market and eat in the room because he says he doesn't trust Tiffany and me to go out by ourselves anymore.

Apparently Joe the Realtor wanted to press charges, even though Tiffany offered to give him his money back (minus the cab fare since she'd already spent that) and Agent Brody proposed reimbursing him for their dinner (which turned out to be double the amount Tiffany stole, mostly due to the bar bill) but Joe the Realtor refused.

Tiffany admits that in retrospect it was a mistake for her to tell the police officer that she and Joe the Realtor hadn't had sex the night before because "he got so drunk he passed out before I could even get his belt off." The police officer, who is a friend of Joe the Realtor's, started ribbing him mercilessly. Agent Brody's take on it is that Joe the Realtor insisted on pressing charges just to save face.

"Tiffany, I don't understand. Why would you offer up that information? Did the cop actually ask you if you had sex with him?" It seems like an inappropriate question to me.

"No," she admits. "But it was true."

"So? You didn't tell the cop you drugged the guy, and that was true too."

She balls up her napkin and throws it at me. "It's all your fault. You keep telling me people are going to get the wrong idea about me because of the way I dress, like they're going to think I'm a prostitute or something. And I started worrying that the cop might think that too. So I wanted him to know that there was no sex last night."

"No sex," Agent Brody says, "just petty theft and drug use. Ah well, it happens."

He's on his fourth beer now and it has definitely mellowed him. He's even stopped referring to us as the "idiot sisters."

"Don't worry," he continues. "I still think you both have bright futures in law enforcement, especially you, Tiffany."

"Thanks," she says and smiles at him.

"Law enforcement?" I say. "Don't you mean as criminals?"

He shrugs and swallows the remains of beer number four. "Two sides of the same coin," he says before burping loudly.

I am *so* glad I didn't sleep with him.

"So how did you manage to get her released?" I ask.

He pops the top off beer number five and takes a swig. "The old-fashioned way, Nina. Bribery."

"You bribed the local cops?" I can't believe an FBI agent would do something like that. It has to be illegal.

He shakes his head. "No, Joe the Realtor. It wasn't hard. I just reminded him that Tiffany still had lots of friends back in New York whose rich mommies and daddies weren't going to want to buy property from some shmuck who presses charges against one of their teenage daughters for playing a harmless prank. That and the extra couple of hundred I added for his troubles convinced him." He points his beer at Tiffany. "And you're paying me back every cent."

She nods and says, "Absolutely," in her most sincere voice

before she turns to me and winks. Apparently the experience hasn't chastened her at all.

It's hours later when we finally catch a break.

54

———

Tiffany and I are lying on the bed together watching an old black-and-white gangster film on TV when Agent Brody's computer pings. He left his computer open on the desk while he went to use the bathroom, so I get up and check the screen. It's a new email with the subject line *Starlight*.

"Read it," Tiffany whispers, but in our new spirit of trust and cooperation, I refrain. Instead I knock on the bathroom door. "I think you just got an email from your hacker friend."

Agent Brody emerges shaking water off his hands. "What does it say?"

"I don't know. I didn't read it."

"I would've," Tiffany pipes up.

"We already know you're ethically challenged," he says as he dries his hands on his chinos before heading to his laptop. He scans the email but his expression gives nothing away.

"Good news or bad news?" I ask, but he ignores me and continues to stare off into space. I call his name and get no response, so I slam the laptop shut. That gets his attention.

"What the hell?" he says.

"Good news or bad news?" I ask again.

"Bad news on the Starlight front, at least in terms of finding your father. Although it may help you, Tiffany."

She mutes the television and sits up. "How can it help me?"

He opens the laptop again and turns the screen toward her, although I doubt she can read it from twelve feet away even with her twenty-twenty vision. He points to the columns of numbers on the screen. "There's over four hundred grand in that account, but only one withdrawal—two thousand dollars was wired to the US a couple of weeks ago, and was withdrawn the next day from a bank in LA."

Tiffany jumps up from the bed and joins us at the computer. "You mean that's Raylene's account?"

Agent Brody nods. "I'm guessing not even your father knows about it."

"I can't believe her! She told me she was broke."

"Don't be too mad," Agent Brody says, closing the attachment and minimizing the screen. "That money's probably her retirement savings. It's not like she's got a 401k."

"Well, it's not like I've got one either."

"You're young," he says, taking in her voluptuous body, clad only in short-shorts and a double tank top. He can't help himself. Most men can't. "You've got plenty of mileage ahead of you. Your mother's best years are behind her. Frankly I'm surprised she doesn't have more."

"Maybe she does," I say. "Or maybe she did and you took it." I try to keep the bitterness out of my voice, but I can tell from Agent Brody's expression that I'm not successful. He looks as if I just slapped him across the face. Admittedly it isn't Raylene's money I'm upset about. I used to have a trust fund before it was confiscated by the Feds—all the money in it, according to the government, could be traced back to my father's crimes.

"Possibly," he says and turns away from me. "The Marshals did confiscate a few accounts in her name."

"Will she get that money back once we prove my father's innocent?" Tiffany asks.

I'm fairly certain it's not Raylene's money she's concerned about either. My father set up a trust fund for Tiffany too.

Agent Brody glances down. "I don't know, Tiffany, that's not my department."

I collapse onto the chair with my head in my hands. "So Starlight has nothing to do with my father and we're back to where we started—which is nowhere."

Agent Brody cracks a smile. "Not necessarily."

55

"My hacker knew better than to disappoint me again so—"

Tiffany lets out a laugh. "And what'll you do if he disappoints you? Shoot him?"

Agent Brody smirks. "Let's just say he could be facing a long prison term or a short one, so it's in his best interests to give me what I want."

I shake my head in disgust. Agent Brody's right—criminals and law enforcement are two sides of the same coin. But of the three of us, I seem to be the only one who's bothered by this fact.

"The point is," Agent Brody continues, "when he realized Starlight was a dead end, he started searching Nevis bank records for any unusual activity."

"You can do that?" I ask.

"I can't. Not without a warrant. But he can."

I shake my head again but Tiffany is practically giddy. "That is so cool. Do you think you could get your hacker to teach me?"

I turn to my ethically challenged sister. "Tiffany, this hacker is obviously in a lot of trouble."

"That's only because he got caught on the wrong side of the law," Agent Brody says. "On the right side, a good hacker can write his or her own ticket."

Tiffany sticks her tongue out at me and reminds me again that she is still a child. "See, it is a good idea. Even Jason thinks so."

If I thought Tiffany was going to be a law-abiding citizen I'd have no problem with her picking up a few hacking skills. But I know sooner or later, and probably sooner, she'll end up on the wrong side of the law too. One convicted felon in the family is enough.

But I'm confident I can put a quick end to this fantasy. "Tiff, you do know that hackers spend all day every day in windowless offices staring at computer screens, right? These people aren't cool. They're social outcasts, pariahs, nerds without a friend to their name. When they make a movie about your life, it won't be Jennifer Lawrence playing you; it'll be some mediocre looking comedic actress who never would've made it if she wasn't funny, and then they'll put some really uncool glasses on her so everyone thinks she's a dog."

She presses her lips together and considers it—for about two seconds. "Yeah, you're right. Sorry, Jason, it's not for me."

He shrugs, then gives her another appreciative eye sweep. "You'd probably make a better field agent anyway." Then he turns back to his computer screen and starts typing again.

"So are you going to tell us what your hacker found?" I ask. "Or are we just supposed to guess?"

"I don't want to get your hopes up. It might turn out to be nothing."

"Our hopes are already up, so you might as well tell us."

He stops typing and looks up. "He found a very well-funded account with a few large transfers around the time of your father's disappearance. And more recently smaller wires at regular intervals from that same account to a bank in Nicaragua."

"Nicaragua?" Tiffany and I say in unison. "Why would our father go there?" I ask.

"Yeah," Tiffany says. "Isn't that, like, a really poor country? Why would our dad go there when he could've gone anywhere?"

"It's the poorest country in Central America," Agent Brody replies. "But it's not true that your father could've gone anywhere. Remember, there was a worldwide manhunt for him —and still is. If he'd checked into the Four Seasons like you thought, we would've captured him the first day."

Then I realize why my father might've chosen to hide in the poorest country in Central America. "Is Nicaragua one of those places that doesn't have an extradition treaty with the US?"

Agent Brody smiles at me. "Good guess, but no, they do. You're on the right track though." We stare at him blankly until he says, "Just because a country has an extradition treaty doesn't mean they enforce it."

"They can do that?" I ask.

"It's a sovereign nation. They can do what they like. But if your father has made a . . . how shall I say this . . . a sizeable investment in the local economy..."

"You mean bribed the right people," Tiffany says.

"Yes," Agent Brody replies, "then certain officials might look the other way. Especially if he's keeping a low profile and no one knows he's there."

"Like the US government," I say.

"Yes, like the US government. Now if your father's clients included Latin American drug dealers, then Nicaragua would not be a good place to hide, but we never found any evidence of that."

"And the Russians?" I ask.

"They don't have a big presence in Central America. But that's why we knew your father couldn't have gone to Europe; they'd have hunted him down there for sure. Your father's no idiot."

I move behind Agent Brody so I can get a better look at his computer screen, but the long columns of numbers are still meaningless to me. "Well, he can't be that smart if your hacker friend was able to find him in a day." Not that the search had been easy. Or legal.

"Don't count your chickens, kiddo. We haven't found him yet."

Tiffany throws her arms up in the air. "Then what are we waiting for? Let's go to Nicaragua."

"It's not that simple, Tiffany. Nicaragua is a lot larger than Nevis. About the size of New York—that's State, not City. And we're not even sure he's there. This is just one of several suspicious fund transfers in large accounts that my guy found."

"But it's the one you told us about," I say, "so you must think it's promising."

His expression turns dour. "It's a hunch. It could easily turn out to be just another false lead. We've had plenty of them since your father disappeared. There's a reason the Marshals put this on the back burner."

"Well, it's on our front burner," Tiffany says. "And we know Dad's not on Nevis."

"We don't know that," I say, infected by Agent Brody's negativity. "Just because no one at the Four Seasons has seen him doesn't mean he's not here. There are other hotels on the island, Tiff. And rental properties. Or he could've bought a house here through one of those shell corporations. We have no idea, and no way to find out."

The hopelessness of this endeavor overtakes me again. What were we thinking? If the US Marshals couldn't find my father after their massive manhunt, how are we supposed to?

Tiffany punches both me and Agent Brody in the shoulder. "What is wrong with you two? Look how far we've come. We can't give up now!"

"Let me guess," Agent Brody says. "You were a cheerleader at that fancy prep school?"

"Yeah, for about five minutes before I realized how dumb it is. But I still went to their parties because they always have the best drugs."

"Tiffany!" This would be one of those times when I want to slap her.

"What? I didn't say I took any."

Right. She just went to the parties with the best drugs because they're there. Of course she would never take any. Does she think I'm an idiot? And hello, her buddy Jason is an FBI agent. Maybe not the best person in the world to admit your drug use to.

She gives me the hands-on-hips stance. "Good drugs means hot guys, and if you weren't such a dork, you would know that." She shakes her head. "I swear, sometimes I can't even believe we're sisters."

"Half sisters. Thank God."

Wound inflicted. Mission accomplished.

"You're such a bitch sometimes."

"Better a bitch than a—"

Agent Brody jumps up and stands between us as if this altercation could turn physical at any moment. He really should've figured out by now that girls fight with their words, not their fists. At least sisters do. "Whoa, ladies, dial it back. What just happened? You two were doing so well."

Tiffany and I glare at each other but say nothing.

Agent Brody sighs. "It's been a long day. I think we could all use some sleep. I'll have my hacker do some more digging overnight and we'll make a plan in the morning."

"Doesn't your hacker sleep too?" Tiffany asks, now as grumpy as me.

Agent Brody shoots her a smug smile. "Not until I tell him to."

Which actually makes me feel a bit better because I'm reminded that, as bad as things are, they could always be worse. I could have Agent Brody deciding my fate.

I'M the second one of us to wake. Agent Brody was the first. It's the glare from his computer screen and the incessant tap, tap, tap of his keyboard that rouse me from the nightmare I'd been having where I was running through the jungle being chased by a madman with a gun. So I'm not unhappy about being awakened in the middle of the night.

"What are you doing?" I whisper from the corner of the room where I'd set up the rollaway bed. Agent Brody hadn't been inclined to give up his full-size bed last night and I hadn't felt like fighting with Tiffany for the other one.

I can see the outline of his smile in the glow from his computer screen. "My hacker came through. He found some small withdrawals from that bank account in Nicaragua at an ATM in San Juan del Sur."

"Where's that?"

"A tourist town on the Pacific."

Surprising since my father never liked the Pacific Ocean—he always said the water was too cold and rough. He preferred swimming in the Caribbean, or better yet, a heated pool. "And you think that's where my father's at?"

His smile fades. "I have no idea. But this is the best lead we've got."

And the only one.

And Benny is expecting his money back in five days.

I silently pray that my father has escaped with enough funds to cover Agent Brody's debt too.

56
___

The flight from Nevis to San Juan, Puerto Rico, is fully booked, so we end up taking a ferry to St. Kitts, then catching a flight to Miami, where we spend another night (and this time I insist we get a hotel room and not sleep on airport chairs) and fly out to Managua, Nicaragua, the next morning. Which means we have exactly four days to find my dad before Benny comes looking for us, or at least Agent Brody, with a baseball bat.

At the airport we rent a four-by-four, which is recommended because of the country's mostly dirt roads, and drive the three hours to San Juan del Sur. The long drive gives us plenty of time to argue about where we should stay when we get there, that is, when we're not marveling at the three-wheel taxis, livestock trucks, and ox carts sharing the lane with us along the Pan American Highway. Nicaragua is cheap by US standards so Tiffany wants to stay high-end. And of course Agent Brody wants to stay at the most inexpensive place in the town. We eventually compromise on a four-star hotel, which is really a three-star property by US standards, but with two-star prices.

We check into the Oceanside Inn, which despite its name is

not near the beach. But if you stand in the parking lot and crane your neck, you can catch a glimpse of the crescent-shaped coastline below. The best I can say about the place is that the air conditioning and Wi-Fi work well, and we're able to get a room with three beds. In other words, Agent Brody's okay with it, Tiffany's not, and I'm too worried to care. We're running out of time, money, and leads. And if we don't find my dad here, I have no idea what we'll do next. When I ask Agent Brody, he shrugs —not confidence inspiring.

It's at least ninety degrees out and what feels like one hundred percent humidity, so after we all shower and change into less sweaty clothes, we drive the five minutes into town, which is all of eight blocks long, and walk along the waterfront in search of a lunch spot.

I'd thought, this being a tiny town in a small, impoverished country, we'd be stuck eating rice and beans our entire stay. But I'm wrong. San Juan del Sur boasts several good restaurants serving everything from gourmet burgers to fresh seafood and even Indian cuisine. I'm now starting to understand why my dad picked this town, if in fact he had. He could live without culture and amenities, but he could not live without good food. He's a foodie at heart.

"So what's the plan?" I ask Agent Brody after the three of us order burgers and beer (no carding in Nicaragua, although Tiffany's fake passport says she's twenty-one anyway).

"We stake out the ATM where the other withdrawals were made. The past few occurred every four or five days, so if it is your dad and he sticks to the same schedule, he's due for another withdrawal today or tomorrow."

"Seriously?" Tiffany says. "*That's* your plan?"

Agent Brody exhales loudly. I've spent enough time with him now to recognize his warning signs and I know he's about to blow. Tiffany should realize it too, and maybe she does, but she doesn't care. She's still angry about the hotel he chose.

"We can take shifts," he says, "so none of us have to spend too long in one place, which in a town this small would arouse suspicion anyway."

Tiffany declares, "That's the lamest plan I've ever heard."

Agent Brody slams his fist on the table and the silverware jumps. "You got a better idea, princess? I'm all ears."

"Yes, I think we should start showing Dad's picture around town, especially at all the restaurants. He can't cook and he loves to eat, so if he's here, someone will have seen him."

I'm about to agree with her when Agent Brody says, "And that's the stupidest idea I've ever heard. If your father is here and he finds out someone's going around town showing his photo asking if anyone's seen him lately, that will immediately send him underground. Then we'll never find him."

"You didn't object when I showed his picture around the Four Seasons."

"Recall you didn't ask me first. If you had, I would've told you not to. But I knew it didn't matter since I was sure your father wouldn't have been stupid enough to show his face there. Too many rich New Yorkers, Tiffany. He could've easily run into someone he knew."

"Well this place is a tourist town too. What's to stop him from running into someone he knows here?"

"Look around, princess. It's all surfers and ex-pats trying to stretch their dollars because they lost their retirement savings in the last market crash or didn't have any to begin with."

"And yogis," I say. I'd spotted a large group of women in their Lululemon workout gear returning to the hotel as we were leaving.

"The point is," Agent Brody continues, "none of these people are likely to know your father personally."

The waiter drops off our burgers and beers and we all concentrate on eating so we don't have to speak to one another. The tension at the table is even thicker than the humidity.

At least Tiffany waits until Agent Brody has paid the bill to announce, "I'm not hanging around outside an ATM all day waiting to see if my father shows up."

"Fine," Agent Brody says, slamming the tip on the table. "Do what you like. Your sister and I can split the shifts."

"Um, I think I'm with Tiffany on this one." Surely we can come up with a better plan than hanging around outside an ATM all day in ninety-five degree heat with one hundred percent humidity and no shade.

Agent Brody gives me his trademark stare, but when I don't blink, he shakes his head, mumbles something I can't hear (and probably don't want to), then screeches his chair against the wood floor as he pushes away from the table. But before he leaves, he wags his finger at us. "Know this, ladies. If you two get yourselves into trouble again, I am *not* bailing you out." Then he turns to Tiffany. "You think our hotel is bad? Wait until you see the inside of a Nicaraguan jail cell. You'll think the Oceanside Inn is the Four Seasons." Then he strides out of the restaurant, knocking over a chair along the way.

Tiffany waits until he's gone to ask, "Who peed in his Cheerios?"

And I find myself in the irksome position of having to defend Agent Brody. "He's worried, Tiff. I am too. What are we going to do if Dad's not here? We have no other leads."

"Well, we're not going to find him hanging around an ATM all day. C'mon, have you ever seen Dad use an ATM even once? When he needed cash he used to send his driver to the bank. And I still think my idea is a good one."

"I know, but I think Agent Brody might be right. If Dad bribed officials to let him into the country, what makes you think he didn't bribe a few locals to let him know if anyone comes looking for him?"

"I guess," she says reluctantly. "But we have to do something!"

I agree, but I have no idea what, and neither does Tiffany. "Whatever it is, it has to be something legal." I'm not one hundred percent convinced Agent Brody would follow through on his threat, but I'm not willing to risk finding out.

"Agreed," she says.

Thank God.

We sit in silence another few minutes, each lost in thought, until I say, "I like your idea about the restaurants though. Dad does like to eat."

She lets out a laugh. "And the man can't cook to save himself. Did you know he almost set the stove on fire once trying to make me a grilled cheese? Juanita was furious. It's the only time I ever heard her raise her voice to Dad."

I hadn't heard that story before. "Where was Raylene?"

Tiffany shrugs. "Who knows. Probably out shopping."

"Of course, he could've just hired someone to cook for him here."

We both frown as we realize that's likely exactly what our father did. If he's in hiding, he's not going to risk eating out at restaurants for every meal. Even if the locals and tourists don't know him personally, someone could still recognize his face. It had been on the news for months. And if the domestic help are as cheap as the hotels, he could afford to hire a different gourmet chef for every night of the week.

When the waiter stops by our table for the third time to see if we want anything else, I realize we've overstayed our welcome. Not that there's a line of people waiting for our table. It's late afternoon and the restaurant is empty, but I assume his shift is over and he wants to go home. As I grab my purse from the back of my chair, I catch sight of a group of women leaving the vegetarian restaurant next door. They're all wearing yoga pants, with brightly colored mats slung over their perfectly straight shoulders.

On impulse I ask the waiter, "What's the deal with all the yogis?" His English is pretty good, so when he gives me a questioning stare, I point to the women outside.

"Ah, yoga people," he says. "They're here for the retreats, and some come for the teacher training."

Teacher training? "You have a yoga school?" I ask, somewhat incredulous that a town of less than fifteen thousand people would have enough practitioners to necessitate a training program.

"*Sí*," he says, "more than one. The Sun Center is most popular with *Americanos*. It's the nicest."

Tiffany immediately starts googling The Sun Center on her phone. "This is where we *should* be staying," she says, scrolling through photos of luxurious bathrooms, carved wood furnishings, and million-dollar views.

I laugh when I see the price—three times the nightly rate of our current hotel. "Good luck convincing your pal Jason to let us switch."

"To hell with him," she says. "We can go ourselves."

I shake my head. "We already lost that battle in Panama, remember?"

Tiffany considers this, probably deciding whether it's worth going to war with him over it again, and ultimately decides not. "Then we should at least go for a yoga class. Look."

She hands me her phone and I'm staring at a photo of a half dozen women standing in mountain pose on a polished wood deck. They're all looking out over a lush green hilltop dotted with red-tile roofs. In the distance is San Juan del Sur's ubiquitous crescent-shaped beach. Unconsciously I start deep breathing and immediately feel my shoulders relax. I shut my eyes and can practically smell the tropical flowers and feel the saltwater breeze. "Let's do it."

Tiffany books us into the sunset class and I justify the expense by reminding myself that I've gotten some of my best ideas on the mat when my mind is quiet and my inner critic lulled into submission by the chanting of "om."

We catch sight of Agent Brody sitting in the air conditioned four-by-four as we leave the restaurant, but decide we'd rather hoof it back to the hotel in the heat and humidity than beg him for a ride.

57

Unfortunately inspiration doesn't strike during downward dog or any of the dozen other poses we contort ourselves into during the hour-long class, but the air is fragrant, there's a gentle breeze off the ocean, and frankly it feels good to be sweating from something other than the humidity. When the class is over, our instructor, Gillian, invites us all to stay for a fruit smoothie and to watch the sunset. Tiffany and I are in no rush to get back to Agent Brody, so we take her up on her offer.

"Where are you girls from?" she asks, joining us cross-legged on the floor of the deck. The other two people who stayed, a middle-aged couple from Minnesota, took their smoothies with them to the lounge chairs in the pool area.

"LA," I say at the same time Tiffany says, "New York." We really need to get our stories straight. "I just moved out to LA," I say. "We both grew up in New York."

"You two are sisters?" she asks.

Tiffany turns to me, daring me to say "half sisters," I think, but I just nod my head.

"My boyfriend's from New York," Gillian says. "At least I think he's my boyfriend. We've only been together a few weeks."

"Surfer?" Tiffany asks. In the short time we've been in San Juan del Sur, we've already determined that all of the cute guys are surfers.

Gillian laughs. "No, an ex-pat like me, although he's taken up surfing since he moved here. Apparently it's required or something. But the two before him were surfers, one from Canada and one from Delaware."

"How long have you been here?" I ask. She didn't look much older than me.

"Three years. I came for a yoga retreat and never left."

We all stare out at the magnificent pink and blue sky with just a sliver of orange left above the horizon. It's easy to understand how someone might come here and never want to leave.

"Where are you from?" Tiffany asks.

"Boston."

She's lost the accent. She could be from anyplace in the US.

"When I left, it was snowing and eighteen degrees. Is it any wonder I didn't go back?"

We laugh and start to reminisce about scraping ice off car windows and walking in high heels through slush-strewn streets. Before we realize it, the sliver of sunlight has disappeared into the horizon and but for the stars and a half moon, the sky has turned black. "Oh shit," Gillian says, glancing at the clock on her phone. "My boyfriend's going to be here any minute and I haven't even showered yet."

The three of us stand and wipe the dust off our clothes. Tiffany turns to me. "We should probably get back to the hotel and see if Jason's forgiven us yet."

"Jason?" Gillian asks.

"A friend," I say, not wanting to explain.

Gillian grabs her yoga mat and workout bag and slings them both over her shoulder. "Is he picking you up?"

I check my phone and see that I have no messages, despite my text to Agent Brody earlier telling him that Tiffany and I were going to a yoga class and he should message me when he's finished his surveillance for the day. "I don't think so. But our hotel's not that far; we can just walk back." It was a hike getting here since it was all uphill, but that means the return trip will be easy.

She shakes her head. "Not a good idea."

"Why not?" Tiffany asks.

Gillian looks up at the night sky and we do too. Clouds must've rolled in because the stars have disappeared and only a sliver of moonlight remains. "It's not safe to walk by yourselves. There are no streetlights here. The roads are barely passable at night even in a car."

"The hotel would probably let us borrow a flashlight," Tiffany says, misunderstanding her concern. "Don't you think?"

"Yes, but that's not going to help you with the *bandidos.*"

"You have bandits here?" Tiffany asks.

Gillian laughs at Tiffany's literal translation. "That's just what we call them. Don't get me wrong, most times I feel safer here than I did in Boston. The locals are nice and super friendly, but there's always a few that ruin it for the rest. It's not considered safe, for women especially, to be walking along these back roads alone at night. I'll have my boyfriend drop you at your hotel."

"You don't need to do that," I say. "We can grab a cab."

Gillian laughs again. "This isn't New York City. You can travel by bus, bicycle, car, and maybe even an ox cart if you time it right, but there ain't no grabbing a cab in San Juan del Sur."

We laugh too. Point taken.

"Come on," she says, motioning for me and Tiffany to follow her. "It's no big deal to drop you at your hotel. Which one are you at?"

"The Oceanside Inn," Tiffany says with obvious disgust.

"You could do worse," Gillian replies. "And we actually have to pass it on the way to my boyfriend's house, so he won't mind at all."

We trail her up the staircase and through The Sun Center's open-air lobby. Just as we're heading outside again, a pair of headlights appears in the circular drive. "Wait here," she says and runs out to meet the beaten-down Range Rover, its lower half covered in a thick layer of mud. The windshield is tinted so we can't make out the driver, but we assume it's her boyfriend since she leans into the rolled-down window and kisses whoever's behind the wheel. When she motions for us to join her, Tiffany and I climb into the backseat as she hops in on the front passenger side.

"P.J.," Gillian says, "I'd like you to meet Nina and Tiffany, my new friends from New York by way of LA. Nina and Tiffany, this is P.J."

P.J. pivots in his seat and his jaw literally drops open. I assume mine and Tiffany's do too. The three of us stare at each other for what seems like an eternity but is probably no more than ten seconds. Tiffany is the first to speak: "Daddy?"

58

———

"Daddy?" Gillian says, then spins around in her seat so she is facing our father instead of us. "You never told me you had kids!"

P.J. is the proverbial deer caught in headlights. "Um, well, Gilly, it's . . . complicated."

"Complicated! What's complicated about telling me you have children? Either you have them or you don't."

"It's not that simple really. The girls and I . . . well . . . we haven't spoken for a while. When their mother and I divorced, we—"

"You and Mom are divorced?" Tiffany cries. "Since when?"

Gillian glares at my father, aware that she is being fed yet another lie. "You are the biggest fucking prick I've ever met in my life," she says, then jumps out of the Range Rover and slams the door shut.

We all watch as she stomps back through the hotel's lobby, her back straight and her head held high, with her workout bag and mat swinging behind her until she disappears from sight.

"Do you want to go after her?" I ask because clearly the man has *a lot* of explaining to do. "We can wait in the car."

But my father just shakes his head and sighs, then shifts the four-by-four into gear. As we bump along the dirt path that passes for a road, our father stares at us through the rearview mirror. And we stare at him too. He looks different. It's not just the clothes—I'm used to seeing him in a suit and tie, not a ratty old T-shirt and cargo shorts—and the hair, which is now mostly gray and hanging down past his shoulders instead of cut short and dyed dark, or even the weight loss—the paunch has disappeared and his shoulders look a bit broader than they used to (maybe it's the surfing). It's his face—it looks different too.

"Did you have work done?" I finally ask. "You look"—I still can't quite figure out what exactly he's changed—"younger." And this is despite the gray hair.

He smiles at me in the mirror. "Eye lift," he says. "It's amazing the difference it's made, don't you think?"

"Your nose looks a little straighter too," Tiffany says.

Now that she's pointed it out, I see it also. His nose used to be crooked—broken during a schoolyard fight when he was a boy—and now it's perfectly straight and a bit smaller to my eyes. This new nose is more befitting a "P.J." than his old one was. Presumably he has a new waspy last name to go with it.

My father's grin turns sheepish. "I figured since I was going under the knife anyway, I might as well fix everything."

"You look good, Dad," Tiffany says.

"Thanks. You girls look good too. And I can't tell you how happy it makes me to see you getting along so well. Vacationing together." He shakes his head. "I never would've imagined it."

Tiffany and I exchange glances. "Um, Dad," I say, "we're not here on vacation. We came to Nicaragua to find you."

He slams on the brakes and the Range Rover skids to a stop, sending puffs of dirt flying in all directions. He leaves the engine running, but he pulls on the parking brake and turns around in his seat. "What do you mean you came down here to find me?

Gillian said you two were here on vacation, that you took her yoga class, and you needed a lift back to your hotel."

"Well, we couldn't exactly tell her why we're *really* here," Tiffany says and rolls her eyes. "Obviously."

Our usually calm, or usually outwardly calm, father is now borderline hysterical. "You two came down here to find me? How do you know you weren't followed? And how did you even know where to look?"

"We didn't come ourselves," Tiffany says. "Agent Brody brought us."

"Agent Brody? You mean Jason Brody, the FBI guy?"

"Of course," Tiffany says. "How many Agent Brodys do you know, Dad?"

"Don't smart-mouth me, Tiffany. This is serious. You two better start explaining yourselves right this instant."

I jump in to try to head off the brewing storm. "Agent Brody came to us, Dad. He told us he found new evidence proving you were innocent, that it was all Chet's doing and he duped you along with everyone else. But he had no way of finding you. The Marshals had pretty much given up. So he came to us for help."

"And how exactly did you two *help* him?"

"That's kind of a long story," I say.

"Then I suggest you start talking."

I'm about to explain about the old photos we found at my mother's apartment and how that led us to Panama when my phone rings.

"Is that Brody?" my father demands.

But before I can answer, he rips the phone from my hand and smashes it against the car's gear shift.

"What the hell are you doing?" I scream, but he ignores my obvious distress.

My father holds out his hand to me. "Give me a paper clip."

"A paper clip? I don't have a paper clip."

"Then a pen or a hair pin or anything with a point on it."

"Why?" Tiffany asks as she starts rummaging through her purse too. She finds a pen in her bag and hands it to him.

"Dad, please tell me what's going on here," I say as he tries to stick the tip of the pen into the side of the phone where the SIM card is stored. The point is too big and he hurls the pen into the backseat, nearly catching me in the eye—not that he seems to care!

"I need your phone too," he says to Tiffany. "Now!" he screams seconds later when she's still fishing it out of her purse. She hands it over and he smashes her screen against the gear shift too, then takes both phones outside and places them under the front tire. He revs the engine and runs over them back and forth a few times, then gets out of the car again. I think he's going to retrieve the phones and hand them back to us, but instead he takes what's left of them and hurls the pieces into the jungle. Seconds later a monkey howls—they're all over the place down here—and I don't know if it's because he's just been hit by a flying phone or he's happy to have found a new toy.

By the time our father climbs back into the car, Tiffany is crying and I'm on the verge of tears too. This is not the reunion either of us was expecting. We thought our father would be happy to see us, especially after we told him we have evidence that proves he's innocent!

"Daddy," Tiffany whimpers, "Why are you doing this?"

He shifts the car into gear and we start moving again. "Jason Brody did not bring you two here because he found new evidence to exonerate me."

"How do you know that?" I ask, now crying too.

"Because I'm guilty!"

59

"That's not true!" Tiffany screams. "I don't know why you're saying that, but I know it's not true. You couldn't have done all those terrible things they said you did."

But I know he's telling the truth, finally, and the weight of that knowledge almost sinks me. "Daddy, how could you?"

He stops the car again and rests his head on the steering wheel. "I'm sorry. I never wanted you girls to know. I'm . . . I need to explain."

"Explain!" I shout through my tears. "What is there to explain? You did it. You're guilty. And when they convicted you, you ran like the coward you are. I can't believe we defended you, we believed you, we even came looking for you. You must think we're the stupidest girls alive."

"No, sweetheart, I don't think that at all. If you just let me explain—"

"No! I don't want to hear any more of your lies. Just take us back to the hotel."

"I can't do that," he says.

"Why not?" Tiffany asks, her voice barely audible.

"Isn't Jason Brody there waiting for you?"

"I guess so." In fact, I have no idea.

"And you think he's going to arrest you?" Tiffany asks.

"No, sweetie, he's not here to arrest me."

My head snaps up in surprise. "Then why has he been looking for you?"

"Money, sweetheart. I owe him money. Your friend Agent Brody is the one who helped me escape."

60

The shocks are so many and so great I can barely stay upright. My head is spinning and I feel like I want to throw up. The father I believed was innocent is actually guilty, and the man I thought wanted justice is actually a criminal himself. Yes, my father has some explaining to do. They both do.

The car starts moving again and I hear my father tell us he's taking us back to his house, but it's as if I'm watching a movie and this is all happening to someone else. I sit in the back of the car with my head banging against the window as we bump along dirt roads. I close my eyes and for a moment it occurs to me that I'll never be able to find my way back to the hotel. Then I realize it doesn't matter. There's no reason to go back to the hotel. Even if Agent Brody is there waiting for us, he's just another lying scumbag too.

And to think after his "confession" in Nevis about his loan shark and the fact that he was searching for my father without his boss's knowledge, I actually did start to trust him the tiniest bit. When he told me he would be honest with me from that point forward, I actually believed him. I shake my head involuntarily. I really am the stupidest girl alive.

Eventually the car stops. My father and Tiffany climb out, but I don't move. *I just want to go home.* Then it occurs to me that I don't have one anymore. I'm not even sure my one non-criminal parent is speaking to me. The last time we spoke, she hung up on me. I might as well just stay where I am.

But Tiffany has other ideas. She grabs my hand and pulls. "Nina, you need to come inside."

But I don't want to go inside. I don't want to hear any more of my father's lies. I don't want to listen to him "explain." I close my eyes again and burrow deeper into the backseat. Maybe if I fall asleep, I'll wake up and this will all have been a bad dream.

But my father walks around to my side of the car and opens the door I'm leaning against. I would've fallen to the ground if he hadn't caught me. He embraces me but I don't reciprocate. I remain limp in his arms, all of my energy drained away. I realize I'm not even angry anymore. I'm just . . . numb.

"Please, Nina. Come inside with us. I need to explain."

I'm a zombie now. When he tells me to sit down on the couch, I sit. When he places a glass of wine in my hand and tells me to drink, I drink. The one thing I won't do is look at him. I can't. It's the one action that can still cause me pain.

I just listen as Tiffany tells him how we found him—how my mother's old photos led us to Panama City, how Enrique led us to Nevis, how Tiffany's snooping led us to Starlight Partners, and how Agent Brody's hacker led us to San Juan del Sur.

"Unbelievable," my father keeps saying over and over again.

When she's done with her tale, Tiffany says, "It's your turn, Daddy. I know you're not guilty, so why are you lying to us? Are you still trying to protect us?"

My father sighs. "It's complicated, Tiffany. The world isn't as black and white as you've been led to believe."

"Then explain it to us, Daddy." She grabs my hand. "We want to understand."

My father pushes himself up from his chair and starts to pace the tile floors of the open-concept living room. "Remember the last market crash? Everyone was panicking and lots of people thought the world was going to end? You were still pretty young, Tiffany, but, Nina, you must remember, don't you? You were in college at the time."

I do remember, but I don't respond. I had a friend who had to drop out of school because his parents couldn't afford the tuition anymore. But it hadn't seemed to affect my dad much. If he'd lost money, he never mentioned it.

"Anyway, a lot of people were really scared, myself included. Luckily we only had a few big redemptions and I was able to cover those. But I kept thinking when the trials start and this whole charade unravels, I'm sunk. And that's when I started moving the bulk of the money offshore. But then it never happened."

"What never happened?" Tiffany asks.

"The hearings, the trials, the long prison sentences. All of these guys—and I'm talking about major players, Tiffany; they make the money I took look like chump change—these guys brought the country, hell, the whole world, to its knees, and instead of sending them to jail, do you know what our government does? They pay them out a hundred cents on the dollar and then give them bonuses on top of it because they're the only ones who can unravel this mess—the mess that they themselves created! The government decides they're all too big to fail, so they don't let them. They prop them up with *our* money and then let the rest of the country go down the drain. I honestly couldn't believe it. Honestly."

"I don't understand," Tiffany says. "What does this have to do with you?"

I'm glad she asked, because I'm wondering the same thing.

Despite myself, I want to hear my father explain. I want some way to justify his actions too.

"Sweetheart, don't you see? I knew then that the fix was in. The whole economy is a sham, a giant shell game. And the only thing my good-for-nothing father taught me before he passed is that only one person ever wins a shell game, and that's the one holding the shell. So that's what I did."

Tiffany still looks confused, but I'm starting to understand. I finally look up at my father, who is now practically manic. "So if the big players can cheat and get away with it, then you should be able to also. Is that it?"

"They didn't just cheat and get away with it, Nina, they got *rewarded* for it. And then the government wants to send *me* to jail? I conned maybe a few hundred people. Those guys conned a *hundred million* people, a billion if you count all the foreign investors too."

"So you really did steal people's money?" Tiffany asks.

"No, sweetie, I never stole. People *invested* with me, and investors always take risks. Of course everyone wants huge returns with no potential downside, but that's not how it works. Did you know the financial industry is the most regulated industry in the nation? You would not believe the disclosures I have to make. It's not my fault people can't be bothered to do even a modicum of due diligence. They just hand over their money and say, 'Here, double it for me so I can send my kid to college or buy myself a boat or retire someday.' And I did! I made a lot of people a lot of money over the years."

"But it wasn't real," I say.

"You still don't get it, do you? None of it is real! It's all just numbers on a spreadsheet, nothing more."

"But money is real," Tiffany says.

Our dad pulls his wallet out of his pocket and slaps a wad of bills onto the coffee table. "Look, Tiffany, it's just paper. It only has value because we say it does. Intrinsically, it's worthless."

Tiffany turns to me and I can tell by her expression that she's scared. And I'm scared too. Our father has clearly lost his mind.

———

61

"Okay, Dad, I understand now," I say, hoping to pull him back from the brink, because at this point I have no idea what he might do. Murder-suicide might not be out of the question if he really thinks this is the end. "What about Chet? How does he fit into this?"

My dad sighs and collapses onto his chair again. "What a pussy he turned out to be. We could've weathered an SEC investigation; we have before. But he found religion last year, the moron, and then gets scared and starts running his mouth off. I still could've kept a lid on it, but then he cut a deal with the Feds and it was game over for me."

"Why didn't you cut your own deal?" Tiffany asks.

"Because the government doesn't cut deals with guys like me, outsiders who know the entire system is corrupt. Remember the Occupy Wall Street movement? They shut those guys down fast when they started gaining a little too much public support. But they knew people were angry and they had to do something. So they found the people a scapegoat, and that scapegoat is me." He lets out a manic laugh. "The government would've hung me from my neck in Times Square if they could have. No, sweetheart, I never stood a chance."

"So Chet's guilty too?" I ask, trying to ground us in reality again instead of letting him fly off into more paranoid delusions.

"Of course he's guilty. You think he would've made a deal if he wasn't? But everyone's guilty, Nina. Don't you understand that yet? Either you're the con or the mark. And I know which one of those two I want to be."

After a brief silence, Tiffany asks, "Does my mother know?"

Our father shakes his head. "I never told her. I never told any of you. I wanted to protect you girls." He jumps up and starts pacing again. "That's what a real man does, Tiffany. He protects his family and provides for them, no matter the cost." Then he suddenly stops pacing and kneels down in front of Tiffany. "You're a beautiful girl, sweetheart. And someday you'll marry and I won't be there for it, which makes me very sad. But I want you to promise me one thing—that you'll marry a man who understands what I'm telling you; that you'll marry a man who knows that his real job is to protect and provide for his family, no matter the cost."

"I promise," she answers solemnly.

And it is those two words that push *me* over the edge.

I jump up from the couch and stare down at her. "You promise? You promise you're going to marry a crook and a con man? Why don't you just start stealing people's money yourself and save the step? Oh, wait, you already did that."

My father stands up too. "Who did you steal from?" Tiffany had conveniently left out that detail from her story.

"Just some boring old guy," Tiffany tells him, then turns to me. "And I didn't steal it, I *earned* it."

"Earned it *how*?" my father asks, his suspicion aroused.

Tiffany redirects her anger from me to him. "Don't you look at me that way. I didn't do anything wrong."

"Then tell me exactly how you earned that money."

"Tell your father, Tiffany," a man's voice calls out. "He has a right to know."

62

———

All three of us spin in the direction of Agent Brody's voice. He's standing just inside the back door, and he's not alone. Gillian is standing beside him, which explains how he found us. But by her fearful expression, her appearance at our father's house is not by choice. She's not crying, but her eyes are swollen and her nose is red, so I assume she has been. But I'm more worried about Agent Brody's gun, which is out of its holster and in his hand.

"Jason," my father says, "I heard you were in town."

"Did you think I wouldn't come looking for you? You owe me a lot of money, Harold."

"I already paid you a lot of money."

Agent Brody smiles. "Two hundred grand? That's chump change to you and much less than what we agreed upon."

"You didn't keep up your end of the bargain. You were supposed to convince everyone I was dead."

"A little hard without a body, Harold. I told you it would be."

"That's not my problem, it's yours."

Agent Brody lifts his gun, which had been dangling at his

side, and holds it against Gillian's head. "Well, it looks like it's your problem now."

Tiffany and I gasp, and Gillian starts begging: "Please don't. I don't know anything, I swear!" My father remains silent while Tiffany says, "It's true. We just met her today," and I say, "Jason, please, just let her go. This has nothing to do with her."

Agent Brody ignores all three of us and stares at my father. "Do I need to shoot her first, or are you going to give me the rest of my money?"

Amazingly, my father doesn't flinch. "Kidnapping innocent women? Threatening to shoot people? This isn't you, Jason. You're a gambler who got in over his head, not a criminal."

"You're a gambler?" Tiffany says.

My dad turns to her. "Didn't he tell you? Your friend Jason likes blackjack. But the cards aren't always kind to him. And there's this loan shark—"

"Benny," I say.

My father spins toward me. "You know about Benny?"

"Yes, Agent Brody borrowed money from him to pay our expenses. We've been flying all over the world looking for you, Dad. That's not cheap, and you know the Feds took everything we had."

My father laughs, which is not the reaction I'm at all expecting. Then he turns back to Agent Brody. "Well played, Jason. But why tell them about Benny at all?"

He doesn't put the gun in its holster, but he does move it away from Gillian's head. I'd like to think that was my father's intention. "I didn't have a choice. Nina picked up one of his calls. I had to tell her something."

"Wait a minute," I say. *More time talking means less time shooting.* "You mean you *didn't* borrow money from Benny to pay our expenses?"

My dad answers for him: "Oh, I'm sure he did, sweetheart.

But he was already into him for half a mill. I guess Benny figured what's a few dollars more. Am I right, Jason?"

Agent Brody shrugs.

"What I still can't figure out," my father continues, "is how you managed to get the guy in Panama—what was his name again?"

"Enrique," Tiffany says. "Enrique Rojas."

My father's expression changes to one of surprise. "President of *Banco Internacional*, Enrique Rojas?"

"You know him?" I ask. I don't know why I'm surprised but I am. Yet another man in my life who's lied to me. I should be used to it by now.

But my father shakes his head. "Only by reputation. I can't believe you got Enrique Rojas to give you information about me. They take their banking privacy laws very seriously in Panama. That was a huge risk for him. If anyone found out he'd—"

"Planning on turning him in to the authorities, Dad? How would that work exactly, seeing as you're a fugitive and all?" How dare he threaten Enrique! It turns out he's the only man in my life who *hasn't* lied to me.

"The authorities would be the least of his problems," my father says to me before returning his attention to Agent Brody. "What did you threaten him with?"

"It wasn't me, Harold, it was your daughter. What can I say, the poor man was smitten."

My father turns to Tiffany, naturally.

"Not me," she says, "Nina."

My dad faces me and I shake my head in disgust. "Not *every* man goes for the buxom blonde, Dad. Some actually prefer intelligent brunettes." Although I'm not feeling very intelligent at the moment.

"You know I think you're beautiful too, sweetheart. Just in a different way is all." He heads toward me with his arms open as if to give me a hug, but I glare at him and he stops midway.

"Spare me, Dad. We all know your type." He dumped my elegant, sophisticated mother for former stripper Raylene.

I can tell he wants to answer me but he swallows it and instead folds his arms across his chest and asks, "How did you get Enrique Rojas to give you information about me?"

"How do you think?" Let him believe the worst of me. I don't care anymore.

"He asked her to be his mistress," Tiffany adds unhelpfully.

"Oh really." My father stares at me. "And what did you say to that?"

"I'm here, aren't I? Not living the high life in Panama. Although obviously that was a mistake. Maybe I should go back and see if Enrique still wants me."

"Nina, the man's twice your age."

I can't believe the hypocrisy, especially with Gillian standing in the room! "Oh, that's rich coming from you, Dad. So it's okay for men to fuck women half their age, so long as the woman in question isn't your daughter?"

"Watch your language."

"My *language*? Agent Brody is holding a gun to your girlfriend's head and you're worried about *my language*?"

"She's not my girlfriend," my father says with a dismissive wave of his hand.

"Since when?" Gillian demands, and we all turn toward her. "I mean, I'm not anymore, but I was until this evening."

Agent Brody laughs. "Good luck getting out of this one, Harold."

And that's when my father lunges for the gun.

63

The gun fires and we all start screaming at once. Gillian runs for the back door, but Agent Brody catches her by the ankle and pulls her down. My father is slumped on the floor next to Agent Brody, a bright red spot spreading across his T-shirt. Tiffany runs to his side, but I choose the opposite direction. I sprint toward the front door—freedom, safety, and help for my family and Gillian. I'm still fiddling with the locks, wondering if my father left the keys in his car or if I'm going to have to escape on foot, when I hear a loud bang and feel the bullet whiz by my ear. An instant later there's a hole in the doorframe and wood splinters everywhere. I spin around and find Agent Brody standing two feet away. This time the gun is pointed at *my* head.

"Step away from the door, Nina."

My heart is beating so hard and so fast I feel like I'm going to have a heart attack at any moment, but somehow I manage to speak. "If you kill me, you won't get your money. My father will never give it to you."

"Sure he will," he says. "He's still got one daughter left."

I'm stunned silent.

"Now step away from the door before I'm forced to do something I'd rather not do."

This time I comply and Agent Brody grabs me by the upper arm, and not gently either, and walks me back into the living room. I join Tiffany, Gillian, and my father on the floor.

Agent Brody points the gun at my father. "Lift up your shirt."

He's having trouble doing it himself, so Tiffany helps him, but she pales at the sight of so much blood.

"You, ex-girlfriend," Agent Brody says, pointing the gun at Gillian again. "Go to the kitchen and get some paper towels."

She stands up and winces. Her ankle is already beginning to swell. As she hobbles into the next room, Agent Brody calls after her: "And don't even think about grabbing a knife. If I see anything in your hands other than paper towels, I'll blow your head off first and investigate later. Understand?"

She nods and continues into the kitchen, not bothering to wipe away the tears, which are flowing freely now.

I'm too terrified to cry.

Tiffany is sitting next to our father holding his hand and obviously trying not to puke, so when Gillian returns with the paper towels, Agent Brody tells her to wipe up the blood. "It's not that bad," he pronounces when he can see the wound. "The bullet just grazed your side. A handful of stitches and you'll be fine. Do you have a first-aid kit?"

"In the bathroom," my dad says. "Down the hall on the left."

"Nina, go get it. And don't try to be a hero. I have no problem shooting Tiffany first if that's what it takes to get you to behave. Understand?"

I nod and run to the bathroom. There's a window above the tub. It's not large, but I could probably fit through it. I consider it for the briefest moment, then dismiss the idea. *He doesn't want to hurt us; he just wants the money. Once my father gives it to him, he'll let us go.* I find the first-aid kit in the cabinet under the sink. I wipe the years of accumulated dust off the box and run back to the living room.

When I try to hand the kit to Agent Brody, he shakes his head. "No, you do it. I'll talk you through it. Ex-girlfriend can help."

I put pressure on my father's wound until the blood slows to a trickle, then Gillian douses it with antiseptic and my father yelps. "You deserve a lot worse than that," she whispers. I agree with her, but not audibly.

"I'm sorry," he whispers back. I don't know if it's meant for her or for me or for all of us. I wipe away the new blood mixed with antiseptic, and Agent Brody instructs us how to close the wound with an old and yellowing but still usable butterfly bandage.

When we're finished, Agent Brody says, "Harold, you look like you could use a drink. Do you have any scotch?"

My father shakes his head. "Rum. Kitchen cabinet next to the fridge."

Agent Brody turns to me. "Nina, go get it. No glasses, just the bottle."

I nod and run to the kitchen. The rum is exactly where my father said it would be—and a butcher block filled with knives is on the counter beneath. I stare at them. *Should I? Shouldn't I? What if he catches me? He threatened to blow Gillian's head off. Would he do the same to me? Damn yoga outfit. It's so tight-fitting there's no way I could hide a knife in my pants.*

I'm still lost in thought when Agent Brody calls out to me. "Nina, what's taking so long?"

"Sorry," I yell back and slam a kitchen cabinet door for effect before sprinting back to the living room, rum in hand. "It was in a different cabinet." *I don't think my father will contradict me—and I'm right.* I unscrew the cap and hand the bottle to my father first. He takes a swig, then hands it back to me and I pass it to Agent Brody, who drinks straight from the bottle too.

He wipes his mouth with the back of his hand and says, "Anyone else want any?"

The three of us shake our heads and he sets the bottle down on the coffee table. "Let's all get a little more comfortable, shall we? Tiffany, help your father onto the couch." When Gillian and I don't move from the floor, he says, "You two go too. I want you all in one place."

The four of us line up on the brown leather sofa—Tiffany, my father, me, and Gillian. Agent Brody sits in one of the two armchairs opposite the couch, the large wood coffee table separating our side from his. He stares at my father. "How much cash do you have in the house?"

"Not much," my father says. "A few thousand."

Agent Brody sighs. "Nina, come here."

I stand up and cross over to his side of the room. "Sit," he says, and I think he means the armchair next to him, but when I try to, he pushes me down to the floor so I'm kneeling in front of him. Then he spins me around so I'm facing Tiffany, my father, and Gillian instead of him. "Let's try this again," he says and places the gun against the back of my head. "How much cash do you have in the house, Harold?"

I silently plead with my father to tell him the truth, or at least tell him what he wants to hear.

"Two million dollars," my father replies.

"Better," Agent Brody says.

"I can wire transfer you the rest," my father continues, "but I'll need to spread it out over several transactions. A three-million-dollar withdrawal will be flagged."

"Not good enough," Agent Brody replies.

"Be smart, Jason. You don't want the scrutiny any more than I do."

"That's not what I meant. The price has gone up. Five million plus another five for each of the girls. That's twenty million you owe me."

Gillian gasps, but Tiffany and I remain silent. If what they said at the trial is true, our father has a lot more money than that.

Harold Rothberg doesn't flinch. "And how do I know you won't come back to me asking for more?"

"You don't," Agent Brody says. "So you better hope my luck holds."

"I don't—"

But before my father can finish his thought, the entire house is plunged into darkness.

64

Tiffany screams, or maybe it's Gillian, and Agent Brody jumps up from the chair. "What the hell is going on here?"

"Power outage," my father calmly replies. "We get them all the time. The backup generator should kick in in about ten seconds."

Ten seconds isn't much time. But maybe I can buy us more. I grab the bottle of rum off the coffee table and swing it at what I hope is Agent Brody's head. I hear the glass break and Agent Brody scream, "What the fuck," so I know I've made contact with some part of his body.

"Run!" I scream as I blindly sprint toward the back door.

I hear movement all around me—feet shuffling, furniture scratching against the tile floor, Tiffany calling out to me, but I don't stop. I wrench open the back door, which I watched Agent Brody close but not lock after Gillian's attempted escape (maybe he'd been planning on using it as his own escape route), and run. I narrowly miss falling into the swimming pool and realize it's all jungle beyond that, so I reverse course and sprint toward the driveway. By the time I make it to the dirt road, the lights in the house are back on. But I keep running as if my life depends on it—because I know it does. And my family's lives too.

I've never been much of a runner, but tonight I'm world-class. It's pitch-black outside and even after my eyes adjust to the darkness, I can hardly see. I fall several times, from rocks, from potholes, from clumsiness, but each time I get back up and start running again. When I get to the bottom of the hill, I make a right. Not because I remember the way back to the hotel, but because I feel the breeze coming from that direction. Breeze means ocean, ocean means town, town means people and, God willing, someone who will help.

I see a light in the distance slowly moving toward me. Then I realize it's actually two lights. Headlights. I run faster, but the lights suddenly stop.

"Help," I scream, still running. "I need help."

I'm still fifty yards away when the driver's side door opens and a figure steps out. "Stop right where you are."

I don't stop. I can't stop. I left my father and sister and Gillian behind with a madman with a gun. No doubt a very angry madman now that I've escaped. Agent Brody knows I'll come back for them. He knows he's almost out of time. He'll be desperate—and desperate people do desperate things. I can't stop. I won't stop. I keep running toward the car.

"I need help. You have to help me."

Then I hear a gunshot and I freeze. It came from what I'm now close enough to see is a large SUV.

"Stop where you are," the dark figure calls out to me. "We're FBI."

FBI? Agent Brody is FBI too. Maybe he called in another favor. Maybe he's not the only one who helped my father escape. Maybe this man is his partner here to kill us all and help Agent Brody flee with the money.

The dark figure keeps talking. "Put your hands on top of your head and turn around."

No, no, no, no, no. It doesn't end this way. It can't. I won't let it. I place my hands in the air and slowly turn around, scanning the area for any means of escape. But there are none—no side streets, no paths, no houses, only a dirt road with jungle on both sides. When I hear footsteps approaching me from behind, I don't think. I just lunge for the jungle.

65

———

I immediately trip over something hard and sharp and tumble down a hill. I stop when I slam into a tree, which must be occupied by a group of monkeys because the howling is so loud it makes my head hurt. But I hurt all over now, and I'm pretty sure whatever scratched my face on the way down drew blood, because I feel a warm trickle of something running down my cheek. I don't know if the FBI guy has followed me down the hill because all I can hear are screaming monkeys and the sound of my own heart pounding in my ears, but I force myself to stand up and start moving again, more slowly this time.

I see light in the distance. A house maybe? Then the sound of another gunshot rings out, piercing even the cacophony of the monkeys.

"Stop where you are. You're surrounded."

Am I? On the road I at least had a sliver of moonlight to illuminate my path, but in the jungle, the lush foliage blocks even that weak light from seeping through. I'm relying more on my hands and my feet to guide me than my eyesight.

I hear the trees rustling around me, but it could just as easily be the movement of monkeys, or whatever other wildlife is living in this jungle that I'd rather not think about, as another human being.

"You said you needed help," the voice calls out. It's definitely getting closer.

There's rustling all around me now. I consider moving again, but if I can hear his movements, that means he can hear mine. It's safer to stay put and hope he passes me by. I scrunch up into a ball, trying to make myself as small as possible. The pounding of my heart is deafening to me, but I doubt anyone else can hear.

"I can help you," the voice continues. "But you need to tell me where you are."

I lift my head and that's when I see the flashlight. Only one. It's headed downhill, but it's twenty feet away from me. If I don't make a sound, it will pass me by. I try to slow my breathing.

I'm so focused on the movement of that narrow beam of light, I don't realize there's a second one approaching me from behind.

66

———

By the time I turn around, the second beam of light is pointed at my face.

"Nina Rothberg?" It's a female voice this time.

"Yes," I say, squinting into the blinding white light.

I raise one arm to try and shield my eyes, and the woman's voice yells, "Hands up."

I assume she has a gun as well as a flashlight, so I place my hands in the air next to my head. I hear rustling behind me and I reflexively turn toward it when the woman shouts, "Don't move." A few seconds later someone grabs me from behind, and before I know what's happening, my arms are no longer in the air but behind my back cuffed together with something plastic digging into my wrists.

The woman steps closer and angles the flashlight upward so the beam of light is no longer directly in my eyes and I can make out the contours of her face. She looks vaguely familiar, but I can't place her.

"Nina Rothberg, you're under arrest for aiding and abetting a fugitive. You have the right to remain silent. Anything you say can and will be used against you in a court of law. You have the right to an attorney. If you cannot afford an attorney, one will be provided for you. Do you understand these rights as I've just read them to you?"

All I'm aware of in this moment is the howl of monkeys in the trees above me and an angry woman staring at me with an expectant expression on her tired face. Am I supposed to answer? Those words are so familiar to me from hearing them on television and in movies that I can't really comprehend that they've been directed at me. *I'm under arrest? How is this possible? I'm the victim here, not the perpetrator.* This can't be happening. It's all so surreal. It must be a bad dream, but I don't ever seem to wake up.

"Do you understand these rights as I've read them to you?" she says again.

I nod.

"I need an audible answer," she says and I whisper, "Yes."

"Good. With these rights in mind, do you wish to speak to me?"

Somewhere in my uncomprehending brain I recall that I'm supposed to ask for an attorney, then stay silent, but the words rush out of me unbidden. "Agent Brody is holding my family hostage. I can show you where, but there's not much time. Agent Brody has a gun. You have to help them."

But she doesn't seem to appreciate the urgency of the situation. Her only reaction is to ask, "Why would Agent Brody do that?"

"Because he's the one who helped my father escape!"

She glances at the man behind me and nods.

Then all hell breaks loose.

67

I thought there were just the two of them, but there are actually many more. The man starts barking orders into a walkie-talkie while the woman hustles me back up the hill. There isn't just one SUV on that road but three, all filled with men, some in dark pants and FBI jackets and others wearing camouflage swat gear. Everyone has a gun but me.

They don't need my help finding my father's house—they already know the way. Have they been tracking him this whole time or did they just find him today? I have no idea.

When we arrive at the house, they leave me in the back of one of the SUVs with a burly guy in an FBI jacket who won't answer any of my questions—what are you guys doing here? Do you know Agent Brody? Did you know he helped my father escape? Why am *I* under arrest?—while the rest of them surround the house. Then someone kicks in the front door and the screaming begins.

I hear a lone gunshot, then a few minutes later, all four of them—my father, Tiffany, Gillian, and Agent Brody—are marched out of the house. They each have their hands tied behind their back, just like me, and an FBI guy pulling them by the arm to one of the waiting SUVs. All except Agent Brody. He has the lone female agent by his side and a bloody towel wrapped around one leg. He's leaning on her for support as he limps toward the rear vehicle.

They bring my father and Gillian to the SUV behind mine and push Tiffany into the backseat with me. Her face is red and puffy from all the crying, and her hair is disheveled, but otherwise she looks as beautiful as ever and gets more than one admiring glance from the swat gear guys.

"You okay?" I ask.

"Sort of," she says and her voice cracks. "You?"

I shrug as well as I can for someone whose hands are tied behind their back.

"How far did you get?" she asks.

"Not far. I was trying to find help. I wouldn't have just left you there, you know. I was coming back for you."

She gives me a weak smile. "I know. Dad knows too. But Jason—"

"Stop talking," the burly FBI guy next to me says.

I think he's mad because he had to stay in the car babysitting me instead of getting in on all the action.

The other FBI guy in the backseat waits until my guy is looking out the window before he leans over to Tiffany and whispers, "It's in your best interests to keep your mouth shut. And if I were you, I'd hire a good lawyer." Then he takes a bird's-eye view of her cleavage before staring straight ahead.

I shake my head. Badge or no badge, they're all the same.

I ASSUME they'll be taking us back to Managua, where we'll catch a flight to the US, but instead of getting on the main highway, we bump along more dirt roads until we come to a stop at an unpaved airstrip where a private plane is waiting. About half the FBI guys escort me, Tiffany, my father, Gillian, and Agent Brody onto the plane, and the other half stay behind with the SUVs. My burly FBI guy is one of the ones who stays behind, and I'm not sorry to say good-bye to him. Tiffany's FBI guy comes with us, and although he won't answer any questions either, he at least cuts the ties holding our arms behind our backs and lets us stretch for a moment before cuffing us again, but this time with our arms in front. He also brings us each a bottle of water and a sandwich, which neither of us eat, but I still appreciate the gesture.

He tells us we should try to get some sleep and I don't think that I can, but eventually the adrenaline rush dissipates and I crash. I wake up as the plane is descending. The sun is shining through the row of oval windows and off in the distance I can see the Manhattan skyline.

We're home.

Sort of.

68

———

Once we land at another private airport—although this one has a paved runway—the FBI agents escort us off the plane and into more waiting black SUVs. They take us to a nondescript office building somewhere in New Jersey. I desperately need a shower, and a toothbrush, but I don't think now is the time to ask. Everyone is extremely tense—not just me and my family but the FBI agents too.

Tiffany's FBI agent is escorting both of us down a long white hallway—white walls, white-and-gray-linoleum floor, even white speckled ceiling tiles—when he suddenly stops and pulls both of us flat against the wall so two other FBI agents can lead my father past us. Our father looks tired, but his expression is neutral. If he's panicking, he's doing a good job of hiding it. I wouldn't be surprised if he's already hatching a new escape plan. As he passes us, he turns and says, "Ask for a lawyer and keep your mouths shut. I'm not—"

But one of the agents escorting him cuts him off. "Eyes front, Harold," he says and gives him a small shove. My father gives us each a pleading look before turning around.

I glance at Tiffany, who's staring at me. I nod and so does she. We're thinking the same. Although I don't trust my father anymore, and I sure hope she doesn't either, I still don't believe he would intentionally put us in jeopardy. He's giving us good advice, or at least believes he is.

After our father disappears down another hallway, a new FBI agent joins us and separates me and Tiffany. My guy brings me to a windowless room with a metal table and four chairs, and I assume the same happens to Tiffany. I have no idea how long I'm left there. It feels like hours and maybe it is, or it could be a much shorter period of time. My watch is still in my hotel room in Nicaragua, or perhaps in an FBI evidence bag by now. In any event, there's no clock in this room, which I presume is intentional.

Eventually the lone female agent, the one who shone the flashlight in my eyes in the jungle, walks into the room. Her hair's combed and pulled back from her face, and her breath smells minty. I'm jealous that she's been able to brush her teeth. I so want to brush mine.

She sits down in the chair opposite me and unlocks the metal handcuffs I've been wearing since I boarded the plane in Nicaragua. "I don't think we've been formally introduced. I'm Special Agent Nancy Margolis."

She holds out her hand to me and I shake it limply. "Nina Roth," I say out of habit, because obviously she knows my name. She raises her eyebrows at the "Roth"—she was probably expecting "Rothberg"—but she doesn't question it. Instead she says, "So, Nina, do you want to tell me what happened?"

I do. Desperately. But I decide to heed my father's advice. "I want a lawyer."

"Why do you want a lawyer? You told me you didn't do anything wrong."

I know she's baiting me, that I should ask for a lawyer again, but I can't stop myself from biting. "I didn't. So why am I under arrest?"

She waves her hand as if swatting at a pesky fly. "We have to do that. It's a formality."

"You have to tell people they're under arrest when they're not?"

"Well, at the time I didn't know what had happened. It was all a bit chaotic as you may recall. We were on our way to apprehend your father and you come running down the road like a mad woman. And when Agent Kelly told you to stop, you ran."

"Because he shot at me!"

She waves her hand in the air again. "No one shot *at* you. It was a warning. You were never in any danger, at least not from us. We're the good guys, Nina."

I finally figure out why her face looks familiar to me—I've seen it on TV. She used to be at the government's press conferences before my father's trial and then again after he disappeared, one of a half dozen or more people on the stage. I only remember her because she was the only woman in the group. *She must be Agent Brody's boss.* Then I remember the rest of his description of her. Obviously he fed me a lot of lies, but what he told me about her still had the ring of truth.

"I want a lawyer," I say again.

"Nina, I just told you, the arrest was a formality. You don't need a lawyer."

"Then I'm free to go?" I say and stand up.

"No," she says and motions for me to sit down. "We still have a lot of questions for you. And there is that matter of you traveling on a false passport. That's a felony punishable by up to ten years in prison, you know. I haven't charged you for it . . . yet. Or you could cooperate and I'll forget all about the passport."

Just as Agent Brody predicted—the carrot and the stick. I

fold my arms across my chest and lean back in my chair. "I'll take my chances with a lawyer, thanks all the same. And aren't I entitled to a phone call? Or is that just on TV?"

69

S he makes me wait a while longer, perhaps hoping I'll change my mind. But eventually I get my phone call. I use it to call my mother, who's frantic. She's been trying to reach me for the last two days because my stepfather has sold the apartment in LA and she wants me to pack and meet with the movers. But all that's forgotten when I tell her where I am and why.

"Don't say one word to anyone, Nina. Not one word. I'm getting you a lawyer."

My parents never agree on anything, but they agree on this, so I know I've made the right decision.

Many hours later a man I guess from the amount of gray in his hair is around my dad's age, who's wearing a tailored suit, expensive shoes, and carrying a briefcase, enters my windowless room, accompanied by Agent Margolis. "I'm Greg Liman," he says and offers me his manicured hand. "Your mother has hired me to represent you. Do you accept my representation?"

"Yes," I say.

"Good." Then he turns to Agent Margolis. "Are you charging my client?"

"Not at this time," she replies. "But we haven't ruled it out. We know your client has committed at least one felony, and possibly more."

"Allegedly," he says. "Nothing's been proven. So if you're not charging her at this time, I'm taking her home. Her mother is very anxious to see her."

Agent Margolis sighs, which my lawyer takes as permission for us to leave. He's already out the door and I'm about to follow him when Agent Margolis calls out to us. "We have a lot of questions for your client, Mr. Liman. She needs to stay in the area, where we can reach her. If I so much as—"

"I'm sure you have many questions," Greg Liman says, cutting off what I presume is intended to be yet another thinly veiled threat. "But we're going to play by the rules here, Ms. Margolis. My client has invoked her right to counsel. The next time you want to speak to her, you call my office and we'll arrange a meeting at a mutually agreeable time and place. If there's nothing else?"

Agent Margolis shakes her head, then glares at me. But in the last twenty-four hours, I've been chased, shot at, and threatened with a gun to my head. Her glare doesn't intimidate me in the least.

As soon as we're out of that room, I start asking questions, but the lawyer hushes me and points to the black half dome in the ceiling. "Camera," he whispers. "I'll let you know when it's safe." I press my lips together so I don't accidentally blurt something out—the urge to speak is that great—and I follow him outside the building and across the parking lot. I wait until we're both inside his black Mercedes, which still smells new, before I speak, but he cuts me off again. He's the one asking the questions now, and he wants me to tell him every word I said to Agent Margolis before he arrived, and then every detail of my interaction with the FBI in Nicaragua.

"Do you mean with Agent Brody too? Because he's been with me and Tiffany since the beginning." Which reminds me, "Where is Tiffany? Is she okay? Are you representing her also?"

"No," he says. "Your mother just hired me to represent you. But I'm sure Tiffany's family hired a lawyer for her."

I'm not. "You don't know Raylene. She's not like my mom."

"If you're really worried, I can make some calls."

"I am."

He nods and starts dialing.

WHEN I SEE the signs for the Lincoln Tunnel up ahead, I know we're not heading to my mother's house but into the city, presumably to Greg Liman's office, where I'll be spending what remains of the day (it's already late afternoon) explaining exactly how I ended up in this mess. I wait until he ends his call before I ask, "Do you think we could stop at a drugstore so I can get a toothbrush and maybe some deodorant?" Between the yoga class, the running for my life, and the overwhelming fear, I'm more than ripe.

He laughs at me. "I assure you, Nina, I've smelled worse. But yes, my office will get you whatever you need."

I'M HAPPILY surprised to find that Greg Liman's offices actually contain a shower in one of the restrooms. He explains that it's for the lawyers to use when they have to pull all-nighters and go to court the next morning, but I suspect I'm not the first client to use it. There's a cabinet filled with an assortment of soaps, shampoo, razors, and other toiletries, as well as towels, and a few magazines.

Even after a very long, very hot shower, I still don't feel entirely clean, but I feel cleaner than I did before. I had intended to climb back into my stinky workout clothes, but when I step out onto the bathmat, I find a pair of khakis and a shirt with The Gap tags still attached waiting for me. The clothes are too big for me and not my style, but I gratefully pull them on and thank Greg Liman's assistant profusely, as she must've been the one who had to run out and purchase them at her boss's request.

She escorts me down the hall to Greg's office, a massive corner suite with floor-to-ceiling windows on two sides and impressive Midtown views. Greg and another lawyer—younger but in an equally expensive suit—are waiting for me. After Greg introduces me to his associate, I accept a bottle of water, pass on the pastries, and take the proffered seat on the couch. Greg sits down in the armchair next to me and his associate sits across from both of us, legal pad and pen in hand. I guess his role here is official note taker.

"Start at the beginning," Greg says.

"The beginning in Nicaragua?" Or Nevis? Or Panama? Or LA? Or before that? There are so many places I could start.

"When did the trouble begin? For you I mean, not your father."

That one's easy. "The day Agent Brody walked back into my life."

"Then start there."

So I do.

EPILOGUE

There's no trial this time. My father was already convicted and sentenced in absentia. He's spending the rest of his life in prison; there's no getting around that.

Greg Liman was correct in assuming that Raylene hired Tiffany her own attorney. The two of them coordinated efforts and neither Tiffany nor I were ever charged with a crime. The government was more interested in locating the missing money and bragging that they'd captured the international fugitive Harold Rothberg than they were in prosecuting his daughters.

That was due to our lawyers' efforts much more than any altruism on the part of the FBI. Tiffany and I never spoke to the press directly (both of our lawyers advised against it), but Greg gave interviews to several well-known journalists who reported the story with his particular slant: Thanks to the efforts of two brave young women, whose only goal was to obtain justice, they were able to accomplish what law enforcement couldn't—track down an international fugitive and turn him in to the authorities.

Obviously that's not exactly how it happened, but the rest of the world doesn't know that. And Agent Brody cut his own deal with the government—a public trial would've been hugely embarrassing for the FBI, Greg explained, so they were happy to plead him out—which means he isn't publicly contradicting Greg's story either.

Several news commentators even proposed that Tiffany and I be given the ten-million-dollar reward for information leading to the capture of our father. The FBI balked at that idea—they were willing to allow us our hero status but not the money. I didn't care because I didn't want it anyway. I told Greg even if they gave it to me I'd just donate it back to the victims' fund, so that became the official story and everyone was happy— everyone but Tiffany that is, who thought we should get at least some of that reward money. I believe her exact words were, "We earned it." Not surprisingly, the FBI didn't see it that way.

My father became a fixture on the twenty-four-hour news channels again for the weeks between his capture and his transfer to federal prison. I only saw him in person one more time. I asked to visit him at the NYC correctional center because I couldn't stop thinking about his behavior the night we discovered him in Nicaragua. My father had been manic that evening and it occurred to me that maybe he has an undiagnosed bipolar disorder.

My father has always been moody. I can recall days when I was young when he was so depressed he wouldn't get out of bed. And other times he'd be flying high. He always attributed the mood swings to work—the stress of managing other people's money and the ups and downs of the market. But what if it's more than that? What if he has a legitimate medical condition that caused him to do what he did?

Yes, I know how pathetic that makes me sound. Despite everything my father has done, I was still looking for a way to justify his behavior. I didn't want to believe that deep down inside he's actually the horrible person everyone thinks he is. Who *would* want to believe that about someone they love?

So I visited him in jail and told him my theory and suggested he ask the judge for an evaluation by a psychiatrist. His response: He laughed at me.

He leaned back on his metal stool, in his orange jumpsuit and shoelace-free sneakers, with his arms folded across his chest, and shook his head at me as if *I* were the one who's the great disappointment in this relationship. "Nina, you still don't get it, do you?"

"Get what, Dad? That the government wants to make you a scapegoat?"

"They've already accomplished that, sweetie, thanks to you and your sister."

That propelled me off my stool like a rocket. I leaned across the table so I was only inches from his face. "Oh no, you do *not* get to pin this on me and Tiffany. *We're* not the ones who stole billions of dollars."

My father stood up too and reached out to me, no doubt trying to calm me down, but when the guard standing a few feet away from us reached for his gun, my father sat back down. No touching—that's the rule. "Nina, please," he stage-whispered, glancing from me to the guard, who was clearly on edge from my outburst.

Since I didn't want to be accidentally shot in a jailhouse scuffle, I sat back down too.

"You're right," my father said, keeping his voice low. "It's my fault for not telling you girls the truth before I left. But I was just trying to protect you. I knew the FBI would question you both and I wanted you to be able to answer honestly that you had no idea where I was or even if I was alive. And if Jason Brody had done *his* job, none of this would've happened. He's really the one to blame here."

And that's when I realized it was truly hopeless. My father will never accept responsibility for his crimes. He'll never show remorse. In his mind, whether that mind is bipolar or completely sane, he is the victim here.

So I walked out of the visiting room and never looked back.

Literally, I mean. I still think about my father and what he did constantly. Some days it's all I think about. For months I laid in bed all day and ruminated for hours on end: Did he set out to be a crook or did he slip into it accidentally? When he was trying to justify his behavior to us in Nicaragua, he made it sound as if it had been the last market crash that set him on this path, but according to the FBI, by that point he'd already been stealing from his clients for years. Although it's not as if I trust the FBI to tell me the truth.

Sometimes I took a break from ruminating about my father to stew over Agent Brody instead. The last time I saw him was when they brought us all back on the plane from Nicaragua, and I have no desire to ever see him again. But my lawyer passed on what he'd learned about him in the course of defending me.

There were never any Russian mobsters. Agent Brody just told us that so he could keep us close. And Enrique never sent any goons to beat him up either—he got those bruises from two security guards at the casino in the hotel where he was caught counting cards. Apparently Agent Brody did receive the message from the Panama City Ocean Club notifying him that his credit card had been declined, and he decided to take a break from tracking Tiffany and me at our dinner with Enrique to try his luck at the tables in the hotel's casino. The real irony here is that if he had won that night, he and my father might never have been caught.

Agent Brody had been telling the truth about one thing: When he tracked me down in LA, the FBI had no idea where my father was. They didn't even have any leads. But they were keeping an eye on me and Tiffany in case our father tried to contact either of us. That was why Agent Brody insisted we travel on fake passports and leave our cell phones at home. But the FBI was tracking my one credit card too, and when I used it to pay for the room at the Panama City Ocean Club after Agent Brody's card had been declined, it sent a ping to some cubicle dweller at the FBI's data center.

According to my lawyer, in that circumstance, the FBI employee would've immediately checked my passport, and when that employee saw that it hadn't been used, most employees would've assumed that my credit card had been stolen and filed the ping away with no further action. Unfortunately for Agent Brody and my father, this ping went to an ambitious cubicle dweller who decided to do a little digging. He started checking surveillance footage at the airports and found an image of me, Tiffany, and Agent Brody going through security together at LAX. He alerted Agent Margolis, who had been under the misimpression that her second-in-command, Agent Brody, was taking a one-month sabbatical to decompress.

Agent Margolis initially thought Agent Brody was just continuing the investigation off-book, which she couldn't officially condone, but she was willing to let it play out in case he turned up anything useful. So she told the ambitious cubicle dweller to keep tracking us, but from afar. It wasn't until Agent Brody's hacker tried to use the information he had given him as leverage to reduce his sentence in a plea bargain agreement that Agent Margolis realized we might actually have a legitimate lead.

At that point she still didn't know that Agent Brody had

helped my father escape—she only flew down to Nicaragua and assembled a team because she wanted to take credit for apprehending my father. She didn't know Agent Brody was involved too until I told her so when she captured me in the jungle.

"It's always those little unexpected coincidences you can't plan for that trip you up," my lawyer told me. And he would know; he's been defending criminals for thirty years.

It was easy to lose entire days thinking about nothing other than my father and Agent Brody—and I did. But my obsessing became so bad that one afternoon my mother walked into my bedroom—I had no choice but to move back in with her and my stepfather; I had nowhere else to go—and handed me a plane ticket to LA.

"You seemed happy living there," she said as I stared at the details of my flight—nonstop, one-way, leaving in two days. "And you're miserable here. You need to build a life for yourself that doesn't revolve around being the daughter of Harold Rothberg. You have a lot to offer the world, Nina. It's time you start."

"But I don't have a job. Or even a place to live."

"I can't help you with the first," she said. "But I can help you with the second. With all the chaos when you . . . came home, I never called the movers. The buyer got frustrated with our delay and backed out of the deal, so we never sold the apartment. It's sitting empty."

"But doesn't Richard still want to sell it?"

She shook her head. "Not after I reminded him that he bought it initially because he thought it would be a good investment—and it still is. Real estate prices in LA rose eighteen percent last year. That's a lot better returns than anyone's getting in the market these days."

"But I thought he needed that money for his business."

"The business will survive without it, but you . . ."

"I can survive without your apartment, Mom. I can get a job and rent a place of my own."

"I know you can, sweetie. And I'm glad you know it too."

So THAT'S what I did—except I moved into their apartment (it seemed silly to leave it empty when I needed one anyway), but this time I pay rent, so my stepfather's happy too. And I was only living in LA for a few weeks before Tiffany decided to join me. She turned eighteen so Raylene couldn't stop her. Not that I think Raylene wanted to stop her. Once Raylene knew with one hundred percent certainty that my father wasn't dead, she divorced him and married Jimmy. It's understandable that she wouldn't want Tiffany around to mess up her new marriage. And she was willing to pay to get her out of the house.

I suspect there's been some bribery by Tiffany with regards to that property in Nevis, which I never told the FBI about (they never asked and Greg told me that I didn't need to offer any unrequested information), but I've never questioned her about it. When Tiffany proposed splitting the rent with me with the money she gets from Raylene, I gratefully accepted. It means I only need to work one job instead of two, which gives me more time to study for my sommelier certification exam. It's not necessary to be certified, but I decided it couldn't hurt, and Wine World offered to split the cost with me.

Yes, I'm working for Wine World again. I'm a hero now, no longer guilty by association for being the daughter of an international fugitive, so when I spotted the online job posting for a manager for their Westside store, I called. I figured since I never filed a criminal complaint against Big Mike, he owed me and I could use it as leverage against him. Borderline sleazy, I know. Call it the corrupting influence of my father or Agent Brody or my lawyer or everyone in the government who went along with our bullshit story to save face. Hell, even Gillian was making the rounds on the morning talk shows to promote her new book: *My life with Harold Rothberg, the Billionaire Who Wasn't.* All I wanted was a job!

Of course when I told Tiffany my plan, she thought it was a great idea: "That man owes you big-time."

"But what if he tries something again?" That was my only real concern, not that I was potentially extorting my ex-boss who'd tried to rape me.

"You make it clear to him that if he ever touches you again, you're not going to bother calling the cops; you're just going to cut off his penis, shove it down his throat, and laugh at him as he chokes to death on his own inadequate manhood."

Ouch.

Thankfully I never had to make that threat. When I called Wine World's corporate offices, the receptionist, who remembered me as the girl with the Louboutin pumps, told me Big Mike no longer worked there and hadn't for several months. "After the heart attack he decided to retire early," she said. I didn't question it. I just told her I wanted my old job back and asked her who was doing the hiring now.

"The owner," she said.

Ugh. I knew he'd lost money because of my father.

"He's coming in this afternoon to go through all the resumes," she continued. "Email me yours and I'll put it at the top of the stack."

I thanked her and hung up, then wrote a personal note to the owner explaining who I was, including the official version of how Tiffany and I had helped the FBI find our father, and asking him for an interview. I didn't really expect to hear from him, but he called me the next day. He said he went back and reviewed the sales figures from the time I had managed the Westside store and decided he didn't need to waste his time meeting me in person—he hired me over the phone instead.

That was six months ago. And my life's been going great ever since. I'm actually feeling optimistic about my future for the first time in years.

A NOTE FROM THE AUTHOR

Thank you for reading *The Billionaire Who Wasn't*. If you enjoyed the book, please spread the word!

If you're interested in receiving exclusive bonus content from me (e.g., deleted scenes, bonus epilogues, etc.) sign up for my newsletter at www.bethorsoff.com. In fact, I wrote a second bonus epilogue for this book. If you'd like me to email it to you then type this link into your browser and sign up: subscribepage.io/qT5qb5

ABOUT THE AUTHOR

Beth Orsoff is an Amazon bestseller and the author of twelve novels ranging from romantic comedies to domestic suspense. Visit Beth online at www.bethorsoff.com. Sign up for Beth's newsletter to receive exclusive bonus content.